D1436134

Return to Blackwater House

ALSO BY VIKKI PATIS

In the Dark
The Wake
Girl, Lost
The Girl Across the Street
The Diary

WRITING AS VICTORIA HAWTHORNE

The House at Helygen

Return to Blackwater House

VIKKI PATIS

HODDER &
STOUGHTON

First published in Great Britain in 2022 by Hodder & Stoughton
An Hachette UK company

1

Copyright © Vikki Patis 2022

A CIP catalogue record for this title is available from the British Library

Hardback ISBN 978 1 529 39452 8
Trade Paperback ISBN 978 1 529 39453 5
eBook ISBN 978 1 529 39454 2

Typeset in Plantin Light by Hewer Text UK Ltd, Edinburgh
Printed and bound in Great Britain by Clays Ltd, Elcograf S.p.A.

Hodder & Stoughton policy is to use papers that are natural, renewable
and recyclable products and made from wood grown in sustainable
forests. The logging and manufacturing processes are expected to
conform to the environmental regulations of the country of origin.

Hodder & Stoughton Ltd
Carmelite House
50 Victoria Embankment
London EC4Y 0DZ

www.hodder.co.uk

For our sisters, who were just walking home.

Prologue

Three little words. They have the power to change everything, to turn your world upside down and make you question your own reality. *I love you. I'm leaving you. I hate you.* The three words that kept me alive when I was a child: *I'm not here. This isn't real.* And then: *I'll save myself.*

And I did. I escaped a childhood I've tried so hard to forget, memories stuffed into boxes, ghosts smothered by the will to survive. Shadows in the corner of the room, fingers reaching out to me like tendrils of smoke, banished by the power of three little words: *I'm still here.* From denial to refusing to be beaten. From fear to defiance. *I'm still here. I'm still here.*

I have worn many guises in my life. Wayward child, victim, survivor. Colleague, friend, partner. So many roles have been forced upon me, so few I have chosen myself. Now I am the concerned stepmother, cast into the role by the disappearance of the girl I love like my own daughter. Another role forced upon me. Another nightmare to endure.

Now, three different words have taken over, turning my world upside down and changing the course of my life, of our lives, forever. It was me who uttered the words for the first time, the breath catching in my throat, my heart pounding in my ears in time with the ocean crashing against the rocks below.

Ava is missing.

Rebecca

1st January 2020

I pace the living room floor, my heart beating in time with my footsteps. Eleven steps, stop, turn, eleven steps, stop, turn. My foot hits the coffee table and I halt, focusing on the throbbing in my toes, relishing the pain. Anything to stop the chaos in my mind, to release myself from the fear. But it is inside me, coiling around me until it is hard to breathe, hard to think about anything other than Ava. *Ava Ava Ava.*

At almost two a.m. this morning, my world was turned upside down by Ava's friend hammering on the front door. The police arrived quickly, blue flashing lights illuminating the garden, but it will still take Daniel a while to get home. I picture his car flying down the motorway from London to Cornwall, his fingers tightening on the wheel as he drives without stopping, desperate to get home. The roads should be clear, at least. It is the first of January, a new year, a new decade, but the sun hasn't even risen and already we are thrust into a new world, one we would never have chosen.

I am standing at the living room window when he arrives; I hear the stones skittering beneath the tyres before his car comes into view. I throw open the front door and stand on the step, hands twisting in front of me, as Daniel slams the car door and rushes towards me. The wind blowing in off the sea is cold, the air full of salt, stinging my cheeks.

He stops before he reaches me, his face pale and eyes wide. I've never seen him like this, fear written so plainly across his face. 'Where is she?' he asks, breathless, his voice small.

'I don't know.'

Three little words. What power they have. His expression changes to something more recognisable. He needs to take control of the situation; it is his way.

He strides up the front steps and past me into the house. 'Are the police here?'

I look up to see Kate's blonde hair disappear through the door at the end of the hall. 'In the kitchen.' I follow Daniel down the hall, remembering the uniformed officers in their heavy boots standing in the hallway hours before, their expressions unreadable as I told them what happened. The helicopter went out a few hours ago, making the whole house vibrate, and I heard them mention the coastguard, but they have found nothing. No sign of her, except the scarf dropped on the grass before the low wire fence at the edge of the garden. Nothing but sea.

She wouldn't have gone over there, I told them. Ava wasn't stupid; she knew it was dangerous to play on the cliffs. But they'd looked at me with a pitying expression, one that told me that they knew better. In their eyes, Ava is a fourteen-year-old girl, a reckless teenager. She is capable of getting on a train or into someone's car of her own volition. Capable of running away. She doesn't know the area, this county we brought her to only three months ago. She might be new here, she might be missing her old friends, but she would never run away. She would never leave me. Us.

Kate, our family liaison officer, is washing mugs in the sink, shirtsleeves rolled up to protect them from the suds. I open my mouth to speak, but then two other officers come in through the back door, their cheeks red with the cold.

'Mr Everley?' the male officer says to Daniel. 'I'm Detective Inspector Allen. This is Detective Sergeant Tremayne, who I understand has already spoken to your fiancée, but I wondered if you might answer some questions as well.'

'What questions?' Daniel demands, and I see something flicker across the officer's face.

'When did you arrive, Mr Everley?' DS Tremayne asks. Her tone has changed since she interviewed me a few hours ago. There is something different in her, a hardness I hadn't noticed before.

'Just now. I left the hotel as soon as Rebecca called.'

'You drove? Weren't you at a party last night?'

Daniel exhales loudly through his nose. 'I didn't have anything to drink. I was perfectly fine to drive. And besides,' he says, his back straightening as his voice increases in volume, 'I think this is more important, don't you?'

I put a hand on his arm, both in support and restraint. He looks terrible, his eyes wide and bloodshot, his face pale, and I'm sure I can smell alcohol coming off him. But he's right: this is more important. 'What else do you need to know?' I ask the officers. 'I've already explained everything.'

'Ava had been having a sleepover in the annex,' DI Allen reads from the notes DS Tremayne must have made when she questioned me earlier. 'It's recently been renovated?' He gestures towards the kitchen window and the building beyond.

I nod. 'It used to be a garage. We intend to let it out to holidaymakers.' I ignore the expression that flickers across his face.

'Five girls including herself, all fourteen or fifteen, were here overnight with their parents' permission,' he continues, then pauses to look up at me. 'We'll need to speak to them all, of course.'

'Of course,' I echo, and he turns to DS Tremayne.

'Uniform has gone out to see them all this morning,' she confirms, and the DI nods, returning to his notebook.

'They ordered pizza, which you picked up from the village, and they were watching movies while you were here in the house alone. Is that right, Ms Bray?'

'Well,' I begin, feeling my cheeks heat up as Daniel turns his gaze upon me. 'A friend popped in for a drink. At around eight? Then I fell asleep on the sofa.' The memory of Poppy banging on the front door, suddenly looking so much younger than her fourteen years, feels like a punch to the stomach. *Ava's gone.* I clear my throat. 'I was woken by Ava's friend Poppy hammering on the door. She said Ava had come into the house to get something, but she hadn't come back to the annex.'

'What friend of yours came here?' Daniel asks at the same time DI Allen speaks.

'And what did you do? Were you immediately concerned?'

I glance at Daniel before turning back to the officer. 'No, not really. I thought she must be somewhere in the house, but I had a look around and couldn't find her. It wasn't until I found her scarf that I started to worry.'

'Her scarf?' Daniel demands. 'Where was her scarf?'

I feel like a pendulum, swinging between the two men, and start to feel sick. 'At the bottom of the garden, by the fence.'

'And you touched it?' DI Allen asks.

'What? Yes. It was so dark . . . Like I said earlier, I picked it up, to see what it was. It was new – I'd bought it for her for Christmas.' Daniel moves suddenly and I flinch, but he is turning towards the sink, filling a glass with water and gulping it down. The FLO, Kate, is standing in the corner now, watching him, her lips pressed into a thin line. She's been so quiet, I'd almost forgotten she was there.

'What happened next?' DI Allen asks. My emotions must be written across my face, because he softens his tone when

6

he speaks next. 'I know you've already gone through it all several times, but if you could tell me again, now your partner is here.'

I try not to think about why it matters that Daniel is here. They're looking for holes, something that doesn't quite add up, or maybe they want to see if I'll change my story now Daniel is here. Whatever it is, I'm not going to give it to them. 'I . . . I checked the rest of the garden, and then the annex, where the girls were. They all said the same thing, that Ava had gone back to the house to get something more than thirty minutes before but hadn't come back. Then I called you.'

'Did you worry she might have fallen?' DI Allen asks, his implication clear. I shiver at the thought of Ava falling into the murky sea beyond the cliffs and shake my head.

'No. No, I told your officers that it was a waste of time look-ing for her down there. She's never climbed over the fence before. She knows how dangerous it is. She wouldn't be so reckless. Her friends all said the same thing, that none of them had been anywhere near the end of the garden. And Poppy said she saw Ava come in through the back door of the house.'

He nods. 'When did the girls' parents come to pick them up?'

'I called Daniel and then I called their parents. I thought . . . I thought they'd want to collect them straight away. The girls were quite upset.'

'And there were just girls here?' he asks. I frown at him, not understanding. 'No boys?'

'Boys?' Daniel echoes. 'Were there boys here?'

'No, Daniel,' I protest, looking to DI Allen for help. 'There weren't any boys. Just the girls.'

'Does Ava have a boyfriend?' the officer asks. I see Kate shift out of the corner of my eye.

'Of course not,' Daniel snaps. 'She's fourteen.'

DI Allen gives me a look and I sigh. Are we just another set of parents who have no idea what their teenager is up to? But I would know if Ava had a boyfriend. She would have talked to me at least, if not her dad.

'Not that we know of,' I say. 'She's new here. We only moved into the area a few months ago.'

'But Rebecca is from here,' Daniel adds. 'Originally.'

'I wouldn't have guessed,' DI Allen says, and I know he is referring to my accent, the accent I shed like a skin when I moved away to Hertfordshire. I wonder what Cornish people hate more – the comers-in, those who move into the area and buy up properties that sit empty for half the year, or those of us who leave and never look back.

I say nothing.

'Rebecca and I knew each other when we were kids,' Kate says, surprising us all. 'We went to school together.'

DI Allen seems to scowl at her as a memory jogs in my mind. Kate had been a couple of years younger than me, and we usually didn't run in the same circles, but I remember taking her back to my childhood home once, something I almost never did. Why did I take her that day? I can't remember, but I can remember the look on her face when she saw the state of that house. I look up to find her staring at me, and I wonder if the same images are flashing through her mind.

DS Tremayne clears her throat and I turn to look at her. 'Do you still have family in the area?' she asks.

'No. My mother is dead and I never knew my father.'

'And you didn't keep in touch with any friends?' She glances up at Kate but she stays silent. 'Apart from Lou Tregenza, that is? The friend who popped in for a drink last night?' I nod and DS Tremayne taps her pen against her bottom lip. 'I know that name. Tregenza Electrical, is it? I think they did a job for me once.'

'That's right. *She* works with her dad,' I say, emphasising the pronouns so that Daniel doesn't jump to the wrong conclusions and think Lou is a male friend.

'Hmm. Small world.' She turns back to Daniel. 'And are all of your family still up country, Mr Everley?'

Daniel frowns at the unfamiliar phrase. I nod. 'Yes. Though, to be honest, he doesn't have much family left either.'

'Just a cantankerous great-aunt,' he supplies. 'Dementia. She's in a care home.'

'And Ava's mother? Any family left on that side?'

I hesitate. 'Yes. She has a grandmother and two aunts, plus their families.'

'Do they see Ava often?'

Not as often as they would like, I think but don't say. 'They used to, when we lived closer.'

'They dropped in at Christmas,' Daniel says. 'Boxing Day, wasn't it, darling?' He squeezes my shoulder. DS Tremayne gives me a look and I try not to react.

'So they weren't here last night?' DI Allen asks.

I shake my head. 'No. They stayed at the hotel in the village for one night, then left in the morning of the twenty-seventh. Aisha, one of Ava's aunts, is heavily pregnant and has young children at home.'

'What happens now?' Daniel demands, his voice so loud I flinch away from him. 'Will there be a search party? A television appeal?'

'The coastguard is going out shortly, but like I said, we're speaking to those who might be able to give us some information,' DI Allen says carefully. 'Poppy and the other girls who were at the party.'

'But what could they tell you? They're *children.*'

'Teenage girls often confide in one another. There might be something Ava didn't want to tell her parents. A secret she didn't want to share.'

'My daughter doesn't have secrets from me,' Daniel says, glaring at the police officers. 'There's nothing we don't know about her.'

Oh, but there is. Ava is very good at keeping secrets. And so am I.

PART 1

I

Rebecca

Before – October 2019

Leaves skittered across the pebbled drive, the wind barrelling into us as we got out of the car and stared up at the house before us. The autumn afternoon sky was dark, the branches on the trees like outstretched fingers reaching towards the clouds, and the sea raged in the background, crashing against the cliffs beyond. Blackwater House, a place I never thought I'd see again.

I took a deep breath. The air was full of salt and the promise of rain, and I caught the sound of a seagull screeching on the wind. It had been more than fifteen years since I left this village, fifteen years of building a new life and trying to forget the old one. And now I was back, with my new family in tow, and I wondered if the ghosts of my past would be hiding in the shadows of our new home.

'We used to say this house was haunted,' I said, peering up at the darkened windows of the house before us. 'That a mean old woman lived here. We used to see her staring at us from the upstairs windows. They said she was a witch.' I regarded my fiancé out of the corner of my eye as he stepped up beside me.

'Poor woman,' Daniel said, laughing. 'I'm sure she was just lonely.'

He has no idea, I thought as I watched him stride towards the front door, overgrown plants reaching across the path to snatch at his trousers. I thought of Gwen then, the one we'd called a witch, who had turned out to be my guardian angel. She hadn't been a witch, of course, and she hadn't been lonely either. She'd loved living in this house, tending the gardens and watching the birds dance across the sky, diving down to the ocean below. Blackwater House had been her sanctuary, and I hoped we would be as happy here as she had been.

Ava, my fourteen-year-old stepdaughter, sidled up beside me, one earphone in, mouth working on a wad of chewing gum. 'Is it really haunted?' she asked, blowing a bubble. 'It just looks like a shithole.'

I frowned. 'Language. And no, of course it's not haunted. It was just a silly story we used to scare ourselves with. The woman who owned it was actually very kind.'

'So kind she had no one else to leave it to?' Daniel said over his shoulder. 'No friends or family?' I frowned, opening my mouth to reply when Ava spoke again.

'I don't like ghosts.' Ava gave a shudder and I put an arm around her shoulders, forgetting how young she still was. She'd shot up in the past year, her long legs making her almost as tall as me, her child's body slowly turning into that of a young woman, but she was still so young, so innocent. She still needed me – us – to protect her.

'There's no such thing,' I said, squeezing her before letting go and following Daniel into the house. But ghosts do exist, just not in the form she imagined. They've been haunting me my entire life.

I closed the front door and leaned against it, swiping an arm across my forehead. It was early October and the house was freezing cold, but I'd worked up a sweat helping bring everything into the house, while Daniel lounged on the sofa and Ava unpacked the boxes in her new bedroom.

'Just leave it, darling,' he'd said as I helped one of the movers carry the dining table in through the French doors. 'This is what we're paying them for.' He gave a huff of laughter and turned back to his phone, thumbs flying over the keypad. The mover had raised an eyebrow at Daniel's words and I tried to hide my smile.

But now, finally, we were in, and I could start unpacking, filling Blackwater House with our lives. It felt strangely normal to cross the threshold of this place, as if I'd come home after many years away.

Ava stomped down the stairs and I smiled brightly at her. 'How's the new room, sweetie?'

She frowned. 'It smells funny.'

'That's just because it's new to you. It'll soon start to smell like home.' I pushed off the door, wiping my hands on my jeans. 'How about some dinner?'

'Can we order pizza?' she asked, jumping down the last step and landing on the floorboards with a bang.

'Careful! That's real wood flooring,' Daniel called from the sofa.

'I don't think anywhere delivers around here,' I said.

Ava grimaced. 'Where the hell have you brought me?'

'There's a pizza place on the corner,' Daniel said, poking his head round the door. 'It's not far – we could go and collect it.'

I peered out at the darkening sky, the clouds heavy with rain. 'It must be new. There weren't any takeaways in the village when I was growing up. Do you think they do gluten-free?'

Daniel was scrolling through his phone again, cursing the lack of signal. Our broadband hadn't been connected yet, and it appeared that this village was still a black spot for modern technology. 'Ah!' he said after a moment. 'Here we are. Yes, they do, and they have a separate oven for it too. You just have to ring up in advance.' He smiled at me as if he'd just won a prize. 'What do you fancy?'

While Daniel ordered dinner, I went into the room across the hall, which would be my office and library. I opened up a box labelled BOOKS and smiled as I pulled them out. I'd been collecting books since I was a child, though most of them had been left in my mother's house when her boyfriend had kicked me out, and I've managed to build up my collection over the years. Last Christmas, Ava bought me a bundle of *Goosebumps* books, which we'd then started reading together on weekends. I've always loved our time together – Saturday morning shopping and slow Sunday afternoons. Now we were in Cornwall, we would have even more time together when Daniel travelled back up to London on the sleeper train for work. I couldn't wait.

I smiled as I stood in the middle of the room. It had been a sitting room when Gwen lived here, the shelves in the alcoves full of books. I wondered where they all were, who had cleared out Gwen's things. Someone must have emptied the house before today, everything packed up and taken to the dump or given to charity. She'd probably set aside some money for the house to be cleared, not wanting to leave it to me to organise. She was like that: thoughtful, considerate. She'd given me the gift of Blackwater House, and the burden of it. But I was excited to get started on our renovation plans.

Although the room needed some work, I already loved it, with its high ceilings and dark wood floors, and I'd already decided how I would decorate. I'd ordered a sofa in dusky pink, which would go perfectly with a dark green ceiling and warm white walls. I would get some gold fittings and had already bought the light, which would hang from the beautiful ceiling rose. There was a huge bay window overlooking the driveway and front garden, which was currently overgrown and rather bleak, but I imagined would look beautiful in the spring. I'd ordered a few bookcases, a coffee table, and two tub chairs, all of which were stacked against the wall, waiting to be assembled, along with a desk, which would go in front of the bay window.

I'd been working as an editor and ghost-writer for years, ever since Ava started school and I'd had more time to fill. I didn't really need to work, as Daniel made enough for us to live comfortably, but I enjoyed it, losing myself in each manuscript as I had lost myself in stories as a child. And it allowed me to build up a healthy savings pot, which also meant I could take a few months off to focus on turning Blackwater House into a home.

I grabbed the toolbox from the hallway and got to work on the furniture, stopping when Daniel came in to tell me the pizzas were ready to collect. I pushed the two assembled chairs against the wall and he moved into the room, running a hand over the back of the one closest to him. 'Why don't you stay here, grab a shower?' he suggested. 'I'm sure you could do with freshening up.' I glanced at my reflection in the mirror and smoothed a hand over my messy hair. 'Ava and I will brave the weather,' he added with a grin. The grey clouds had turned darker and now rain lashed at the windows.

'She'll be furious if her hair gets messed up,' I warned, turning back to him. 'There should be an umbrella in one of the boxes in the hallway. Try the one closest to the stairs?'

He rummaged around, crying 'Aha!' and lifting it in triumph before calling up the stairs for Ava. 'I'll bring back a bottle of wine,' he said, shrugging on his coat. 'To celebrate our new home.'

I wasn't sure the pizza place or the village shop, if it was open, would have the kind of wine Daniel was used to, but I didn't say anything. Instead I smiled. 'Good idea, darling. See you soon.'

The door slammed shut behind them, making the lights flicker, and a memory of the first time I'd been inside this house came back to me. It had been raining then too, my hair and clothes drenched as I'd stood shivering in the hallway, a puddle forming beneath my feet. A warm September day had brought thunderstorms in the evening, the sky turning from a light reddish gold to deep grey. The front garden had been overgrown even then, weeds and thorns tangling together, the grass knee-high, the trees standing like guards to the east. Such a contrast to the back garden, which was orderly and tended. It was almost as if she wanted to warn people away from Blackwater House. But I had found my way through, and it was then that I'd learned the name of the witch who lived here, the woman whose house we'd thrown eggs at on Halloween and whose door we'd knocked on before running away and hiding in the hedges.

But, on that September evening, I wasn't trying to disappear. I was fifteen, cold and wet and bleeding. I needed help, and Gwen – kind, generous Gwen, not the witch I had once imagined – was the only one to give it to me.

Shaking myself out of my memories, I headed upstairs. I grabbed a towel and my toiletry bag from an open box in our bedroom before stripping off and padding into the en suite. The tiles were cold beneath my feet and I wondered if we could have underfloor heating installed, a luxury I had gotten used to in our previous house. The shower was probably older than me, and it took a while for me to find the right temperature, but I sighed as the warm water hit my skin, melting the knots from between my shoulder blades. As I was rinsing the conditioner from my hair, I heard a door slam downstairs, and smiled.

'That was quick!' I called out, but I couldn't hear a response over the sound of the water. I stepped out of the shower, wrapping the towel around me, and hurried into the bedroom to get dressed. I tore open a box labelled REBECCA'S CLOTHES, grabbed the first things I could find and threw them on before heading back downstairs. The hallway was empty, but wet footprints tracked across the floor towards the kitchen. I pushed open the door, expecting to find Daniel and Ava sat at the breakfast bar, pizza boxes open in front of them, but there was nobody there. The room was a mess, with boxes everywhere, some torn open and half-emptied, and a memory of my childhood kitchen flashed into my mind: the filthy counters, the dirty dishes piled in the sink. *It's not the same,* I told myself, turning away. *You've only just moved in. It's not dirty, just untidy.*

I heard a noise and jumped. 'Hello?' I called, the sound echoing in the empty hall. What if there was an intruder? I glanced around for a weapon and found a large torch sitting on top of an open box beside the understairs cupboard. After picking it up and switching it on, I crept down the hall and pushed open the living room door, the beam lighting my way. The room was freezing, the sea air blasting in through the open patio doors at the back. Frowning, I hurried across the room to close them, my teeth chattering with the cold, but before I could get there the doors slammed shut and I jumped again, staring wide-eyed at the woman in the glass before realising it was my own reflection.

2

Rebecca

Before – October 2019

I closed my eyes, trying to control my breathing. I'd always been jumpy. It was something Terry had laughed about, his eyes glinting nastily as my mother sat silently, as she always did, through shame or fear or the drugs she had just taken. Terry was her boyfriend, her drug dealer, her abuser. When he arrived, nobody expected him to stay for long. People often crashed at our house, sleeping wherever they fell, muddy boots and threadbare jackets piled up on the stairs, for as long as there were enough drugs or alcohol to keep them entertained. I rarely learned the names of those people, for they would disappear as swiftly as they arrived, but Terry was different. Sharper somehow. No matter how much he drank or smoked, he was still alert, still ready to strike, like a viper watching its prey.

Forcing myself to turn away from my reflection, I went into the kitchen and started tidying up, unable to shake the memories that were crowding in. With Terry came more people who took up residence in the living room, ranting about how the rest of the country forgot about Cornwall, 'those pricks in Westminster leaving us to rot' in poverty and deprivation. I remember listening to the voices coming from the living room – always men's voices, loud and angry – and not understanding it. But it didn't take me long to understand what fuelled Terry. Power, or the idea of it, usually gained through violence.

He didn't flinch from cruelty, and he had a reputation as being quick to anger.

I often heard him hitting my mum too. He would lay into her whenever she passed out too quickly or took something he hadn't said she could. She would fight back at first, usually with anything she could lay her hands on – empty bottles, an ashtray, the coffee table. That went through the window once, which Terry had to board up the next day. But he was always stronger, and her anger would soon turn to pain, and her pain would turn to acquiescence. By the time I was twelve and Terry had lived with us for over a year, I had seen and heard more than any child should have, and I quickly came to understand that Terry was more dangerous than the others, and he wasn't going anywhere.

I was scrubbing the kitchen sink, the scent of bleach stinging my nostrils, when Daniel and Ava came back, the front door slamming, jolting me back to the present.

'We're home!' Ava sang as she went through to the kitchen. 'I hope you're hungry!'

I turned and took a deep breath. I repeated my mantra in my head, the one I'd learned during my counselling sessions. *Don't let your past dictate your future.* I had to stay focused, keep looking forwards. I had to leave my ghosts behind me. I pasted on a smile and went out into the hall.

'Ah, there she is!' Daniel grinned, handing me a bottle of wine as he wrestled out of his coat. 'Ava, can you hunt out some plates?'

'I can't find them!' she called from the kitchen. I heard something smash and winced. 'Oops.'

'Leave it, darling,' I said quickly, pushing open the kitchen door to find her trying to pick up a broken jar of jam. 'We'll eat from the box, like savages.' Ava grinned and slid onto a stool at the breakfast bar while I cleaned up, inhaling sharply when a piece of glass sliced my thumb. I washed my hands at the sink, wrapping a piece of kitchen roll around the small wound. I'd dig out the first aid kit later.

'Have you been cleaning?' Ava asked, sniffing the air. 'I can smell bleach.'

'Just the sink. There was a nasty smell coming from the drain.'

Daniel wrinkled his nose. 'I hope there's nothing wrong with the plumbing.'

'Oh, I'm sure there isn't,' I said quickly. 'Shall I find some wine glasses?'

'Definitely,' he said, sitting down beside his daughter. 'We're not fifteen, sitting down the park with a bottle swiped from our parents' cupboard. Not that Rebecca ever did that,' he added with a wink at Ava. 'She was a good girl.'

I laughed nervously, turning to reach into another box and pulling out three wine glasses wrapped in newspaper. Becks Bray had never been a good girl.

'Only half a glass for you, young lady,' Daniel warned, raising an eyebrow at Ava. I smiled. We'd decided to introduce alcohol at home instead of letting Ava discover it on a park bench like I had, though Daniel didn't know about that particular aspect of my past. And I intended to keep it that way.

'Yes, Father,' she said with a smile, opening her pizza box and tearing off a slice. 'Yours is there, Becks.' She pointed at a box with GF written on the front. I gaped at her. She'd never called me Becks before. I hadn't been Becks in a long time, had shed that identity when I left. She frowned at me. 'Did you hurt your hand?'

I glanced down at the kitchen roll, now stained red. 'Just a nick,' I said, trying to ignore the buzzing inside my head. I forced a smile and kissed the top of her head. She screwed up her face, wriggling away, and I caught Daniel's eye and smiled. She was growing up quickly – too quickly. She knew more than we gave her credit for, more than we wanted her to. But why had she called me Becks? Had she found something of mine with that name on, something I thought I'd hidden?

Daniel poured us each a glass of wine, then raised his. 'To us,' he said, and I picked up my glass too. 'To our new adventure.'

'To Blackwater House!' Ava piped up, raising her glass to clink against her father's. They both watched me as I lifted my own, trying to ignore the blanket of dread settling over me.

To Blackwater House. And to all the ghosts I left behind.

After dinner, Ava declared that she was having an early night, and Daniel and I exchanged a look. An 'early night' for her meant lying in bed watching something on Netflix, but we didn't mind. She was fourteen, after all. She didn't want to spend all of her time with us.

'I'll be up to say goodnight soon,' I told her as she went upstairs. Riffling through a box, I found a bottle of washing-up liquid and a pack of sponges, and quickly cleaned the glasses we'd used during dinner. Daniel had gone into the living room; the TV had been switched on and muffled voices floated down the hall. After drying my hands on a tea towel and applying a new plaster to the cut, I switched on the torch on my phone and carried the pizza boxes through the utility room and out the back door to where the bins were kept. It was pitch-black outside now. Night had descended like a blanket being thrown over us, and I looked up to see the sky dotted with stars. The view was breath-taking, even in the darkness. Moonlight rippled across the waves, which stretched out as far as the eye could see, until sea became sky.

Gwen had called it her sanctuary, and that's what it became for me too, when she'd opened the door that night all those years ago. Blackwater House had been built in the eighteenth century as a dwelling for the mine captain and his family, back when machines tore tin from the earth across the Cornish coast. It's this part of its history that made us move back here instead of selling when we found out Gwen had left Blackwater House to me. Subsidence due to historic mining meant no bank would lend a mortgage for it, and we'd even struggled to find a decent insurance premium that wasn't through the roof.

But honestly, as soon as I'd read the letter from the solicitors, explaining that I had inherited Blackwater House, I knew I would have to come back. It was the chance of a lifetime, to restore a beautiful house in a historic area, which was surrounded by second homes and holiday lets. Gwen had given me the chance to return to my heritage, and the sea that had always called me home.

3

Kate

Now – 1st January 2020

Kate wakes with a start, her phone vibrating on the bedside table. Light filters through the half-closed curtains, dust motes sparkling in the air as she shields her eyes from the glare. It takes her a moment to realise the light is coming from the neighbours' overzealous security lights and not the sun. Groaning, she checks the time before answering the phone.

'Winters,' she grunts, which is met with a tinkling laugh.

'We don't really answer the phone like that, maid,' the voice on the other end says. 'That's just another lie Hollywood has been telling us about policing.'

Kate laughs despite herself. 'Are you ringing at five o'clock in the morning on New Year's Day just to mock me, Barbara? Do you have any idea how hungover I am?' The sound of the control room buzzes in the background as Barbara laughs.

'Late one, was it? And no, I wish I was, maid.' Her voice turns serious and Kate sits up slowly. 'Missing girl reported this morning over St Agnes way. Fourteen years old. Went missing after a sleepover last night.' She pauses. 'Oscar One wants you as FLO on this one.'

Kate waits for the room to stop spinning before throwing back the covers and heading for the bathroom. 'Why me?' she asks as she wriggles out of her pyjama bottoms and kicks them into a corner.

'He reckons you might know the stepmother. Rebecca Everley?'

Kate pauses, one sock dangling from her foot, the phone pinned between her shoulder and ear. The name doesn't ring a bell. 'Nothing to do with my expertise then?'

Barbara snorts. 'One missing person found safe and well and suddenly you're the expert.'

'Just because your Frank can't find his own house on the way back from the pub, there's no need to be snarky with me.' Kate grins as she remembers having to lead Barbara's husband the twenty yards from the pub to his house, Barbara opening the door in a dressing gown and slippers, her hair in curlers, tutting loudly as she dragged him inside.

'When will you let me forget that?'

'Maybe next year.' Kate glances at her appearance in the mirror and decides she can scrape her hair up into a half-decent bun to avoid washing it. She thinks of her wife's curls and curses her own straight blonde hair, which is too fine to do much with. 'Where am I going?' she asks.

'I'll send you the address. Uniform is with the family now. I believe a search is being conducted at the property as we speak. They've had the chopper out already, but no joy.' Barbara exhales loudly. 'And, Kate? Don't step on any toes. You're being brought in because Oscar One thinks you're the right woman for the job.'

'Me, step on toes?' Kate pretends to be offended, but she's touched by the older woman's concern. Kate qualified as a family liaison officer last year, and she is already known within the Devon and Cornwall Police to be ambitious – though *ruthless* was the word she overheard being used to describe her recently. Unfairly, she might add. There's nothing wrong with being ambitious, though lately she's been wondering where her career might lead.

'I'll be on my way within twenty minutes,' she says, hanging up and jumping into the shower. In the bedroom, she pauses by her wife's side of the bed as she's buttoning up her shirt. Lauren has been away for a few days, taking care of her dad after he had an operation, and Kate knows she'll still be sleeping soundly, miles away in Hertfordshire.

'Lucky sod,' she murmurs as she grabs her phone and hurries downstairs.

Less than an hour later, Kate is driving down the narrow lane towards the old tin mine, which sits proudly on the edge of the cliff. A memory of her mum clambering barefoot up the rocks makes her smile in the gloom. Sunrise is still a couple of hours away; the sky is a pale purple with an orange hue.

What a start to the new year, she thinks, then realises she's driven past her turning. Swearing, she reverses and swings the car down the drive towards Blackwater House, a place she hasn't thought about in years. Another memory rises up as the house comes into view, this time of the old woman who'd lived here when Kate was growing up. What was her name again? She can't remember. People used to say she never left the house; that she was either a witch, a hermit, or a ghost, or maybe even all three, but Kate used to see her walking into the village at the crack of dawn to do her shopping. They would smile and say good morning to each other as Kate carried her paper-round bag out to her bike. 'I'll take the paper now,' the woman had said once. 'Save you coming all the way out to me.'

She had struck Kate as kind, her hair tied back in a neat bun and her grey eyes crinkling at the corners as she smiled. As her car rumbles up the drive now, she remembers the local kids targeting this house on Halloween, climbing over the gate and throwing eggs and toilet paper at the front door, and she feels a tug of guilt as she remembers the year she went along, hiding in the bushes with the others, trying to fit in.

Parking up, Kate gazes through the windscreen at the front of the house. It hasn't changed much since she was last here, but the wrap-around garden looks neater and the garage seems to have been converted into something. *Rebecca Everley*, she thinks, trying to place the name. The old woman must have moved on or died, and now this Rebecca Everley was making Blackwater House her home.

A throbbing has started behind her left eye and she curses herself for her stupidity the night before. With Lauren up in Hertfordshire, Kate had spent the evening down the pub with a few colleagues, succumbing to peer pressure and staying far later than she'd originally intended. Popping open the glove-box, she finds a packet of paracetamol and swallows two with a gulp of water before getting out of the car. It's freezing cold, and she notices a frost on the grass as she crunches her way across the drive and raises a gloved fist to knock on the door, ignoring the video doorbell attached to the wall beside it. She steps back to check for other cameras when the door opens to reveal a uniformed police officer who had been at the pub with her the night before.

'Morning,' PC Smith says with a grimace. 'You look how I feel.'

'Have you been to bed at all?' she asks with a chuckle, stepping inside and wiping her boots on the mat.

'I probably managed an hour or two,' he says, covering a yawn with the back of his hand. 'The baby woke up at four and wouldn't settle back down.'

'So you're on night feeds then?'

'Yup. Almost glad to be called out, but don't tell my wife that.'

Kate flashes him a grin before looking around. The hallway is bright, all white paint and pale wood, the stairs opening up straight ahead to reveal a wide landing. 'Nice place. I've never been inside before. When did they move in?'

'October time. She's from here, apparently, but I don't recognise her.'

'How old is she?'

The PC shrugs. 'Thirties?'

'And how old are you?'

'Twenty-one.'

'Well, that explains it then. You were probably a babe in arms when she left. Where did she go?'

'Up country somewhere.'

'Very specific.' Kate pokes her head around the living room door, scanning the empty room. The Christmas tree is still up, the lights looping through a series of patterns. Her left eye twitching, Kate looks away.

'She's in the kitchen with DS Tremayne,' PC Smith says as Kate peers into what looks like an office on the other side of the hall, the room blissfully dark.

Kate suppresses a groan. Of all the officers on call, it had to be DS sodding Tremayne. 'Right you are. You coming with?'

'I'm to go down and meet the coastguard.'

'Coastguard? Do they think she went down there then?'

The PC shrugs again. 'The back garden is open to the sea. Well, there's a low fence, but she easily could've climbed it.'

'Jesus. All right, thanks. Drink plenty of water.'

'Yes, Guv.' He gives a mock salute and Kate pretends to swat him before making her way down the hall towards what must be the kitchen. The door is open a crack and she can hear voices now. As she pushes open the door, she sees the DS standing by the sink while a woman sits hunched over on a stool, her face in her hands. Tremayne offers Kate a nod, almost looking relieved to see her.

31

'Ah, good,' she says, and the woman looks up. 'Rebecca, this is your family liaison officer, Kate Winters. I'll, uh, leave you to it.' To Kate's relief, she strides out into the garden.

The woman's face is ashen, her eyes rimmed with red. Kate offers her a small smile as she takes in her crumpled clothes and her wild, tangled hair. She notices that the woman is wearing odd socks. 'Ms Everley, I—'

The woman interrupts. 'It's Rebecca. Rebecca Bray.'

Suddenly it clicks, and Kate struggles to hide her surprise. Becks Bray. She recognises this woman as the girl she went to school with, who'd lived in what was known as the rougher part of the village. She focuses on keeping her voice level as she speaks. 'Hi, Rebecca. Do you know who I am?'

Rebecca nods, and Kate sees recognition flash across her eyes. 'Kate Jones.'

Kate smiles. 'It's Winters now.' She thinks back to the notes she'd hastily made from Barbara's message, wolfing down a slice of toast as she scribbled. 'As DS Tremayne said, I'm your family liaison officer. Do you know what that means?'

Rebecca nods slowly, her gaze unfocused. 'I . . . I think so.'

'I'm here to support you. Whatever you need, day or night, you call me.' Kate rummages through her pockets and comes up with a slightly creased card. 'I'm going to do everything I can to help you through this difficult time.'

'Thank you.' Rebecca's voice is barely above a whisper. She clears her throat. 'It's nice that . . . well, I mean. I'm glad to see a friendly face, I suppose.'

Kate fights to keep her expression neutral. *Friendly* isn't how she would describe them; she hasn't seen Rebecca in over fifteen years, and they had hardly been friends when they were kids. *But that's why you're here,* she reminds herself silently. *To make friends. And to find out the truth.* 'Can you tell me what happened?' she asks gently. 'Your stepdaughter has gone missing?'

Rebecca blows out a breath. 'Ava. She . . .' A tear rolls down her cheek, and Kate reaches out to grab a square of kitchen roll from the holder on the side. 'Thank you.' She wipes her eyes before continuing. 'Daniel, my fiancé, he's . . .' She trails off again, staring into the distance.

'He's driving down from London now, is that right?'

'Y-yes. He was there for new year's. I called him as soon as . . . as soon as I knew Ava was gone.'

'Can you take me through that? How did you discover that Ava was missing?'

'She had a sleepover. Here, in the annex.' Rebecca gestures towards the window and the converted garage beyond. 'She had four friends over for the night, and one of them came to tell me that Ava had left to get something but hadn't come back.' She glances up at Kate. 'I've told the police all this. They've been here for hours.'

'I know. I'm sorry you have to keep going through it, but it's helpful for me to build up the full picture so I know how best to support you.' Kate smiles. 'How about a cup of tea?'

Rebecca blinks. 'Oh. Yes, thanks.'

Kate flicks on the kettle and opens a cupboard for mugs. 'Sugar?'

'Two please.'

They are silent while the kettle boils, the only noise the clink of the spoon against the side of the cups as Kate adds sugar. She has found that the ritual of tea-making can be soothing for both her and the person she is interviewing. Because that's what this is, an interview, where Kate must gather the facts to compare with whatever Rebecca said earlier. She isn't just there to support the family, she's there to look for holes, for clues, for anything that might help the investigation. This is the hardest part of her role, having to maintain a distance from the family whilst being in their home, in their life, for the duration. Having to keep an open mind and not be blinded by any sense of loyalty. *This is a test,* she realises as she pours hot water over the teabags. *And I need to pass it.*

'When did you move in?' Kate asks, placing the mugs on the counter and sitting down opposite Rebecca.

'October,' she says, and Kate adds a mental tick to the information PC Smith shared. 'We, uh, well. Do you remember Gwen? The woman who lived here when we were growing up?'

That's the one. Gwen. Kate nods.

'Well, she . . . left it to me. When she died.'

Kate stares at her. 'Blackwater House? Gwen left Blackwater House to you?'

Rebecca nods. 'I'm not really sure why. I lived here, for a while. I don't know if you knew? My home life was difficult and, well, she gave me a place to stay.'

Memories are coming back to Kate now, of the one and only time she'd seen Rebecca's house, her mum passed out on the sofa. The dirt, the smell. She struggles to keep her expression neutral. 'Did you keep in touch? With Gwen?'

'A bit. I always got the feeling she was pushing me away, you know? Not in a bad way, but more like, encouraging me to get away from here. To start a new life.'

'But then she left the house to you?'

'I know, it doesn't seem to make sense. Maybe she knew I'd never have anything to inherit from my own parents.' Rebecca wraps her hands around the mug in front of her. 'I don't know how much you remember, but my mum . . . she had some problems. Drink, mostly, and drugs. She kicked me out when I was fifteen and Gwen took me in.'

Kate tries to hide her surprise. 'Was it ever official? I mean, were social services involved?'

'God, no. I suppose that seems strange to us now, doesn't it?' Rebecca gives a small smile. 'But you know what it was like around here, like a cocoon the outside world could rarely penetrate.'

Kate nods. Many places in Cornwall can be quite insular, and this village is no exception. There's no train station, two pubs and a smattering of bakeries, cafés and restaurants, many of which are closed or run on reduced hours during the off-season. It's why Kate had moved away as soon as she could, though not as far as Rebecca had.

'Whereabouts in Hertfordshire did you live?' she asks. 'My wife is from the area.' Kate watches for a reaction as she often does, expecting the worst, but Rebecca's expression doesn't change.

'East Herts, around Ware and Hertford. We lived in Stanstead Abbotts before moving here.'

Kate doesn't recognise the place names. Lauren is from Hitchin, which is where she is right now, seeing in the new year by looking after her dad while he recovers after an operation. Kate had texted at midnight but hadn't got a response, and knew Lauren was probably asleep. *She's probably still asleep,* she thinks ruefully. 'So you moved here because Gwen left you the house?' she asks, forcing herself to stay focused.

Rebecca nods. 'We thought it would be nice. A fresh start, you know, somewhere nice and safe for Ava to grow up.'

'It's a great place to raise kids, or so I'm told.'

'Do you have any?'

'No.' She doesn't add the usually expected *yet* on the end. Neither she nor Lauren have any intention of having children, and Lauren's dad is content with Kiana as his 'grandkitty'. They make an odd but happy family: Kiana glaring at his dog Dash whenever they visit, Dash staring at her as if she hung the moon. Kate remembers finding them curled up together on the rug one morning, Kiana's head resting on Dash's tail, and smiles. 'Just one rather demanding cat. Though my wife has been going on about getting a dog lately.'

'Ava wants a dog too. She—' Rebecca suddenly stops, her head jerking up like a hound that has caught a scent. Kate opens her mouth to speak but Rebecca is up and hurrying through the hallway towards the front door. She follows, watching as the other woman opens the door and goes out onto the porch. She can see a car pulling up, tyres skidding on the gravel, and a man emerges from the driver's side.

'Where is she?' the man demands, and Kate sees Rebecca shrink back a little at his approach.

'I don't know,' she says.

4

Rebecca

Before – October 2019

'Ava! Come on, darling, it's time to go.' I heard my voice echo around the hall as I stuffed my feet into boots and pulled on my coat. Ava slammed her bedroom door and stomped down the stairs. 'All set?' I asked her.

'Yes. Wait! No. My lunch.' I reached down to pick up a lunchbox from the floor and held it out to her, trying not to laugh as she grimaced. 'Don't we have like a plastic bag to put it in or something?'

'And kill the planet to save your pride?' Daniel said, chuckling as he came out of the kitchen, holding a mug of coffee. He was barefoot despite the cold, his tracksuit bottoms damp at the ankles.

'Have you already been for a run?' I asked as Ava joined us in the hallway.

Daniel nodded. 'Got up bright and early to watch the sun rise over the old tin mine. It was incredible. We should go exploring more.' He took a sip of his drink.

I tried to hide the way the mention of the tin mine made me feel, the memories it evoked. But I had to face them sometime. 'Yes,' I said, forcing a smile. 'You're right, it's so beautiful here.'

'Don't forget the plumber is coming today to discuss the bathrooms. He should be able to have a look at the boiler too.'

'Oh, thank God,' I said, pulling my coat tighter around me. Although the boiler seemed relatively new, the house was freezing day and night. I'd ordered some heated blankets for our bedrooms, but a house of this age wasn't built for keeping in the warmth.

Ava made a face. 'I am *not* going out at sunrise,' she whined. 'That's *so* early!'

'Not at this time of year. It's practically midday!' Daniel joked.

I smiled and smoothed a hand over Ava's hair. I have always loved the corkscrew curls she'd inherited from her mother. As soon as I met her, I wanted to learn everything about her, and so we spent a lot of time together in those early days. She was a thoughtful child, the kind to offer around the biscuit tin before she took one for herself. She was quiet and creative, happiest when her fingers and clothes were covered in paint. She was fond of catching spiders and keeping them in her room, though she would burst into tears when I scooped them into a glass and set them free, until I explained that spiders preferred to live in the grass, not the beds of little girls.

'Mr Spider is off to see his friends,' I said as we crouched in the grass, watching the spider scurry away. 'They'll be pleased to see him.'

Ava stood, cocking her head to one side in that way of hers. 'Am I your friend?' she asked.

I hesitated, wanting – needing – to get it right. 'You're my best friend,' I answered finally. She slipped a hand into mine, her palm soft against my skin, and I exhaled. Now in many ways, she felt like my own daughter.

'Come on,' I said now, glancing at the clock. 'We're going to be late.' I grabbed my keys from the hall table and pecked Daniel on the cheek.

'When can I get the bus?' Ava asked as she trailed behind me, waving goodbye to her father before slamming the door behind us.

I tried not to take her need for independence personally. She was growing up, that was all. She needed to spread her wings. 'Next week. We're waiting for them to send your bus pass.'

I pulled out of the driveway, gravel crunching beneath the tyres, and set off for Ava's new school. I could hardly believe she was already in Year 10 and working towards her GCSEs. She'd done half a term back in Hertfordshire, looking simultaneously too young and too grown up in her smart uniform, but today I got a flash of the woman she would become, with her dark, fiery eyes and quick wit. I glanced at her as we made our way out of the village. Daniel often said that Ava was 'too much', that she should be quieter, but to me, Ava was always exactly as she should be. Smart, beautiful, kind. She had her whole future laid out before her, and I intended to make sure she got it.

I glanced at her again as she typed on her phone, thumbs flying furiously over the touchscreen. 'Are you nervous?' I asked, and she paused, her thumbs going still.

'Not really,' she said after a moment, lifting her eyes to the road ahead. 'I miss my friends though.'

'I know,' I murmured, 'but you'll make new ones. And maybe your old friends can come and visit, once the house is in better shape. Would you like that?'

Ava grinned. 'Yes!' she cried, and for a moment, she reminded me of the little girl I met all those years ago, her personality big enough to fill a room. 'That would be amazing.'

'Cool,' I said, and I caught her rolling her eyes. 'What? Don't people say *cool* anymore?'

'No, Becks,' Ava said, her lips twitching with a smirk. '*Cool* isn't cool anymore.'

I stopped by the village shop on my way home from dropping off Ava, picking up milk and a bottle of red wine. I had decided to cook pasta tonight, dipping into my precious stash of gluten-free fusilli, so I picked up some peppers and an onion, glaring at the pitiful 'free from' selection, which mostly consisted of digestive biscuits that tasted like dust.

I was diagnosed with coeliac disease when I was at university, finally dragging myself to the doctor after almost two weeks of throwing up and feeling like I was going to die. Up to that point, I was the healthiest I'd ever been since I'd left my childhood home, being well looked after by Gwen and then eating at least two meals a day, getting what nutrients I could with my meagre student loan. The doctor had frowned when I said I'd only been managing to eat dry toast and ordered me to go gluten-free straight away, just in case.

By the time I received the test results back – positive – I was almost back to normal. It had scared me, that fortnight of watching the weight I'd carefully put on drop away, my nails losing their strength again, my hair becoming greasy and lifeless. I remembered staring at myself in the mirror and seeing Becks, the neglected child I was trying so hard to forget, not Becca, the new me I was still trying to create.

Being gluten-free was not easy on a student budget. Even the basics like bread and pasta could be almost triple the price, but I managed, for the most part. Whenever I slipped up and used the communal toaster or failed to check the ingredients in a meal my housemates cooked, I paid a heavy price, and so I learned the hard way how to manage the condition. And I wondered now if I'd always had it, if the cheap and nasty food I lived on as a child had only been making me worse.

'Hello there,' the shopkeeper said as I made my way to the till, peering at me above half-moon glasses. He was dressed like a librarian, with a heavy woollen jumper and a grey shirt underneath. He could be the same shopkeeper from when I was a teenager, the man who chased me up the road once after I'd nicked a bottle of Lambrini. I smiled vaguely and placed my items on the counter. 'You've just moved into Blackwater House, haven't you?'

I stared at him for a moment, the frustration of living in a small village suddenly rushing back. I nodded, breaking his intense eye contact and scanning the shelves behind him. I asked for a pouch of tobacco and his eyes widened.

'We've just got those "e-liquids" in,' he said, making air quotes with his fingers. 'There's so many flavours, and they're supposed to be much better for you, you know.'

I didn't want to get into a discussion with a shopkeeper in a tiny Cornish village who may or may not have once chased me out of his shop, shaking his fist and calling me a 'thieving toerag', about the benefits of vaping versus smoking. I'd heard enough of it from Daniel over the years. Despite my upbringing, I found the smell strangely comforting. I gave a tight smile and shook my head. 'Just the tobacco, please.'

A gust of wind buffeted me as I stepped out of the shop. I pulled my coat tighter under my chin and jogged back to the car. I hadn't realised how difficult it was to park in this village, and the house was only a few minutes away. I would walk from now on, I vowed. Start doing more exercise as Daniel was always urging me to. I turned down the private track that led home and the sight of it still took my breath away.

I parked next to a van with BC Plumbing stamped across the side. Letting myself into the house, I called hello to Daniel, shopping bag dangling from my wrist.

'Upstairs, darling!' he shouted down the stairs. 'Come up, will you? We're in the en suite.' After depositing my shopping in the kitchen, I joined Daniel and the plumber, who introduced himself as Bradley, in the bathroom across the hall to our bedroom where he was measuring the shower enclosure.

'What colour tiles did you want again, Rebecca?' Daniel asked, indicating the booklet laid open on top of the toilet.

I picked it up, flicking through before finding the right page.

'These,' I said, pointing at the white metro tiles, 'covering these two walls and the shower enclosure.' I could see it now, the white sparkling tiles against the blue walls, the marble counter-top and dark tiled floor. I'd spent hours on Pinterest and Instagram over the past few weeks, ever since we'd told Ava that we were moving. Daniel hadn't been keen on the idea at first, worried about having to commute back to London, but so many people worked from home these days, and besides, what was the point in being the boss if he couldn't enjoy the benefits?

Daniel owned an accountancy firm in London, which had started small and ended up expanding beyond even what he had imagined. He'd spent much of his adult life – and Ava's fourteen years – working long hours, trying to build up his company. He deserved a break. Once he'd settled things at the office, we'd broken the news of the move to Ava, who had also had reservations, but she was a smart girl. She'd soon seen it for what it was: an opportunity, a fresh start. And so I had the entire renovation planned out, a project I could really sink my teeth into, and I was excited to get started.

'I'd like a roll-top bath there,' I told Bradley, pointing at the old, yellowing bath. 'I can text you the link to it.'

'And underfloor heating,' Daniel added. 'In both bath-rooms, actually.' He turned to me. 'Shall we show him the other one?'

When I was growing up, I'd never once considered that I would live in a house with more than one bathroom. The two-up, two-down ex-council house we'd lived in was tiny and neglected, the walls yellow with cigarette smoke, the bath-room tiles covered in mould, the carpets stained and foul-smelling. I'd promised myself that Ava would never know that life. She deserved so much better.

5

Kate

Kate listens to the exchange between DS Tremayne and Daniel, watching Rebecca flinch when her fiancé barks at her. He is imposing in a way, reminding her of one of those men who jogs right behind you on the pavement, pretending to knock into you as he overtakes, grinning like it's all a big joke. The kind of man who laughs at an idea you suggest at a meeting then presents it as his own. The kind of man who likes to be in control.

We are emotionally aware. I treat others with respect, tolerance and compassion, she tells herself as she watches the scene unfold.

She sees the flash of irritation in DI Allen's eyes when she steps forward to tell her colleagues that she and Rebecca grew up together, and winces. *Don't step on any toes,* she reminds herself, fading back into the shadows as he continues to interrogate Rebecca. She is taking it well, Kate thinks, considering she'll have spent the past five or so hours being asked the same questions over and over again. It can seem like a waste of time, especially when someone is missing, but sometimes you can find out a lot from those left behind. Sometimes, a member of the family knows more than they're letting on. As Kate watches Daniel, she wonders if he is the one who knows something about his daughter's disappearance, something he isn't sharing. Yet.

Her ears perk up at the mention of the coastguard, who her drinking buddy, PC Smith, has gone to meet. It's not beyond the realms of possibility that Ava and her friends had been mucking about on the clifftop, despite how adamant Rebecca is that Ava wouldn't do such a thing. She remembers again the time she'd found herself throwing eggs at Blackwater House with the others, how easy it was to be pulled along by the tide of your peers. Ava is fourteen, and no fourteen-year-old is immune to peer pressure. *No thirty-odd-year-old either,* she thinks, her hangover still lurking in the corners.

'Have you called Sierra?' Daniel is asking Rebecca. DI Allen has gone back outside, apparently satisfied with their answers. For now.

'Not yet,' she replies quietly, her eyes on the floor. Kate is about to slip out of the room to see if she can catch DS Tremayne and ask about Sierra when Daniel glances at her with something like dislike, and she feels her skin prickle.

'Sorry, who are you?'

'This is Kate,' Rebecca says quickly. 'Our family liaison officer.'

'Kate Winters,' Kate adds, offering a hand for Daniel to shake, which he ignores.

'And what do you do, exactly?'

I manage relationships and partnerships for the long term, sharing information and building trust to find the best solutions, she thinks, forcing a small smile onto her lips. 'I'm here to support you throughout this investigation, Mr Everley.'

He grunts and turns away, already dismissing her. 'I'll be upstairs,' he says to Rebecca and leaves the room. Kate sees Rebecca's shoulders drop as soon as he is gone.

'Do you mind if I go out for a cigarette?' Rebecca asks Kate, surprising her.

'Of course not. I'll come with you – I can have a look at the garden. I don't suppose you've been able to do much out there yet?'

Rebecca fumbles in the pocket of a coat hanging in the utility room, finding a packet of tobacco and rolling a cigarette. She lifts the pouch to offer Kate one, who shakes her head. 'No, not yet,' she replies, digging around for a lighter before slipping the coat on and stepping into a pair of wellies. 'Gwen let it get a bit wild. She must not have been as mobile as she once was.'

The sun is coming up now, weak light breaking out over the horizon. They step out into the garden, and the first thing Kate notices is the view. There are thick trees and hedging on either side, giving the garden a high level of privacy, but the rear is open to the ocean. The second thing she notices is the police tape across the low fence, one end flapping in the breeze. *Anyone could climb over that fence,* she thinks as they head towards it. She can see ivy creeping across the ground beyond, a few large rocks just visible, and then – nothing. A sheer drop into the sea below. She shudders at the thought of Ava falling through the air, the black water opening up to swallow her whole.

Is that what happened? Had Ava been messing about with her friends, climbing over the fence and slipping into the water below? The girls had all said they hadn't been down there, but teenage girls stick together. Were they all keeping the same secret?

'It's a lovely view,' she says to break the silence. 'Peaceful.'

'They won't find her, you know,' Rebecca says, blowing smoke into the sky. 'Not down there. It's a waste of time.'

Kate glances at her out of the corner of her eye. 'You're probably right, but nothing is a waste of time if it can help us find Ava. Everything is worth doing, if only to rule something out.'

Rebecca nods and they continue walking in silence until they reach the back fence. She grips the wood with one hand, knuckles turning white. 'I can't believe this is happening. It all feels like a bad dream, like I'm going to wake up any second.'

'We're doing everything we can,' Kate says softly, trying to remember her training. On more than one occasion, Kate has wondered whether she is the right person for the FLO role. She always imagined them as people like her mum, dressed in loose, patterned skirts and sandals, come rain or shine, with wide smiles and gentle voices. She is known to have a 'resting bitch face', according to Lauren, and her own wardrobe is somewhat sterner in comparison: black trousers and dark-coloured shirts, but, just like her mum, Kate appears to create in others the desire to confide, and it is this strength that she must use to her advantage. That, and her ability to make a good cup of tea. But she's already played that card once this morning. 'Tell me about her,' she says instead. 'Ava.'

Rebecca takes a deep breath, eyes on the horizon. 'Ava is . . . She's just amazing. I don't know anyone else like her. I've known her since she was small, this tiny person with such a huge personality.' Rebecca smiles, a faraway look coming into her eyes. 'And even huger hair. I've always loved her curls.'

Kate nods, remembering the description she'd been given of Ava. *Fourteen years old, mixed race, dark curly hair. Approximately 5 foot tall, 49kg. No distinctive marks, not known to police. Links to London and Hertfordshire.*

'And her father? Do they get on well?' she asks. Something flashes across Rebecca's face, something fierce and . . . what? But the look is gone before Kate can analyse it properly.

'Oh, yes,' Rebecca says, still staring out across the water.

'What subjects does Ava like at school?' Kate asks, changing tack. She purposely uses the present tense, remembering her first case as an FLO and her use of the past tense during a meeting with the parents of a missing child, which resulted in a mug being thrown in her direction. And she'd deserved it.

'She's taking GCSE English; she's always been a reader. But what she loves the most is art. She wants to be an artist. Ever since she was a child, that's all she's wanted to be.' Rebecca looks at Kate then, her head cocked to one side. 'Did you always want to be a police officer?'

Kate considers the question for a moment. 'Not until I was older,' she says eventually. 'When I was a teenager, I wanted to be an artist like my mum. She made ceramics in the small shed at the bottom of the garden to sell to tourists at extortionate prices. Paintings too.' She smiles. 'I was rubbish though. I'd love to see some of Ava's work. What did her mum do?'

Something flickers across Rebecca's face before she speaks. 'She was a lawyer. Well, she qualified. But she fell pregnant with Ava and then ...' She trails off, her eyes darting up to meet Kate's. 'Well, she died when Ava was still just a baby. Drunk driver.'

Kate feels the lurch the loss of a young life always gives her. It reminds her too much of her mother, and the cancer that killed her when Kate was eighteen. 'How long have you known Ava?' she asks, forcing herself to focus. 'How old was she when you met Daniel?'

'Oh, I met her when she was about two.' Rebecca's smile is back again, and Kate wonders how exhausting it must feel to be pulled between emotions in this way. 'She was a lovely child, always wanting *just one more story* at bedtime.' She gives a small shake of her head. 'She was so good, genuinely. She had her tantrums like every other child, but she was always so kind and thoughtful. Always ahead of her years. Sometimes I think I fell in love with her before I fell in love with Daniel.'

Leaving Rebecca in the utility room with a load of washing Daniel brought back with him, Kate decides to have a nose around upstairs. She knows that uniform has already searched the house to make sure Ava isn't hiding somewhere, but Kate needs to get a feel for this family, to understand them better. She admires the flooring as she climbs the stairs, the way it's been sanded to give it what Lauren would call a *shabby chic* look. At the top of the stairs, the hall opens into a U-shape with doors leading off either side, bending around the staircase to create a type of balcony that overlooks the front garden, with a little window seat covered in plump cushions. Another staircase sits to the left, leading to the second floor.

The first room is small and seems to be a dumping ground, a desk taking up most of the back wall. Boxes are stacked to the left, a few paint tins and rollers left on the floor. After pulling the door to, Kate crosses the hall and pushes open the next door. A large bed with a pink duvet cover and white bedframe dominates the room. The light fitting is one of those fluffy ones Kate has always considered a dust trap, and there's a white rug spread out on the floor at the end of the bed. It is tastefully decorated but quite untidy, which is exactly what Kate would expect from a teenage girl. A dressing table sits against the window, a vanity mirror set to one side. Cosmetics litter the surface, and Kate inches open the top drawer to find yet more bottles of nail varnish and lipsticks.

She glances up, catching sight of a collage of photos hanging above the bed, and moves further into the room, peering at the images. Ava features in almost all of them, her thick curls reaching the middle of her back, her skin clear and fresh. Some of the photos were clearly taken at school, and she notices a different uniform in some of them. They must have been taken at Ava's old school in Hertfordshire. She makes a mental note to see if the head teacher there has been contacted, whilst taking out her phone and snapping a picture of the collage. Her attention is caught by one particular photo, smaller than the others and faded, as if it has been cut out from a newspaper. A woman holding a baby on her hip, the child's fist bunched at her neck. Her mother, perhaps, not long before she died.

Ava's bedside table is loaded with a Kindle, a lamp, a tin of Vaseline, two pens, and a couple of chargers. Sliding open the top drawer, Kate notes a blister pack of pills amongst the otherwise innocent detritus of a teenager's bedside table and turns them over to read the brand name. Kate wonders if Rebecca – or Daniel – knows that Ava is on the contraceptive pill. *She's only fourteen,* Kate thinks, then mentally reprimands herself. She hears Lauren's voice telling her that *you're never too young to have safe sex,* and reminds herself that plenty of people take the pill to regulate their periods. She pictures Lauren's packet on her bedside table, wondering how old Lauren was when she started taking it to manage her own horrendous cycles. Perhaps Ava just suffers in a similar way.

After closing the drawer, Kate opens the next one, which is stuffed with exercise books. Eyes flicking back to the pens on top of the table, Kate wonders if having a physical diary is too old-fashioned. That's what social media is for these days, she supposes.

'Having a good nose around, are we?' A voice from behind her makes her jump. She spins around to find Daniel standing in the doorway, arms crossed, his feet planted hip-width apart. 'You won't find her in here,' he says.

'I'm just trying to get an idea of who Ava is,' she says carefully. She nods towards the photo collage. 'She has a lot of friends.'

Daniel's face softens a fraction. 'She does. She always makes friends, everywhere she goes. Nursery, school, dance club. Even when she was little, when we just popped out to feed the ducks or to the shops. She'd find someone to make friends with.'

'Does she enjoy school?'

'As much as any teenager, I suppose.' Daniel unfolds his arms and sighs. 'She's very bright. She always gets good grades, and she loves art.' He nods towards the open drawer behind Kate. 'Those are her sketchbooks. She fills them faster than she can pinch them from the stationery cupboard.'

Kate lets out a breath. Sketchbooks, not diaries. She should have known that these would have already been checked by uniform. Daniel moves into the room and takes out the top book, flicking it open to show her. Rough drawings fill the pages – flowers, animals, trees, houses – but they're good. Kate nods.

'She's talented,' she says as Daniel closes the book. She takes in the purple rings around his eyes, his chapped lips, and something inside her releases. 'I didn't mean to pry.'

'It's your job,' he says, sitting down heavily on Ava's bed and running a hand over his face. 'I'm just so . . . I can't believe this is happening. Ava. *My* Ava. She's never run off or anything like that. She's just a normal kid. She's happy. And moody, sometimes,' he admits, smiling ruefully. 'But that's normal, isn't it?' He sighs again, his shoulders slumping.

Taking the sketchbook from him, Kate flips it open again, pausing as she catches a glimpse of one of the drawings. It looks like a sketch of the photo pinned to the wall, the one of Ava and her mother. But a large M has been drawn on the woman's chest, the pencil having been pressed so hard the paper is almost scored through. She stares at it, a flicker of discomfort creeping over her.

'She would never leave me,' Daniel says again, more quietly this time, and his words send a shiver down Kate's spine.

6

Rebecca

Daniel went back to work the following Sunday, driving to Truro and getting on the sleeper train to London. He wouldn't be back until Friday morning, his week full of meetings and lavish dinners. My days would be full of painting and sanding, my hair covered in dust, my limbs aching. But I loved it, and it meant I could spend the evenings with Ava, just the two of us. The internet was finally hooked up and so we ate dinner on the sofa, taking it in turns to choose a film each night. The living room hadn't needed much work, just a lick of paint and some accessories to make it feel more homely. I'd gone neutral in here, painting the walls a chalky white with a hint of pink, which went well with the mid-grey sofas and light wooden floors. The boiler had been fixed and the bathrooms were both coming along, the plumbers working away as I focused on other areas.

One evening, Ava helped me put together a new coffee table to replace the one that had been broken in Hertfordshire before we moved, and afterwards she helped me choose some curtains for the patio doors.

'Green?' she exclaimed when I showed her the ones I'd been looking at. 'Do you know of any other colours, Becks?'

I gave her a look. 'Pink and green should always be seen.'

She rolled her eyes, a smile playing on her lips. 'Did you see that on Instagram?'

'Maybe.'

'Here, these are what you want.' She tapped on a square and swiped through the photos of some white voiles. 'Light and airy, and they wouldn't block the view either.'

'But you could still see in,' I said. 'From the outside.'

'So? Who's going to be looking, a whale?' She nudged me with her elbow and I smiled, trying to cover my anxiety. 'There's nothing but sea out there, Becks.'

Nothing but sea. Gwen had said something like that to me once. After that dark September day, when she ran me a bath and gave me clean clothes to change into, I'd hoped she would let me stay. I had nowhere else to go, and although I was used to summers spent outdoors, winter was fast approaching and I didn't fancy my chances against the elements. I tried to make myself useful, making Gwen cups of tea and scrubbing the bathroom until it shone. I even tried to cook, but my knowledge was limited and I burned almost every dish to begin with. I'd expected her to be angry when I melted the handle of a colander by having it too close to the hob or dropped a plate into the sink and chipped it, but she never was. She let me make mistakes, a luxury I'd never been afforded before, and she helped me learn from them.

I never really understood why she took me in. Everyone in the village knew a cantankerous old woman lived in this house, but it wasn't until I turned up on her doorstep, shivering with fear and pain, that I found out who she really was. She had been eighty-nine when she'd died, according to her solicitor, so she must have only been in her sixties when I met her, but she had always seemed old, like she'd been here since the beginning of time. She was wise, and while she didn't like children throwing eggs at her front door or knocking at all hours of the night, she wasn't really cantankerous. Funny, how we build pictures in our minds without knowing the facts.

I wonder who started the stories about a woman living alone in a house on the cliff, why they took a dark turn. Whether she knew about them. How cruel children can be when they put their minds to it.

'Becks?' Ava waved a hand in front of my face and I blinked. 'Where did you go?'

'Oh, nowhere. Sorry, I'm just tired.' I smiled at her. 'These curtains are perfect, darling. I'll order them tonight.'

We went upstairs together, Ava pausing at the top of the stairs to kiss me on the cheek. As she pushed open her bedroom door, I suddenly remembered that it was the same room Gwen had let me sleep in all those years ago when I was around Ava's age. And that Daniel and I now slept in hers.

I woke with a start, heart pounding, to a pitch-black room. Shapes crouched in the corners of the room, boxes turned to monsters in the shadows. I blinked, trying to listen for what had woken me. We had no neighbours, our private lane leading nowhere but to our house and the sea beyond, and the nearest dwelling was a caravan park and tearoom across the fields, closed for the off-season. We were alone up here. Isolated.

I switched on the bedside lamp, the bulb casting a warm glow over the room as I got out of bed and quietly opened the door. The windows were shut tight against the chill, the heating off for the night, and the house was silent. Our bedroom was on the second floor, up a half-flight of stairs from where Ava's room was. From the top of the stairs, I could see out through the large picture window, which looked over the front garden and the fields beyond. Ava's room had the view of the sea. *Nothing but sea*. At Blackwater House, it was easy to believe you were the last person on Earth, the world beyond a gaping void. *My sanctuary,* Gwen had said, and she was right.

I only hoped it would be the same for Ava, a place for her to feel safe and loved, a home for her to return to once she flew the nest. Things I'd never had, until Gwen had taken me in, and Blackwater House became my sanctuary too, right when I'd needed it most.

I was born on a hot, airless day in June, unexpected and entirely unwanted. My mother, Gemma Bray, was only sixteen when she fell pregnant, still living at home with her parents at the time, and my father had been a stranger in the pub one night, an older man who forced himself on my mother and left her with nothing but a painful memory. And me, of course. He left her with me.

She didn't realise she was pregnant until it was too late. I was born on the bathroom floor of my mother's childhood home, and I went with her when she was sent on her way the following day, wrapped up in shame.

I know all of this because she told me, more times than I can count. *Child of rape,* she called me. *Burden. Unwanted. Unloved.* Three little words. She didn't need to tell me these things, though. For as long as I could remember, her actions had made her feelings perfectly clear. I had believed – wanted to believe – that she tried her best to begin with. She'd suddenly had to take care of someone else – a tiny, helpless thing she never asked for. It must have been hard for her, young and homeless and poor, trying to keep me fed and clothed. But I never asked for it either, and any sympathy I might have had for her disappeared as the years went by.

She began to try less and less, until she abandoned me alto-gether. She started to pay the rent by selling drugs for the landlord and swiftly succumbed to addiction herself. One of my earliest memories is of my mother sprawled against the wall at the bottom of the stairs, her eyes wide and sightless, a needle hanging out of her arm. And then the people came, other waifs and strays searching for their next high and some-where to crash for a while.

I learned from an early age that crying got me nowhere. I had no safe home, no warm bed, and often no food for days on end. I took refuge in school – free school meals and a library filled with books to escape into – but the weekends and holidays always came too quick. Long, endless days spent huddled in my bedroom, rereading the few books I'd borrowed over and over again, hiding them beneath my mattress in case someone found them and they got damaged. They liked to destroy things, those men and women who frequented our house, usually anything they could get their hands on and themselves most of all, and so I learned how to be invisible, silent. A ghost.

By the time I was eight years old, summer was spent almost entirely out of the house, sleeping on the beach or hidden in the heather. I was safer out there, the blanket of stars protecting me from above, the whooshing of the waves like a lullaby. At home there was nothing but danger, and a mother who didn't care. I was rarely missed and spent days at a time out there by myself, alone but never lonely. And, once, I saved a life.

One hot evening when I was eleven, I heard a scream, high and piercing, carried on the breeze as I clambered over the rocks towards the beach. I scanned the sand below, then the sea, the green-blue water sparkling in the sun, boats drifting across the horizon. Another scream rang out, and then I saw it. Her. A girl waving her arms above her head, her head going under as the current dragged her beneath the waves.

Cars were starting to leave the car park. People still stood on the beach, rolling up their towels and taking down their windbreakers as the tide edged closer, but nobody was look-ing at her. She bobbed up again, her head barely breaking the surface before she was pulled back under. I scrambled down the rocks, taking the shortcuts across the heather only the locals knew, the danger of snakes forgotten in my panic. I had to help her. Desperation pushed me on as I jumped onto the sand and ran, kicking off my shoes as I splashed into the water.

I was a strong swimmer, even then. I probably looked about seven years old, my body too small and skinny, but I had always been good at swimming. I spent half my life in the sea, learning her ways, treating her with the respect she deserves. Never fully trusting her, though she held my life in her hands. The sea is a wild thing, deceptive and alluring. On the shore, calm, foam-tipped waves gently lap at your ankles, cooling your toes, the siren's song filling you with a sense of peace, but out there, beneath the shimmering water, lies a wild, untamed beast, a beating heart that is ever patient, ever hungry, waiting to take what it needs.

I plunged into the waves, opening my eyes beneath the water. Seaweed drifted past, tickling my legs as I swam towards the girl. I could see her pink swimsuit, her legs kicking furiously as she tried to suck in air. But she was tiring, and soon the sea would take her.

A wave engulfed us as I surfaced beside her, my mouth filling with water. The sea roared in my ears as I took her arm, and a current snatched at my legs as if to drag me under. *She is mine,* the sea hissed, but I couldn't leave her. She was tiny, even to me; she couldn't have been older than two or three. Her eyes were closed, her mouth gaping open, and her body hung limp in my arms. I tried to hold her face above the water as I fought against the current, kicking my way back to the shore. The sea tried to drag me down; I thrashed as it tugged at my legs, and the girl went under again.

No! We burst through the waves, sea foam filling my eyes, and, suddenly, I felt sand beneath my feet. I scooped her up and ran, pebbles cutting into the soles of my feet, and collapsed onto the sand. I laid her down, bending to press my ear against her chest, but my own heart was pounding in my ears. 'Help!' I screamed, the word ripping its way out of my throat, the salt from the sea burning. 'Help! Please!' Figures came running and I scrambled back, fear pushing me towards the water. The sea was a wild thing, but so were men, and I knew which I trusted the most.

I shivered as the men bent over her, their hands pressing down on her chest so hard I thought she would snap in half. I edged back towards the surf, the waves crashing around me, luring me back to its embrace. More people arrived; a woman shrieked as she fell to her knees beside the girl, her hands fluttering around her head like nervous birds. Then the girl spluttered, her eyelids flickering until they opened, and in an instant they found mine. As the adult heads began to turn towards me, I fled, scurrying up the rocks barefoot and disappearing into the sunset. The sea called to me as I climbed towards the old mine, birds shrieking above, but still I ran.

I didn't know then that Gwen had seen me that day. She had been watching from the cliffs and saw me run towards home, where I hoped to find comfort. But there was never any to be found there.

'This can be your home,' Gwen had said not long after I moved in. 'Blackwater House will always be here for you, when you need it.' And although that had been true for a few years, Gwen had always encouraged me to move away, to start a new life elsewhere. At first I'd been hurt, but I soon realised that she was right, and that she only wanted the best for me.

I'd never expected to return to Blackwater House, to Cornwall. I'd told myself that I had built a new life, that I could leave the past behind. As I stood at the window, staring out at the darkness beyond, I realised I'd always known that was a lie.

7

Rebecca

Before – October 2019

Days ticked by, and half-term was suddenly upon us. Daniel took the week off work and the weather was surprisingly warm, so we decided to do some exploring. We walked into the village for breakfast in the local café, which served a delicious gluten-free lemon and blueberry cake, before heading down towards the beach. The village is built on a hill that leads you up to Blackwater House and the tin mines, and the beach loops around the bottom, curving around the village like a protective embrace. The autumn sun shone down on us as we picked our way down the uneven path, tree roots shifting the earth beneath our feet, sticking out between the old cobblestones. At one point I tripped, knocking into Daniel and almost sent us both flying.

'Careful!' he snapped, holding on to my wrist tightly as I fought to keep my balance. Ava looked back at the noise, a worried expression on her face.

'Sorry, darling,' I said, directing my smile at her. 'You know me – I'm so clumsy.'

Ava turned around, head down in the way people do when they're staring at their phone, and no one said anything until we emerged onto a road opposite a shop.

'Why is everything closed here?' Ava asked, moving over to the window and peering inside, her hands cupped over her eyes.

'It's the off-season,' I said. 'April to October is when places like this get really busy, but in between it's usually just the locals, so businesses keep shorter hours.'

'It's weird.'

I moved to stand beside her and looked in through the window. 'I guess not many people need to hire wetsuits or paddleboards in the winter.'

'Come on,' Daniel said brusquely. 'The news said it might rain later. I don't fancy getting caught out in it.'

We continued on down the road, the beach coming into view a few moments later. It was beautiful, dazzling in a way only the ocean can be. The waves glittered in the sunshine like it was sprinkled with diamonds, and seabirds whirled over-head, twisting together in an elaborate dance. I breathed in the salty air and felt a sense of peace settle over me. Since I left all those years ago, I'd never once visited the English coast. We'd holidayed in France and Spain and even seen a few Greek islands, and as someone who had never owned a passport before, I'd loved visiting these new and exotic places, but if I had been able to choose a holiday destination, it would have been Cornwall. It would always be Cornwall.

'It's beautiful, isn't it?' I murmured to Ava, putting an arm around her shoulders.

To my surprise she nodded. 'It's so empty, peaceful. I like it.'

I smiled. 'Wait until it gets to August, and every scrap of sand is taken up by screaming kids and sunburnt dad bods.'

She laughed. 'Dad bods. You are funny.'

'What's a dad bod?' Daniel asked, and Ava and I laughed, our heads touching like friends sharing a secret. As soon as I met Ava, I knew she would be a friend for life. It was tricky at first, what with her being so young and Daniel working so much, I often fell into the role of mother, but I tried not to step into Meghan's shoes. When Ava's mother had died in a car crash, she left behind a grieving husband and a six-month-old baby, and although I knew Ava would have no memories of her mother, I never wanted her to forget her either. Which is something Sierra, Ava's grandmother, had realised early on and, I hoped, respected me for. She had been the first of Meghan's family to open her arms to me. I liked to think she saw how much I loved Ava, how I tried to give her a good life, despite everything.

Ava's aunts were a different story. Aisha had given birth to her first child around the same time Meghan had, and the loss of her sister must have hit her hard. Cass was still a teenager, a Fresher at Cardiff University when I first moved in with Daniel, so we didn't see much of her at the beginning. But it was always important to me that Ava knew her family – her whole family. Daniel had no one left on his side, and I had lost contact with my mother after I'd moved in with Gwen and she'd encouraged me to go to university up country, but Meghan had had family enough for all of us.

Aisha went on to have four children, and regularly picked Ava up for soft play or swimming or, later, shopping days with her only female cousin, Cora. She went to Sierra's every other Sunday and always came back with something – slices of cake, made gluten-free for me, or a new toy. As Ava got older and her artistic side started to make itself known, Sierra bought her sets of paints and pencils and they would sit together in her North London garden, sketching the flowers and the clouds in the sky.

I'd known she would miss them when we moved to Cornwall, but we'd invited them to visit at Christmas. I hoped the house would be ready enough by then, but even with the garage renovation completed we wouldn't have had enough room for them, so they were going to book somewhere in the village. A builder had quoted for bricking up the door and making it look more like an annex and less like a garage, and he was due to start the week after half-term. I wondered what Gwen would think, part of Blackwater House being rented out to tourists. I'd rarely heard her say a bad word about anybody, so I hoped she wouldn't mind. Although she'd been old, Gwen had really looked after the house over the years. It had been modernised where it mattered – double glazing, central heating – and most of the walls were in such good nick, we hadn't needed to replaster as we'd expected. I hoped she would be pleased with our efforts to put our own stamp on the place.

The kitchen was my next project. After our walk, Daniel went to the gym and Ava and I painted the cupboard doors, painstakingly removing them from their hinges and labelling them so they didn't get mixed up. They were in good condition, so they only needed a light sand and away we went, listening to a podcast on Cornish folklore as we worked, something Ava's English teacher recommended after she expressed an interest in the history of the area.

'The giant Bolster fell in love with a girl called Agnes on the North Cornwall coast,' the narrator said. 'He terrorised the village and was known to have a foul temper. Despite already having a wife who he mistreated, Bolster pursued Agnes tirelessly, until one day, irritated by his attention, the girl asked him to prove his love by filling a hole in the cliff with his own blood.'

'Gross,' Ava said, wrinkling her nose, and I smiled as the narrator continued.

'The giant thought this would be an easy task considering his large size, but what Agnes failed to mention was that the hole went all the way down to the sea. His blood continued to flow like a river into the ocean below, and the giant eventually died.'

'So she killed him because she didn't like him?' Ava asked, pausing the podcast and turning to me with a frown.

'Well, I think it was his ego that killed him,' I said. 'He assumed his love would be welcomed, and when it wasn't, he continued to pester her. He wouldn't take no for an answer.'

'No is a complete sentence,' she murmured. 'It's something Aunt Cass told me.'

I considered her words for a moment before nodding. 'And the absence of a no doesn't mean yes,' I added, trying to ignore the discomfort creeping through me as memories lashed at my mind. Ava pressed play and the narrator moved on to another story.

Later, after three coats of paint and a TV break, we reattached the first of the cupboard doors and stepped back to admire our work. We'd gone for an off-white to pair with the terracotta tiles, and it totally transformed the space. The utility room would have to wait for another day though. Daniel had been to the shop on his way home from the gym and picked up a whole roast chicken from the deli.

'Protein for my hard workers,' he said with a grin. It was still warm, so I made a quick coleslaw and chopped cucumber and spring onions, throwing them with some leaves into a large salad bowl. The table and chairs we'd brought from Hertfordshire were too small for this garden, but it would do for now. We ate outside, watching the sun set over the horizon, the sea calm and glistening. It reminded me of all the evenings I'd sat on the cliffs a little further along, alone and unwilling to go home.

I wondered if Gwen had ever noticed me then, with my chin resting on my knees, my coat too small for me, my boots too big. I wondered what she'd seen in me when she'd asked me to stay. She'd been lonely – that much was clear to me now – but she hadn't needed to be so kind, so welcoming. She'd treated me like her own granddaughter, feeding and clothing me, encouraging me to go back to school, to open my mind to a world bigger than this village, this county. This life. I owed her so much, and the only way I could repay her was to love Blackwater House as she had. And to make it a safe home for Ava as Gwen had done for me.

'Here we are,' Daniel said, wrapping a blanket around my shoulders after Ava went up to bed. I was already bundled up in a thick jumper and scarf, but the temperature had dropped while we sat outside, cheeks flushed from the red wine he'd bought.

'Thanks, darling.' I smiled at him as he sat back down beside me and picked up his glass. 'We were lucky with the weather today.'

'Hmm. They'd said it would rain.'

'They're often wrong. Cornish weather has a mind of its own. You'll get used to it.'

He half-turned towards me, something flickering across his face. 'I'm sure I will, Rebecca.'

I sipped my wine, turning my attention back to the sea. It was dark now, the moon hanging low in the sky, clouds gathering in the distance. Days like this would be rare now, I knew, as October came to an end. We were staring winter in the face, and I only hoped we would be strong enough to withstand it.

8

Kate

Kate leaves Blackwater House that afternoon with a heavy feeling settling over her. She's exhausted, both from the night before and the emotionally draining day, and is looking forward to a quiet evening at home complete with an early night. She picks up a takeaway for dinner and eats it on the sofa in front of the TV, rewatching old episodes of *Friends*, before running a bubble bath. She is sitting cross-legged on the bed, wrapped up in her dressing gown, when her phone rings.

'Evening,' she says, cupping the phone with her shoulder as she flips the page of her yearbook. 'How's the patient?'

Lauren laughs on the other end. 'He keeps telling me to "stop fussing", so he must be on the mend.'

'You do like to fuss,' Kate says with a smile, then remembers how frantic Lauren had become on Boxing Day as she prepared to rush up to see her father after his girlfriend called to say he'd collapsed with a hernia.

'How dare you. Next time you're in bed with a cold, you can get your own damn tea.'

'Now that's fighting talk!' Kate laughs. She hears the sound of Lauren's vape in the background. 'Still not smoking?'

'Nope. Six weeks now. Though heaven knows how I cope with you two in my life.' Lauren exhales, her voice thick with vapour. 'How are things there? Is Kiana behaving?'

'Kiana never behaves; she's a born rebel.' Kate looks through the bedroom door. 'She's currently sitting on top of the washing basket. It's her new spot.'

'Is that because it's full of clothes?'

Now it's Kate's turn to pretend to be offended. 'How dare you. I put a load of washing on yesterday morning, I'll have you know.'

'Is it still in the machine?'

'It is not.'

'Is it still in the tumble dryer?'

'It might be.'

They both laugh. Kate puts the yearbook aside, searching the box of photographs instead for Rebecca. She was a few years above Kate at school, but she remembers seeing her at parties and around the village. Age gaps didn't mean much in Cornwall, with kids of all ages thrown together on the beach or at functions, used to fending for themselves.

'So what are you up to?' Lauren asks. 'Did you have an exciting new year's?'

'It was very exciting. I went to the pub with some guys from work, had half a lager, and was tucked up in bed by eleven-thirty.' This isn't strictly true, but Kate knows Lauren will have spent most of the night looking after her dad and she doesn't want to rub it in. Besides, Kate can still feel the remnants of her hangover, despite the chow mein and the bubble bath, and she doesn't want Lauren to rub *that* in.

'You absolute wild child,' Lauren says.

'And you?'

'I went to the pub too actually, just for a couple of hours, with the girls.'

Kate pictures the group of young women Lauren had reconnected with in recent years. 'How are they?'

'All good. They said hello. Natalie came for a bit, but she had to get back.'

'For the cheel? How old is he now?'

'Nearly one.' Lauren sniggers. 'Cheel. Bleddy Cornish.'

'Bleddy emmet,' Kate fires back.

'Do emmets live in Cornwall?'

'All right, comer-in then.'

'That's a new one.'

'Used to be one of Mother's favourites.' The wave of grief Kate feels is brief yet sharp, and it sparks a memory. 'Here, I've got a case at the moment of a missing girl.'

'Shit,' Lauren says, sobering.

'Yeah, but that just reminded me that Mum used to know the family of the stepmother.'

'Small world.'

'Even smaller down here,' Kate says. 'I think her parents were alcoholics, and I'm sure Mum warned me to stay away from her, though of course I didn't listen. I've been looking through my memory box to try to . . . Ah! Found her.' She holds the photo up to her face, peering at the low-quality version of teenaged Rebecca, her eyebrows plucked too thin, eyelids coated in blue eyeshadow. She stands beside two other girls Kate barely recognises, both of them wearing leather jackets and faded jeans. The expression on Rebecca's face is serious, her lips pressed together in what looks like a grimace, while the other two smile widely, arms around one another. Kate wonders how she got this photo, and where it was taken.

'Were you friends?' Lauren asks.

'Not really. I just knew of her, you know. Saw her around. Though I went to her house once.' Kate hears a kettle boiling in the background and the sound of Lauren making tea. 'Good idea, I'm parched.' She unfolds her legs from beneath her and makes her way down to the kitchen, patting Kiana on the head as she passes. She places the photo face down on the table while she makes tea then slides onto a chair, phone still pressed to her ear. Lauren is telling her about her walk with Dash, her father's dog, and meeting a golden retriever down the park earlier today.

'She's called Lucy and she is huge!' Lauren laughs.

'What kind of a name is Lucy?'

'I thought the same, but Dad said you could call her Lucy Pup, you know? Lucy Pup. It has a ring to it.'

'It does, actually.'

'Anyway, she jumped straight up at me, and her front paws nearly rested on my chest! She's only nine months old, her owner said.'

'You are also the size of a child.'

Lauren huffs. 'Ha-ha.' She pauses, moving her mouth away from the phone as she calls, 'Yes, Dad, I'll tell her.'

'Tell me what?'

'That you need a new joke.'

'Ha-ha,' Kate mimics, smiling at their ability to make each other laugh, no matter what is going on in their lives. Kate is often stressed at work, and Lauren has her own demons to contend with, but together they can always find something to laugh about. Lauren is her life raft, her tether to the normal world outside of policing, and they steady one another, hands clasped tightly as they face the world together.

'No,' Lauren continues, 'he said he found that painting you were looking for.'

'Really?' Kate feels a rush of excitement. 'How? Where?'

'eBay, would you believe. Someone in Shropshire was selling it.'

The smile drops from Kate's face. 'Was? Did someone buy it?'

'Yeah. Him. He says Merry Christmas.'

Kate laughs, relief flooding through her. She looks up at the wall above the sofa, picturing her mother's painting hanging there. It had been a special commission for someone local, depicting the rugged Cornish cliffs and the tempestuous sea, but it had been lost when the owner died and the family, no longer living in Cornwall, had had the house cleared. And now David has found it for her and it can come home, where it belongs.

'Tell him thanks, really,' she says, her throat tight with emotion.

'You can tell him yourself,' Lauren says. 'He says he's coming down as soon as he's allowed out of bed. He thinks the sea air will rejuvenate him, like he's a Victorian lady with consumption.'

'I *can* see the resemblance,' Kate quips, and Lauren laughs. 'When are you coming back?'

'Soon. I think he's milking it, personally. Likes to be waited on hand and foot.' Kate hears David shout something in the background and Lauren makes an outraged noise. 'He says I can leave now if I want, since my tea is crap anyway. The ungrateful git.'

Kate smiles as she listens to Lauren telling her about her day. She loves the relationship Lauren has with her father, their light-hearted banter reminding her of her own child-hood. Unlike many of her peers, Kate and her mum had been friends as well as mother and daughter. They'd rarely argued and had truly enjoyed spending time together: snuggling on the sofa under a warm blanket, sharing a packet of Maltesers, or taking trips out into the countryside or to the beach, her mother barefoot, tracking her way across the sand.

She thinks of Rebecca then, and how her face had lit up when she'd spoken about Ava. She had seemed genuine, Kate thinks. You couldn't fake love like that, could you?

9

Rebecca

Before – November 2019

With Ava back at school and Daniel back at work, the house felt strangely empty. When Ava texted one lunchtime to ask if she could go to a friend's house after school, I agreed with a private stab of jealousy. I'd avoided venturing out too often into the village, afraid of who I might recognise – or who might recognise me – but I was beginning to feel quite lonely. Autumn was slowly merging into winter, but the sun was still warm and so one lunchtime I decided to visit the local pub. I already knew they served gluten-free options as I'd booked a table for Christmas lunch, and I was looking forward to the walk into the village – and not having to cook for a change.

The pub was busier than I'd expected, with a group of tradesmen eating fish and chips and a few women clustered at the bar, but I found a seat in the corner and opened Instagram on my phone. I'd started following some interiors accounts and had toyed with the idea of setting one up myself, but decided that Ava would probably never forgive me. I double-tapped a few posts as I ate – steak and ale pie with surprisingly good gluten-free pastry – before flicking over to Ava's account. Her last post had been uploaded the day before, and it showed a portrait she had sketched of her mother. I felt a swell of pride as I looked at it. Though she couldn't remember her mother, I knew she still wanted to find some way to connect with her. Ava really was a talented artist, and I knew she was destined for great things. Nothing – and nobody – was going to get in her way.

My plate empty, I glanced around the room and caught the eye of a tall woman with ice-blonde hair sitting at the bar. As the corners of her mouth curved up, I could feel my cheeks start to flush and looked away. *It's not her. It can't be.* But it could be. This was the village I grew up in, and not everyone would have moved away. In fact, barely anyone left a place like this, moving into houses down the road from where they grew up, sending their kids to the same schools they'd gone to themselves. I recognised the woman staring at me from across the room as Elouise, a girl I'd once called a friend.

Memories suddenly threatened to overwhelm me. I made for the bathroom, ducking my head as I passed the bar. Seeing Elouise – or Lou – transported me back to the last time I saw her in 1999, when I finally lost control. I hadn't thought about it in such a long time, but there was something about being here that was bringing it all back. I sat on the toilet, my fingers gripping my scalp as I remembered Elouise's eyes, wide and rimmed with red, as my fist connected with her face, my blood fizzing with adrenaline and alcohol.

I learned a lot growing up in my house. I learned how to turn an empty Pepsi bottle into a bong; how to blow smoke rings; how much vodka I could drink before throwing up. My mother taught me how to throw away your life, and Terry taught me how to blame everyone but myself. And I learned how to fight, to curl my fingers into a fist and turn almost anything into a weapon. And that night, Elouise had been on the receiving end of it.

Terry was throwing a party to 'celebrate the end of the world'. Y2K didn't faze him in the slightest; it was as if he'd been waiting his whole life for the world to implode. Maybe then it would match his own reality. I escaped to my friend

Stacey's house, a bag full of bottles and packets of tobacco swiped from the kitchen slung over my shoulder. By the time Terry discovered they were missing, the house would be full of people, every one of them a suspect, and his fifteen-year-old stepdaughter would be at the bottom of the list. Or so I hoped.

'There she is!' Stacey shrieked when she opened the door, makeup on only one eye, half her hair piled on top of her head. 'Just in time!' I followed my friend upstairs, the bag heavy on my shoulder. The vodka bottles clinked together and Stacey threw me a grin. 'I see you came prepared. What you got?' I opened the bag to show her and she squealed again. 'Won't he know?'

I shook my head as I dropped the bag onto her bed. 'He's fucked already. I think they've been at it since first thing this morning. Or since last night.'

Stacey laughed and sat in front of the full-length mirror to finish her makeup. S Club 7 blared out of the CD player; I skipped until I found Britney Spears. Stacey frowned at me and I stuck out my tongue, humming along to the music as I opened a bottle of vodka. The door opened and I looked up to see Lou and Georgie come in.

'Woo!' Georgie shrieked, jumping on the bed beside me, giggling. 'She's here! Becks is here!'

'Careful!' I laughed, holding my bottle in the air. 'This is precious.' They were the first real friends I'd made, and every encounter was a balancing act, making me feel as if I was walking a tightrope. I was slowly coming out of my shell, discovering who I was away from my childhood home. I was becoming a different person around my friends, trying to mould myself into someone who could join them, some semblance of a normal teenage girl. I saw in them a way to escape, and it was at that point that I turned away from the sanctuary of the sea and towards the bottle that had ruined my mother's life. I wanted to grow up, to become an adult as quickly as possible and escape into my own life, and this was the only way I knew how.

Her makeup finished, Stacey sat beside me, dumping her makeup bag between us, and pushed my hair out of my face. She ran a brush through it, gently teasing out the tangles, and arranged it around my shoulders. The eyeshadow brush was a blur, sweeping across my eyelids, glitter falling onto my cheeks. I rarely wore makeup and didn't have any of my own except for a tinted lip balm Stacey had given me, and it always made me feel different, like I was becoming someone new.

'Do me next, Stace,' Lou said, lighting a cigarette and blowing smoke out of the open window, Georgie beside her.

'All right, bossy.' Stacey applied a second coat of lip gloss to my lips before sitting back and assessing me. 'What are you gonna wear, Becks?'

I took a sip of vodka, relishing the fire burning down my throat, feeling the stickiness of my lips. I glanced down at my black skirt and tights, the plain white top. 'This?'

Lou laughed. 'No way! You *cannot* go out like that. We've got a reputation to uphold.'

'What's wrong with it?' I asked, perturbed and embarrassed. Fashion was not a word I was familiar with, and I relied on my friends to steer me in the right direction.

'It's boring!' Georgie giggled, smoke coming out of her nose.

'You look like a *waitress*,' Stacey declared, pointing the lip gloss wand at me. 'No, it won't do.' She went over to her wardrobe, pulling open the double doors and standing with her hands on her hips, her head moving from left to right. 'Ah!' She pulled something roughly from its hanger and threw it at me. I caught it in mid-air, tucking the vodka bottle between my thighs to hold the garment in front of me.

'I'm not wearing this!' I snorted, staring at the light blue fishnet crop top. 'It's below freezing outside!'

'We'll be inside, silly,' Georgie said, throwing her cigarette butt out of the window.

'Besides, drink enough of this,' Lou put in, pinching the bottle from between my legs and taking a gulp, 'and you won't feel the cold.'

'Oh, go on, Becks!' Stacey whined. 'It'll look *amazing* on you. I could never pull it off.' She pouted, pulling at her non-existent love handles.

'Don't be silly, Stace!' Georgie said loyally, while I frowned down at my near-skeletal legs, my knees protruding painfully through the tights. I tried to remember the last time I'd had a vegetable or a full meal, and envied those girls their concerns about eating too much food.

'Yeah, I *wish* I could wear that skirt!' Lou moaned, raising an eyebrow at Stacey's outfit hanging up on the wardrobe door. 'I'm *way* too short.'

We threw compliments at one another in a way we would never compliment ourselves. Because that's what you do, isn't it? You find fault with yourself in every way imaginable – my skin is too pale, my boobs too small, my arse too big – pinching at your belly in the mirror, hating yourself, while pouring all the love you should be giving yourself into those around you. And round and round we go, on this merry-go-round nobody wants to be on, but none of us know how to stop.

But oh, how I wanted to be one of those girls. What I wouldn't have given to swap places, just for one day. With Georgie and her protective older brothers; with Lou and her dad who did Elvis impersonations; with Stacey and her happy family, her gymnastics and Sunday roast every week. What I wouldn't have given to be someone else.

'What colour bra are you wearing?' Stacey asked me, reaching over and pulling up the back of my shirt. 'Beige! Who the hell wears beige? How old are you, Becks, ninety-four?' The others giggled and I refrained from telling them that it was the only one I owned. I never let on to the girls how bad it was at home, not really. They knew Terry was a twat and that Mum liked a drink, but they didn't know about the stale loaf of bread hidden in my wardrobe, the only food I'd eaten for two days. They didn't know about the people who practically lived in our house, sleeping wherever they fell, off their faces on drugs. They didn't know the truth. They'd never been invited to my house and they never would be, not after the last time I'd taken someone home and almost died from the shame.

'I've got a black one, hold on.' Stacey rummaged in her underwear drawer and pulled one out.

'That's not going to fit me!' I protested, holding the lacy bra up against my flat chest.

'Just stuff some socks in it,' Lou said, grabbing a pair of Stacey's socks and throwing them at me. 'No one will know!'

My cheeks burning, I stood and tore off my T-shirt, turning to the wall as I unclasped my bra and put Stacey's on. Georgie came over and tightened the straps until the bra almost fit, and I tried not to think about how my ribs would be sticking out, my skeletal body sharp and unsightly. I stuffed in the socks and pulled the fishnet top over my head before turning towards the girls.

'Well? Will I do?'

'Yes!' The three girls chorused in unison, before dissolving into fits of giggles. I caught a glimpse of myself in the mirror and barely recognised myself, with my glossy hair and heavy makeup. My glittery eyeshadow almost matched the top, and my lips were plumped and shiny. I looked like someone else, but I knew that was as far as it could ever go. I was still me inside.

'Becks?'

The voice brought me back to the present with a jolt. I jumped, splashing water on my top as I turned away from the sink towards the voice. Lou was standing in the doorway, a half-smile on her lips.

'I thought it was you. When did you get back?'

'Oh,' I said, turning off the tap and drying my hands on a paper towel. 'Recently. I moved into—'

'Blackwater House. Yeah, I know.' She tilted her head to one side. 'Do you remember me?'

Images flashed through my mind. Blood on my knuckles, a tear in the borrowed top, Lou's eyes wide with shock and pain and fear. Why had I hit her? I couldn't remember, and that seemed worse somehow. 'Y-yeah, of course. How are you?'

She smiled. 'I'm good. I married Mateo, you remember him?'

'The most exotic person in the whole county?' I joked, and she laughed, tipping her head back.

'Strange, isn't it? He was born in Bristol, for fuck's sake.'

'That's nice though. I'm happy for you.'

'We should catch up. It's been such a long time – I'm sure we could chat for hours!'

I nodded, simultaneously nervous and eager. Had that party been the last time I'd seen Lou? It must have been. I'd left afterwards, mascara streaking down my face as I ran home, towards a solace that wasn't there, had never been there. She leaned against the doorframe now, apparently at ease. Did she remember that night as I did? 'You're renovating the place, aren't you?' she continued. 'I'd love to see it.'

I nodded again. 'Just updating it, mostly. Gwen kept it in good condition.'

'Who?'

'Gwen. The woman who lived there before.'

'Oh.' Lou screwed up her face. 'I didn't realise she had a name.'

What a strange way to put it, I thought. Not *I didn't realise that was her name*, but *I didn't realise she had a name*. Of course she'd had a sodding name.

'Well, anyway,' she said, flapping a hand, 'I'd love to see it. I bet the views are stunning.'

'Oh, they are. It's so peaceful.' The door opened behind Lou and a woman gave a little squeak of surprise to find us standing there. Giggling like we were fourteen again, we moved out of the way and went back through to the bar.

'Look, here's my number,' Lou said, scribbling it down on a bit of paper and handing it to me. 'WhatsApp me; we'll arrange something.'

'Sure, that'd be nice,' I said, a truth and a lie at the same time. On one hand, it might be nice to catch up with Lou, to find out who she is now. But on the other hand, did I really want all those memories being dredged up? The memory of the girl I was.

The house felt strange when I got home. I went to call out for Ava, but it was too early for her to be back. Sighing, I kicked off my shoes and hung my jacket up before going into the kitchen. The builders were due the day after to start work on converting the garage into an annex, and I needed to finish clearing it out, but the sky had clouded over and I didn't want to get caught in the downpour. I emptied the dishwasher and made myself a cup of tea, sitting at the breakfast bar and looking out the window at the garden. The fence needed repairing on that side, the old wooden posts rotting in the damp ground. I sighed at the prospect of having to replace it all entirely.

Daniel was planning on selling the house in Hertfordshire, which would help replenish our savings after paying to renovate Blackwater House, but I worried constantly about money. I suppose it was a consequence of growing up the way I did. I'd worked throughout my time at university, in pubs and restaurants and clothes shops, trying to make sure I could cover all of my expenses year-round. Most people went home during the holidays, but after the first year, I stayed in my student accommodation, spending Christmas alone. Gwen had drilled it into me that it was a fresh start, an opportunity to make a new life for myself, and leave the past behind. And I tried. I really did try.

The heavens opened then, fat raindrops splattering against the glass. *Good for the garden.* I heard Gwen's voice and smiled. She was such a keen gardener, and even had a little vegetable patch and a few fruit trees. I hoped I could keep it all going, but I'd never been very good at keeping things alive. But maybe things would be different here. Maybe we really could be happy in Blackwater House, and make this place our home.

A bang startled me out of my reverie and I turned towards the back door. A woman stood in the doorway, her raincoat dripping onto the wooden floor. I gasped as she smiled at me and the mug fell from my grasp, smashing against the tiles.

'Hey, Becks,' my sister said. 'It's been a long time.'

10

Rebecca

'Ashleigh.' I stared at her as her eyes swept around the room before she settled her gaze on me.

'Nice place,' she remarked, her eyes glittering. 'When did you move back?'

'Why are you here?' I demanded, ignoring her question. 'How did you know I was here?'

'You know what this place is like,' she said with a chuckle. 'News travels. And when you didn't show your face, I thought I'd better come to you.' Her eyes darkened and I suddenly remembered the last time I saw her, the fire in her eyes when I'd screamed at her to leave me alone. I'd tried not to think about my sister since I left her behind in Cornwall to build a new one. Out of sight, and almost out of mind.

She looked so different now. Her dirty blonde hair was long and wavy, darkened from the rain, and she was taller than me. Her skin was pale, cheeks and nose reddened from the cold, and her eyes glittered like the ocean beneath the setting sun. She rubbed her hands together and grinned at me, and suddenly she was that little girl again, the child I left behind. ''Tis bleddy freezing in here,' she said. 'Don't you have any heating?'

I hadn't realised how the house had grown cold around me. I unlocked my phone and opened the app to turn up the heating, mercifully fixed by the plumber, before folding my arms across my chest and staring at her. Seeing her again was like seeing a ghost, and I wasn't ready for it. I shook myself again. I couldn't let myself go back there. I couldn't let myself remember. 'How did you get in?' I demanded, aware of how I sounded, unable to change it.

She cocked her head, staring at me. 'I'm here to see you,' she said, and I felt a shiver as my eyes locked with hers. Then she smiled again and the moment was broken. 'And the door was open. I know this is Cornwall, Becks, but you really should be more careful.'

'My name is Rebecca.' My words were like a whip but she didn't react. She was still staring at me, a strand of hair falling in front of her face. When she spoke, it sounded as if her voice was coming from inside my own head.

'Mum's dead.'

The words hit me like a wave of cold water. 'Dead?' I repeated.

'Dead. She died a while ago, actually, but I didn't know where you were. You'd disappeared.' She opened her fingers to imitate a puff of smoke, her lips curving into a slight smile. 'She didn't leave you anything. She didn't leave anything full stop, except for some debts with some of the more delightful people around here.' She rolled her eyes, and I caught a glimpse of the young woman my sister had become. She must be eighteen by now, I realised, nearly nineteen. Almost two decades of living in the same house as our mother, the woman who barely deserved the name. Two decades of enduring hardship and poverty. Just like I had.

I felt Ashleigh's revelation settle on my shoulders. *Mum's dead.* Two words, just two little words, and yet I felt as if all the air had left my body. 'How?' I asked, trying to read Ashleigh's face, but she wasn't giving anything away.

'I'd like to tell you it was cancer, or even a heart attack, something natural, you know, but . . . well . . .' I held my breath as she paused, clasping her hands between her knees. 'She was attacked, probably by someone she owed money to. They slit her throat.' I winced, trying and failing not to picture it.

'And Terry?'

Ashleigh frowned. 'He died years ago. Now that *was* a heart attack. I found him in the bathroom, trousers round his ankles.' She shook her head. 'I think I was nine or ten.'

Guilt flowed through me as I pictured Ashleigh pushing open the door, finding Terry's face pressed against the filthy tiles, his eyes wide open. 'I'm sorry,' I said quietly, and she smiled.

'Don't be. That was the best day of my life.' Nausea rose and I took a deep breath, slow and controlled. 'Nasty way to go,' she continued. 'But I can't say I mourned him much.' I stared at her and she gave me a look, as if my thoughts were written all over my face. 'You escaped a long time ago, sis. You have no idea what it's been like.'

I couldn't argue with her. I'd spent years blocking out the worst of my childhood, and from the age of fifteen I was here, in Blackwater House. By eighteen I was gone, up to Hertfordshire for university, and I stayed up country, leaving everything behind. Including Ashleigh.

She moved towards me, reaching out to put a hand on my shoulder. 'Sorry. It must be a shock.'

'Where is she buried?' I asked.

'Buried?' She sounded surprised. 'She's in the sea, maid. There wasn't any money for a funeral or the like. Once the police released her body, they took her straight off to be cremated. I tipped her out down Chapel Porth.'

Tipped her out? I stared at her, my mind whirring, trying to process her words. Terry and Mum, both dead. Why had Mum never told me about Terry? I could have come back, helped her with Ashleigh. Helped her get clean. She'd had a decade to get her life sorted, if not for me then for Ashleigh, the youngest child who still needed a mother. But she hadn't. Even then, she'd chosen booze and drugs over her children.

Then again, I reminded myself, she hadn't known where to find me. Not even Gwen knew about Daniel and Ava. We'd kept in touch by letter when I first moved away, but I changed my student accommodation every year and we lost touch by the time I graduated. I'd disappeared, as Ashleigh had said.

She cleared her throat, wrenching me from my thoughts. 'Better go. See you around, sis.' And before I could speak, she was gone, disappearing out the back door and into the night. I got up to close it behind her, making sure I heard the lock click before moving back to stand at the window. I stared out at the rain, wondering what kind of person my sister had become, and whether I wanted her back in my life.

I I

Kate

Now – 2nd January 2020

The next morning, Kate parks on the road outside Blackwater House. PC Smith is in the passenger seat, a half-eaten McMuffin balanced on his knee. 'You'd better not leave that wrapper in my car,' Kate says, glaring at him.

PC Smith grins, picking up the rest of the muffin and taking a bite. 'You're just grumpy because you didn't get one.'

Kate makes a face as the rest of the muffin disappears into PC Smith's mouth, ignoring the rumble in her belly. 'Good job you're always on that bicycle of yours, else your poor diet would show.' She nods towards the fold-up bike resting on the back seat. 'How's the baby?'

'He never sleeps. Ever. I'd be amazed if I wasn't so bleddy exhausted.' He pops the last morsel into his mouth and wipes his hands on a napkin. 'There, the offending item is gone.'

Kate shakes her head, a smile on her lips. 'Here, have a chewing gum. You can't go in stinking of sausages.'

'What are you thinking?' he asks as he pops the gum into his mouth. 'Did she fall over the edge?'

'I don't think so. The coastguard didn't find anything, and the girls are all saying the same thing: they were in the annex, and Ava went into the house.'

'Teenage girls though. They could be covering for her. Maybe she went to meet a boy or something.'

Kate sighs. They're still waiting for the data on Ava's phone to come through, but nobody has mentioned a boyfriend. It doesn't feel right. Kate's gut is telling her something, to keep looking closer to home. 'I don't trust the father,' she says after a moment. 'Especially not after what Tremayne told us yesterday.'

PC Smith grins. 'I've been looking forward to making him squirm all morning.'

They cross the driveway, stones crunching beneath their boots. PC Smith leans his bike against the wall and raises a fist, but before he can knock, Daniel flings open the door, dressed in a pair of jogging bottoms, his hair damp. 'Is there news?'

Kate glances at PC Smith before responding. 'No, I'm afraid not. Can we come in? PC Smith here has some more questions.'

Daniel opens the door wide, gesturing for them to go into the living room where Rebecca sits, her hands twisting in her lap. She looks up and goes to rise, but Kate waves for her to stay seated. PC Smith takes the armchair and Kate perches on the footstool beside him, suddenly feeling as if she is acting as a barrier between them.

'More questions? What on earth could there be left to ask?' Daniel demands, sitting down next to Rebecca.

Kate looks at him, taking in his appearance again. He seems disgruntled rather than distressed, more like an overzealous neighbour complaining about an over-pruned hedge, not the father of a missing girl. *It could just be his way of coping with the stress,* she reminds herself. *I seek to understand the thoughts and concerns of others even when they are unable to express themselves clearly.*

PC Smith clears his throat. 'Mr Everley, I understand you were staying at a hotel in London on the night of the thirty-first of December?'

'That's right. It was a hotel in Kensington. I've told you this.'

'And why were you there?'

Daniel blows out a breath. 'For a New Year's Eve party. A client's party – I had to be there.'

'And did you stay at that hotel?'

'Yes.'

'What time did you go to bed?'

'Late. After two, I think.'

'Did anyone see you go to bed?' Smith asks. Kate can almost hear the additional unspoken words – *did anyone go with you?* – and by the way Daniel's eyes narrow, she can tell that he hears them too.

'We all went to bed *separately*,' he says evenly. 'Everyone left the party at about the same time, I think.'

'So how do you explain leaving the hotel much earlier that night?' PC Smith asks, and Kate watches as the words hit Daniel like a blow.

'W-what?' he stammers, seeming unsure for the first time.

'There was a room booked under your name,' PC Smith continues, 'but CCTV shows you leaving at quarter to ten. Where did you go?'

'I . . . I went home.'

Kate turns her attention to Rebecca, who is staring at her partner with a look of alarm. Her mouth opens as if to speak but she remains silent.

'Home?' PC Smith echoes.

'To my house in Stanstead Abbotts.'

'And what time did you arrive there?'

'I'm not sure. I didn't . . . I didn't go straight home. I went somewhere else first.' Kate waits, watching as Daniel appears to gather himself, straightening his spine and controlling his features. 'I went to the crematorium. To visit someone.'

'Meghan,' Rebecca breathes.

'Meghan?' Kate repeats. 'Ava's mum?'

Daniel nods. 'She . . . She died on New Year's Eve. I try to visit her every year. She has a plaque there, at the crematorium.'

Rebecca is staring into the distance, a faraway look on her face, but before Kate can ask, PC Smith begins to speak.

'So when did you leave the crematorium?'

'It's hard to say. I heard fireworks going off in the distance, so possibly around midnight. It's only about ten minutes away from home.'

Home. Kate wonders why he keeps calling it that, as if he hasn't moved down to Cornwall with the rest of his family. Did he not want to come? Is that why he's rarely here?

'What do you plan to do with the house up there?' she asks as PC Smith scribbles down some notes.

'Why?' Daniel demands. 'What is the relevance of that? It's my house.'

Like Blackwater House is Rebecca's, Kate thinks. This is not a couple who shares everything, she realises. 'Why did you lie about spending the night at the hotel?' she asks.

Daniel glances at Rebecca before responding. 'I didn't think it was relevant. And . . . Ava and I usually go together, on New Year's Eve. It's something of a tradition, I suppose.'

Rebecca's head snaps back towards him. 'Do you?' Their eyes meet and a silent communication seems to pass between them, something Kate can't interpret.

'Did anyone see you at the crematorium?' PC Smith asks. Daniel shakes his head. 'Did you go anywhere else, anywhere you might have seen someone else? A petrol station?'

'No. I left the hotel, drove to the crematorium, then went home to bed. There might be CCTV at the crematorium, but I didn't see any.'

'We'll check,' Kate says. 'Can you give us the address?' PC Smith writes down the address Daniel reels off.

'But why does it matter? You surely can't suspect *me* of—'

'Nobody is accusing you of anything,' Kate says quickly, noting the flash of anger in Daniel's eyes. *He's definitely hiding something. But what?* 'We just need a full account of everyone's whereabouts that night.'

'Did Sierra Bird meet you at the crematorium?' PC Smith asks.

'No,' Daniel says shortly. 'She didn't.'

'So why did she call you just after midnight that night?'

'I don't know. I didn't pick up.'

He's lying, Kate thinks, remembering the call log pulled from his phone. *But why?*

His eyes narrow, and Kate can see that his patience is wearing thin. 'Again, I don't understand the relevance of this.'

'Everything is relevant, Mr Everley. We're trying to establish a timeline.'

'But not *my* timeline. Ava's, yes, but not mine.' He looks between the two officers. 'Surely you don't suspect that I had anything to do with what happened to Ava?' He gives a bark of laughter, which makes Rebecca flinch. 'I was nowhere near here, or Ava. How could I have taken her?'

'So you believe she was taken?' PC Smith says.

'Oh, for fuck's sake!' Daniel explodes, getting to his feet. Rebecca cringes back but Kate mirrors him, and for a moment Daniel stares at her as if he is sizing her up. *I don't trust you,* she thinks. Could he have made it down to Cornwall in that time? With clear roads and no stops, maybe. There's something lurking beneath the surface, a shadow barely concealed behind his eyes, and she waits, muscles tensed, for his next move. Then he strides out of the room, and Kate feels herself deflate.

'I'm sorry,' Rebecca whispers, her eyes wide and brimming with tears. She takes a deep breath, appearing to try to compose herself. 'He's just . . . We're very upset, as you can imagine.'

'I know,' Kate says, surprised by her urge to reassure her. 'Have you tried calling Ava's phone again?'

Rebecca nods. 'It's still switched off. Would you know if . . . ?'

'If it's switched on, we'll know about it,' Kate tells her.

Tucking his notebook away, PC Smith nods to Kate. 'All right, thank you for your time,' he says, giving Rebecca a brief smile.

Kate walks him to the door. 'Where are you off to now?'

'Tremayne wants me with her when she speaks to one of the girls from the sleepover. You know what she's like with children.' He gives a wry smile.

'Or people in general,' Kate adds. 'Is she picking you up?'

'It's only in the next village – I'll cycle over.' He unfolds the bike with one fluid movement.

'Impressive.'

'You should see my Lego building skills.'

Kate rolls her eyes as he mounts the bike and cycles down the drive. When she returns to the living room, she notes that Rebecca's eyes are fixed on the front windows.

'It's so lovely in here,' Kate says as she looks around the room, noting how clean and tidy it is. Even the Christmas tree looks as if it's been professionally dressed, with its perfectly placed baubles and twinkling lights. Rebecca catches her eye and smiles.

'It's totally different, isn't it? To my mum's house.' Rebecca gives a shake of her head. 'Do you remember it? I think you came over once.'

'Weren't we all going to the beach or something?' Kate remembers splitting off from the large group of teenagers to accompany Rebecca back to her house. But why had she gone in? The memory hits her with a sudden force and she feels her cheeks heat up. She had been twelve, that first year of secondary school when she'd still felt like a child but her body was starting to change into something she hadn't understood. Becks had noticed the blood first, had pulled Kate's towel from her bag and wrapped it around her waist to cover the stain. Kate remembers feeling her cheeks redden, the idea of having to walk the entire length of the village back to her house to get changed suddenly feeling insurmountable.

'My house is round the corner,' Becks whispered, telling the others that they'd catch up. 'Let's find you something else to wear.'

Kate recalls the overgrown front garden full of rubbish, the smashed window, the peeling paint on the front door. It had been quiet inside, the hallway dark and unwelcoming. She'd followed Rebecca up the stairs to her bedroom, the door locked behind them before Becks opened her wardrobe and dug through her clothes to find something for Kate to wear. She pulled out a pair of faded shorts with a small hole in the waistband and held them out, her expression unreadable.

'Do you have a towel?' Becks asked, and Kate had looked down at the towel wrapped around her waist before realising what she meant. She nodded. 'Good. Do you want to get changed in here or in the bathroom?'

'In here is fine,' Kate said. 'I don't ... My mum never showed me.'

She looks at Rebecca now, who sits with her hands clasped around her knees, her head tilted forwards, and tries to reconcile her with the Becks Bray from back then. She remembers her patiently showing her how to stick the sanitary towel into her underwear. She'd turned her back while Kate got changed into the shorts, and then they had left, creeping back out of the house and down towards the beach.

'I never returned them,' she murmurs, and Rebecca looks up.

'What?'

Kate thinks of the girl Rebecca was, who'd had so little but hadn't hesitated to offer help to someone in need. And Kate had never bothered to return those shorts, had never been able to face going back to that house again. Despite the shared intimacy, or perhaps because of it, Kate had distanced herself from Rebecca, and never repaid her kindness. 'Nothing,' she says, suddenly ashamed of herself.

'God, that house was a shithole,' Rebecca says, blowing out a breath. 'So different to this place.'

'What was it like living in Blackwater House? Before, I mean. With Gwen.'

'Oh, it was actually quite nice. Gwen was kind and it was just so ... peaceful. After growing up in that house ...' She shakes her head. 'How's your mum? I swear I saw a painting of hers in a shop window the other day. You know the little art shop?'

Kate smiles, thinking of the painting Lauren will be bringing home with her. 'Oh, yeah, it probably was one of hers.' She clears her throat. 'But she, erm, she died. When I was eighteen.'

'Oh, no. I'm sorry. How did she die?'

'Cancer.' The loss of her mother is still too hard, over a decade later, and she doesn't want to talk about it, not now, but she can feel herself being drawn in. *You're on a job,* she reminds herself, surprised at how easily she can slip back into her teenage self, looking up to Becks Bray. Although she knows she was a child, she wishes she'd done more at the time to help her. She's surprised at how much she wants to go back to those early years, to find out what happened to Rebecca, and to stop it.

*

Kate yawns as she unlocks the front door, shrugging off her jacket and hanging it on a hook in the hall before slipping off her boots and walking through to the kitchen. Lauren is standing at the sink, rinsing a saucepan. She turns at the sound of Kate's footsteps and smiles.

'There she is,' she says, wiping her hands on a tea towel. 'And just in time for dinner. For once!'

Kate smiles back, reaching out and pulling Lauren close. 'You're back,' she whispers into her hair. Although she has only been gone a week, Kate has missed her. Lauren pulls away and grins at her.

'Captain Obvious.'

Kate tugs on one of Lauren's curls, recently cut to sit above her shoulders. The new look suits her. 'What are we having? I'm starving.'

Lauren rolls her eyes. 'You're always starving.' She opens the oven, moving her head away from the burst of hot air before it can steam up her glasses. 'It's chicken and leek pie. With mash.' She nods towards the hob. 'You can start mashing.'

Kate rolls up her sleeves and joins Lauren at the hob, rummaging around in the cutlery drawer for a fork. 'We really must get a masher,' she says, frowning as she fights the lumpy potato.

Lauren laughs. 'You say that every time, and yet—' she holds her hands in the air '—we still do not have a masher.'

Kate sticks out her tongue, then speaks to the smart device sitting on the console table. 'Add potato masher to my shopping basket.'

'I just added stainless steel potato masher, black handle, to your Amazon basket,' the Echo replies. Lauren shakes her head, smiling.

'What?' Kate protests, turning back to the hob. 'You're

the one who loves all this "smart" technology.' She remembers the video doorbell on the front door of Blackwater House and wonders if the lab has managed to pull any footage yet.

'So how was your day?' Lauren asks, leaning against the counter. She takes a pull on her vape and Kate frowns.

'Over the food, really?'

'All right, grumpy,' Lauren says good-naturedly, taking three steps to her left and opening the window. 'Happy now?' She blows the vapour out of the window. 'Anyway, you can talk. You're the one who lets Kiana walk all over the kitchen counter.'

As if on cue, the tortoiseshell cat pads down the stairs and into the kitchen. She meows once, then leaps onto the table and begins cleaning her paw.

Kate starts mashing the potato with a fork, her thoughts full of Daniel and his lies. *What else is he hiding?* The pan almost tips over and she swears under her breath, suddenly noticing how hard she had been gripping the fork.

'Steady on, what did that potato ever do to you?' Lauren says with a laugh, but when Kate looks up, she sees she is frowning.

'Oh. I'm just a bit . . . distracted, I guess.'

'How old is the missing girl again?' Lauren asks, as if reading Kate's mind.

'Fourteen. They moved here a few months ago. Rebecca used to live here, then she went up country for uni.'

Lauren shuts the window and moves closer to inspect the mash. 'Where did she go?'

Kate pauses, cocking her head. 'Hertfordshire, actually. She went to Hertfordshire University. Where is that? Is it near your dad's?'

'Hatfield. It's not far. What did she study?'

'Psychology. Apparently she's a ghost-writer now, works from home.'

Lauren lets out a laugh. 'Okay, this is getting spooky now. It's like we switched places.'

Kate pauses, the block of cheese held against the grater. Although Lauren has a day job in HR, she has recently started writing a novel, following in her dad's footsteps. 'Yeah. It is a bit weird, now you mention it. I wonder why she went all that way for university.'

'Why did I go all the way from Hitchin to Plymouth?' Lauren shrugs, nabbing a piece of cheese from the counter and popping it into her mouth. 'To escape.'

12

Rebecca

Before – November 2019

I threw myself into the renovation. I'd cleared my work sched-
ule until February, and I intended to get the annex up and
running before then so we could advertise to tourists for the
peak season. The builders were efficient, creating a new front
door and cutting out spaces for windows, then levelling out
the floor and plastering the walls before erecting a partition to
block off the bathroom. I'd taken their advice on replacing the
garage door with bifold ones too, which would look out over
the sea. Although it had been quite a large double garage, we'd
had to get creative with the space, so we ended up with one
bedroom on the mezzanine, one bathroom and an open-plan
kitchen and living space, but it would be enough, and the
location alone would attract visitors. I intended to fence off
some of the surrounding grass and lay a patio outside the
bifold doors to create a private garden space for guests, which
I started on while the kitchen and bathroom were being
installed. The weather grew colder but stayed dry for the most
part, so I ordered sand and slabs and got to work. It kept me
busy, and my mind off the past. Seeing Ashleigh again had
brought up so many memories, and I couldn't help wondering when she was going to appear next.

The renovation reminded me of when I'd moved into my
own flat after graduating. It was rented of course, but the
landlord decided to redecorate before my tenancy began and

I persuaded him to let me do it. I'd never done much decorating before, but how hard would it be to paint a few walls and change some light fittings? He'd knocked a bit off my first two months' rent, which just about covered what I'd spent on paint and supplies, but it was worth it as a way to fulfil my mantra: *make yourself useful.* And I'd enjoyed it. It was the first time I'd ever had my own proper space, my own home, where I didn't have to worry about cross-contamination or strange men in the bathroom. I'd wanted to make it special, my very own sanctuary, and I felt the same about Blackwater House. The holiday let was a way of making it pay for itself, and give me what I craved the most: security.

Daniel was impressed by the progress when he returned home one November weekend. Despite his best intentions, he didn't always make it back on Fridays. But I'd always known he was passionate about his business and besides, there was very little to bring him back to Cornwall in the dead of winter – except for us, of course. We would have more time together come the spring, I told myself as I watched his car bump down the track. When life settled into a more regular rhythm.

'It looks amazing,' he said, his voice echoing slightly in the empty room of the annex. The kitchen units had been installed, though the oven still had its stickers on and the sink hadn't yet been hooked up. 'It must be nearly ready?'

'The plumber is coming back on Monday to finish up,' I told him, 'then the electrician will do his second fix.' I was getting used to the lingo and liked to show off, according to Ava. 'Then it's just the flooring before we can decorate and fill it with furniture.'

I paused at the suggestion of more money being spent – like me, Daniel had always been conscious of his spending – but he only grinned. 'I can't wait to see it,' he said, pulling me to him, and I sighed. I'd missed him, I realised with some surprise. Although he often worked late and came home after I'd gone to bed, we'd seen much more of each other when we lived in Hertfordshire. I hoped we weren't losing any of our closeness, or, at least, we would get it back when the renovations were finished.

'Ava's going to choose the paint tomorrow,' I said. 'Since she'll be using it when guests aren't staying. We're going to head into Truro. Do you want to come?'

Something flickered across his face and I tensed in his arms. 'I'd quite like to relax, actually.'

'Oh, yes, of course. Of course you would. We'll go, and we'll bring back something fun for dinner.' My words rushed out, tumbling over one another in my haste to placate him. I was so thoughtless; he'd been working hard all week, and then spent half the day on a train. Of course he wanted to relax.

'Something fun?' he said, and I looked up to see his eyes sparkling with humour. 'I'll hold you to that.'

'Poppy's invited me for a sleepover,' Ava said after dinner that night.

'Oh?' I said, taking a sip of wine. I tried to limit my alcohol intake during the week, since Daniel loved a drink and I had a hard time saying no whenever he poured me a glass. 'When?'

'Next Friday. Can I go?' I raised an eyebrow at her and she cupped her chin in her hands, batting her eyelashes at me. 'Please?'

I smiled, looking at Daniel. 'What do you think, darling?'

'Hmm?' He looked up from his phone, and I realised with a pang that he hadn't been listening.

'Ava's new friend Poppy has asked her to stay over next Friday.' I turned back to Ava. 'Is she the one who does ballet?'

Ava nodded. 'And tap. She's very into fitness. You'd like her, Dad.'

Daniel put his phone down and smiled at his daughter. 'Where does she live?'

'Truro,' Ava said, getting up and moving around the table to pick up our plates. She always loaded the dishwasher when her father was home, but during the week I tended to do it myself. She had enough to do, with homework and her art. 'Her mum would pick us up from school and then bring me home the next day.' She gave me a look before going into the kitchen, and I realised Daniel had picked up his phone again.

'It sounds like a good idea,' I said to him. 'For Ava to make some new friends.'

'She wouldn't have had to make new friends if we hadn't moved,' he said without looking up. I held my breath, waiting for him to speak again. When he did, his eyes met mine and I tried to smile. 'I won't be here anyway, so it's fine by me.'

I held the smile on my lips, feeling like I'd been frozen in place. 'Great,' I said brightly.

'Great? That I won't be here?'

'Of course not, darling. I only meant—' His hand darted out and grabbed my wrist, fingers tightening around it. He twisted my arm towards him, the pain making me gasp, and opened his mouth as if to speak, but then his eyes fell on Ava in the doorway and he dropped me as if I had burst into flames.

'You can go,' he said, grinning at her. 'But no drinking, and no boys, okay?'

'Okay,' Ava said, her eyes darting between us before her mask settled in place. 'Thanks, Dad.' She bent down to peck him on the cheek, her eyes fixed on me. I gave a small shake of my head. 'I'm going to do my homework now.'

'Okay, sweetie,' I said, forcing myself to smile. 'I'll bring cake up later.'

'Cake?' Daniel exclaimed, reaching out and poking a finger into Ava's tummy. 'I don't think so. Maybe you should join Poppy in her dance classes.'

Hurt flashed across her face before she turned away, her footsteps loud but not quite stomping as she went upstairs. She knew better than that. We both did.

13

Rebecca

Before – November 2019

I didn't see Ashleigh again until the day of Ava's sleepover, and I had to admit that I was relieved she hadn't appeared while Daniel was home. It was Friday, Daniel was staying in London, and I knew I had a blissful weekend ahead of me. The air was crisp but the sun was out and I was warm from a morning of garden work, so I'd ordered a pizza for lunch and sat in the garden, admiring my handiwork. I'd put together the sleepers and carved out a larger area for growing fruit and vegetables on the west side of the garden, and I couldn't wait to start planting in the spring.

The plumber had been back to finish in the annex, so we now had light and heat too. Ava and I were going to start painting after her sleepover. She'd chosen a beautiful light blue with green undertones for the open-plan living space, and a bold cobalt for the bedroom ceiling, which could be seen from the ground floor.

'It'll be like they're underwater,' she'd said with a confident grin. I trusted her judgement. As much as I loved decorating and seemed to have an eye for colours, Ava was the artist in the family. The annex, which I'd said she could come up with a name for, was her space to be creative. 'The Hideaway,' she'd announced after some consideration. 'Let's call it The Hideaway.' She was going to make some custom signs for the gate and over the door to the annex using leftover wood and vinyl stickers, something she'd seen on YouTube and wanted to try. I ordered the sealant she'd requested on my phone, then pulled the blanket tighter around my shoulders and took a sip of wine, looking out across the ocean. I would never tire of this view.

I remembered sitting here with Gwen, mugs of hot chocolate cupped between our fingers, listening to the crash of the waves below. It was where I had told her everything, piece by piece, stitching together the story of Rebecca Bray and how she had ended up on the doorstep of Blackwater House, in need of shelter.

'Tell me,' she'd say, and I would speak, the words flowing from me like a river, gushing, desperate to be released. I told her about my mum and the drugs, Terry and the people who stayed at the house, the empty cupboards and filthy rooms. I told her about that party in 1999, when I'd punched Lou then ran away, ran towards more danger. Towards the event that would change my life forever.

'Hi, Becks.' I turned, inhaling sharply as Ashleigh materialised out of the shadows. The evening was closing in, the skies darkening earlier and earlier as winter took hold. She was pushing a bike along beside her, which she rested against a tree before making her way over and sitting down beside me. She glanced at the pizza box and grinned. 'Got any spare?'

'It's gluten-free,' I said as she lifted the lid. 'But then, it *is* hereditary.'

'What is?'

'Coeliac disease.'

'Well, Mum drank enough beer to float that there ship,' Ashleigh said, nodding towards a passing vessel on the horizon. 'So I reckon I'm safe.' She picked up a slice and bit into it, made a face. ''Tis fine.'

'"Tis free,' I said, mimicking her accent. She grinned and took another bite. 'What are you doing here?'

'Charming,' she said with a snort, finishing the slice and dusting crumbs from her fingers. 'I just came to see how you are. Catch up, y'know. Hang out.'

'Hang out,' I echoed, raising an eyebrow.

'Yeah. It's been years, sis.'

For good reason, I thought but didn't say. This was the reason I'd stayed away. Cornwall held too many memories for me, too much pain. But Gwen had wanted me to return. Why had she left Blackwater House to me? Was there something I didn't know, something she wanted me to do? Or maybe she'd thought I would be ready to come back, that the years away had dulled the pain and I could start again. I glanced at Ashleigh and knew I could never escape my past entirely. She was a painful reminder of where I had come from, of what had happened to me. But she wasn't to blame for any of it, I reminded myself. She was so young, still just a child when I left. She wasn't responsible for our childhood, for our mother. She didn't deserve any of it. Just like I didn't.

'Have another.' I pushed the pizza box towards her. She took a slice tentatively, as if I was going to snatch it away at the last second, and I felt a pang as I remembered that exact feeling. That everything was temporary, every reprieve transient. Every meal I'd had at a friend's house, every tenner I earned from cleaning a neighbour's car, every quiet evening. It could all be snatched away at a moment's notice with the sound of the front door slamming and a voice in the hallway. Every time I caught Mum rifling through my coat pockets, searching for money or cigarettes. Every time I had to go home from somewhere else, that feeling of contentment slipping with every step.

'Thanks,' she said when she'd finished eating. 'Not sure I'd order it myself, mind. It definitely tastes different.'

'You get used to it,' I said with a smile.

She looked up at the house behind us. 'How are you getting on here? Was there much to do?' I followed her gaze, surprised by her questions, but then I supposed she'd never had a real home of her own, somewhere to be proud of. I hoped she would eventually find it, as I had.

'Not as much as there could have been. Gwen kept it ticking over, for the most part. A lot of the work was cosmetic. It was a blank canvas really, though the bathrooms were quite outdated.'

'Bathrooms, plural? Nice.' She nodded towards the annex. 'And that? Didn't it used to be a garage?'

I nodded. 'We're going to rent it out during the peak season. Tourists.' I caught the look she gave me and smiled again. 'Emmets.'

Ashleigh shook her head in mock reproach. 'I wondered if it was for Ava. A studio or something, for her art.'

I looked at her sharply. 'How did you know she was an artist?'

'You must've said.' She stood up, brushing down the seat of her jeans. 'Give me a tour then. I want to see where the emmets will be staying.'

She started walking towards the annex, so I had no choice but to follow. After unlocking the door, I went in and switched on the lights. I hadn't been in there in the dark since the electrician had been, and as the lights flicked on I realised the bifold doors turned into mirrors, obscuring the garden and sea beyond. I would have to get curtains for in here too.

'We're going to paint in here this weekend,' I said as Ashleigh went into the kitchen, trailing her fingertips across the counters. 'A sofa will go along that back wall there, a TV on the wall opposite, and I need to get some stools for the breakfast bar.'

'Nice. Is the bedroom up there?' Ashleigh pointed towards the mezzanine above our heads. I nodded and she headed for the stairs, poking her head into the bathroom on the way. It was small with no space for a bath, but we'd managed to fit a shower enclosure along one wall. It would do. 'It's so big,' she said as we emerged on the first floor. 'Bigger than it looks from down there.' She leaned over the railing, her hair falling forwards, and I felt my heart lurch. We'd met all the necessary building regulations, making sure the railing was high enough to prevent people from climbing or falling over it, but still I wanted to reach out and drag her back. I closed my eyes, fighting the image trying to play inside my head: Ashleigh falling, the ground below transforming into sea, waves parting to swallow her whole.

'Becks?' I opened my eyes to find her right in front of me, her forehead creased as she stared at me. 'Are you okay?'

'Fine. I'm fine. Let's go back down.' Our footsteps echoed on the wooden stairs as we descended. I switched off the lights as we went, ushering Ashleigh back out into the night.

'Where's Daniel?' she asked as I locked the annex door behind us.

'Hmm? Oh, he's in London. At work.'

'He still works up there even though you live here now?'

'He has his own business. He tends to come back on Fridays and leaves again on Sundays.' She gave me a look and I sighed. 'Not *every* Friday. He has a . . . thing, tonight. A client dinner. He'll be back next week.' We started walking back through the garden, the solar lights flicking on as we passed. Daniel was big on security: he'd had a video doorbell installed on the front door and a security camera overlooking the back garden.

I shuddered, suddenly wondering if he was watching us now as we made our way across the grass. Would he ask about Ashleigh? What would I tell him? He knew very little about my childhood, only that I'd grown up here and moved away for university. I'd told him both my parents were dead and I had no other family, which is why Gwen took me in when I was fifteen. I was glad I'd been honest about that, at least. It meant he hadn't looked too closely when Blackwater House had been left to me.

'Is Ava here?' Ashleigh asked, cutting into my thoughts. 'I'd love to meet her.'

I glanced at her in surprise, suddenly realising that she and Ava were closer in age than she and I were. How strange, that Ashleigh had been born just four or five years before Ava, though in very different circumstances. I thought of Ashleigh's tiny fingers reaching for me from her makeshift bed in the chest of drawers in my old bedroom. During the years I'd lived in Blackwater House, I'd visited my sister as much as I could, slipping in through the back door, which was never locked, creeping up the stairs and tapping three times on the door, our secret code. I always took her food, fruit and crisps and anything that could be kept in the wardrobe. I taught her how to use the lock I'd installed on the door, making sure it was secure when I left, before sneaking back out. I rarely saw my mother, and she never saw me.

Sometimes I wondered why I hadn't taken my sister with me. Lying in bed in my student accommodation, I'd tortured myself with images of Ashleigh in that house. I'd begged Gwen to look out for her when I was gone, and she'd looked at me sadly before pressing her lips against my cheek and folding me into her arms. That was the thing about Gwen: she never demanded anything of me. She gave me the space to speak, to tell her everything I wanted to, everything I needed to, and never pressed for more. Sometimes it was like she knew what I was going to say before I opened my mouth.

'She's at a sleepover,' I said, picking up the empty pizza box and carrying it over to the bin. 'Maybe next time.'

'Hi, darling,' I said as Ava came up the drive the next morning. I smiled as I realised she was wearing her dressing gown over her pyjamas. 'Is that Poppy's mum?' I lifted a hand as she expertly turned the car around. She was clearly used to the narrow lanes and tight parking spaces in Cornwall. The woman waved back before the car disappeared back down the track.

'Yeah, she had to go. Poppy's got a dentist appointment.'

'Oh, no problem. Maybe she can stay for tea when Poppy stays here next time.'

Ava looked at me with an unreadable expression. 'I'm not sure . . .'

'When your dad isn't here,' I said, winking at her. 'We could have a girls' night. I could cook.'

She smiled then, her face clearing. 'Yeah, that sounds nice. I'll ask her.'

I followed her into the kitchen where she grabbed a carton of juice from the fridge, and shook my head when she offered me one. 'Did you have a nice time?'

'It was good. Poppy has an amazing room – it's *so* big. And they have this TV that looks like a framed picture.'

'Really? That sounds nice. Maybe we could get one for The Hideaway.'

Ava's eyes widened. 'Really?'

'I don't see why not. I think it'd look really good in there. Send me a link.' I filled a glass with water and took a sip. 'Are you still up for painting today?'

She nodded. 'I'll go get changed in a minute. Is there anything to eat?'

I almost teased her for always being hungry, then remembered the way Daniel had made fun of her the other night, his finger poking into her flesh. She hadn't wanted to eat the slice of cake I'd taken up to her later. 'I could make us bacon sandwiches?' I offered. She grinned and went to the fridge, pulling out a pack of bacon and both tubs of butter. We had duplicates of many things – jam, butter, even a second toaster – so I could avoid cross-contamination. I watched as she opened the freezer and grabbed my gluten-free bread from the top drawer, popping it into my toaster to defrost. She was so thoughtful, always taking such care to make sure I was catered for, though I supposed it was all she'd known since I came into her life, bringing my own toaster and labelling jars in the fridge from day one. She caught me watching her and smiled.

'What?' she asked, head cocked to one side.

'Nothing,' I said, knowing she wouldn't want me to make a fuss, but being unable to stop myself. 'Thank you for being so helpful, darling.'

She turned away with a shrug, taking her phone out of her dressing gown pocket and opening Instagram to hide her embarrassment. Lately, it was as if she was struggling to accept praise, and I hoped she wasn't losing her self-confidence. As a child she'd been so at ease with herself, but I supposed she was at the age now when things started to get more complicated.

After we'd eaten, Ava and I went to get changed. As I was making my way back downstairs, I heard a clatter and paused outside Ava's room. Through the crack I could see her kneeling beside her bed, her hair falling into her face as she peered at something on the floor before her.

'Ava, are you—?' I pushed open the door and she jumped, shoving whatever she had been looking at beneath her bed.

'Ever heard of knocking?' she snapped, and I frowned. For a teenager, Ava wasn't often moody and she almost never spoke to me like that. She reached out to grab a hairband from her dressing table and flipped her hair over to pull it into a high ponytail. When she straightened, her expression had changed, a smile blossoming across her face. 'Come on, Becks, we're losing daylight!' she said, ushering me out of the room and closing the door behind us. I followed, trying not to over-react in my mind. She was fourteen; she'd probably been hiding her diary or something. If kids still *had* diaries. But she didn't have any secrets from me, not really.

There was nothing to worry about, I told myself as we made our way over to the annex to get started. The flooring hadn't been laid yet, but I draped dust sheets over the kitchen counters to protect them from paint splatters before taping up around the doorframes, then Ava came in and helped me carry the ladder up the stairs. While she assembled the extendable roller, I mixed the paint and poured it into a tray.

'I love this colour,' she said, making sure the roller was evenly coated. 'It's going to look so good.'

I watched as she applied the first strokes. 'It's so vibrant. Have you decided on whether you want all the walls painted this colour or just the one where the TV will go?'

'Start with that one,' she said, flashing me a smile as she rolled the paint across the ceiling. 'Then we can see.'

'Good plan.' I jogged down the stairs, pausing at the bottom to look up from the living room area. It already looked great up there, the blue such a contrast to the white, adding depth to the space. It was beautiful, and exactly the right choice.

I poured the blue-green paint into another tray and started cutting in, being careful where the wall met the edge of the kitchen cupboard and breakfast bar. Although I'd taped up, my hand wasn't as steady as Ava's, and I was nowhere near as confident. She came down as I was rolling the second half of the wall and stood back, hands on her hips.

'I think we should leave it at this wall,' she said decisively. I finished the section and joined her, standing roughly where the sofa would be.

'And keep the rest white?'

'Yeah.' She glanced at me. 'What do you think?'

I smiled. 'You're the boss here. But I think you're right.'

'What if we painted the radiator too?' Ava suggested as we sat on the floor, backs against the breakfast bar, sharing a bag of crisps. She nodded towards the vertical radiator that sat on the wall opposite, in the space between the two areas.

'Can you? With this paint?'

'I saw it on Instagram.' She tilted her head, eyes still on the wall. 'Do you trust me?'

'With my life.'

She smiled, and I watched as she selected the right brush, deftly applying the paint onto the radiator. We'd agreed that Ava could use this space whenever we didn't have guests, as a place to have sleepovers or to enjoy a bit of independence. She was growing up and was starting to need her own space, but I wanted to keep her close for as long as possible whilst equipping her with the skills she'd need in the outside world. It was a balancing act, raising a teenager, but I hoped I was doing an all right job.

'Will this place be finished by New Year's Eve?' she asked when she'd finished the first coat, turning to smile sweetly in the way she did when she wanted something. 'Maybe I could invite Poppy, and a few other girls from school, for a sleepover?'

I thought for a moment, trying to remember what was left to do. The flooring wasn't being laid for another three weeks, which would take us to the week before Christmas. Daniel's office was closed from the twenty-third December until the sixth of January, which meant we'd all have a solid couple of weeks together. Would he mind if Ava invited some friends over for one night? He hadn't told me of any plans, though I tended to avoid New Year's Eve parties, preferring to stay at home while he went out to fancy London restaurants and bars. Thankfully, this year we were looking forward to a quiet one at home.

'You'd have to help me build the furniture,' I said. 'It's all on order, but we can't put it together until the flooring goes down.'

'Couldn't we just put the stuff for the bedroom together? The floor upstairs is done.'

She was right. The mezzanine had wooden floorboards, which the builders had sanded down, unlike the ground floor, which had needed another layer of concrete to even it out. 'Oh, yes. That would work. We could do the upstairs furniture next weekend; it should all have arrived by then.'

Ava clapped her hands together. 'So . . . it's a yes?'

'Well, I need to ask your dad.' Her face fell. 'I'm sure he won't mind. In fact, I'm sure he'd prefer a sleepover to be here than in the house. You know what he's like.' Her eyes met mine and I tried to smile encouragingly. 'Don't worry, I'll sort it out.'

She nodded, and I felt something pass between us. She really was growing up, and she saw everything.

14

Kate

Kate stares up at the ceiling, the digital clock displaying the time above her head – 00:43. Her mind refuses to switch off, her tangled thoughts full of the missing girl. She considers what she knows about her. Ava. Fourteen years old. Mixed race. Father Daniel Everley, stepmother Rebecca Bray. Mother died when she was a baby. Two aunts, some cousins, one grandmother, all still living in or around London. Disappeared from a sleepover on New Year's Eve from Blackwater House, where she had been living for almost three months.

Lauren fidgets beside her, rolling onto her side and letting out a snore. Her words from earlier ring inside Kate's head. *To escape.* Kate knows what Lauren was escaping from, the painful events from her childhood which still haunt her, but what was Rebecca running away from? Was it just her shitty mother, or did something else happen to her in that house?

Kate tries to remember the last time she saw Rebecca when they were teenagers. She tries to picture Rebecca back then, when they were still so young and preparing themselves for the world. She sees Rebecca's blonde hair and thin body, and grimaces as a memory of her own early noughties' haircut floats before her eyes, the dodgy fringe she'd convinced her friend to cut for her and instantly regretted. Rebecca must have been about fifteen when she went off the rails, so Kate would have been about thirteen. Was she just being a normal teenager, pushing boundaries, taking risks? She frowns as she remembers a house party they'd both gone to; it was possibly Kate's first one, her mother a bit of a worrier when it came to her daughter despite her otherwise carefree nature. She smiles as she remembers her mum putting a plate of spaghetti in front of her. *Never drink on an empty stomach.* She'd smiled, placing two small bottles of WKD on the table. *That's all you're having, all right? You're still just a cheel.* And she was, Kate thinks now. She was just a child, and so was Rebecca. And so is Ava.

Kate remembers seeing Rebecca that night, sitting or standing next to a boy Kate didn't know. He'd looked older than the rest of them, and spent the entire night sprawled in an armchair, sipping from a bottle of vodka, Rebecca hovering around him like a moon around a planet. Kate hadn't understood his pull. He wasn't particularly good-looking, though she admits now that she was probably biased, glancing across at Lauren whose curls have fallen across her face, the shorter layers coming loose from the ponytail on top of her head. Kate brushes the strands away before returning to her memories.

No, the guy hadn't been attractive at all. In fact, he'd oozed danger, his eyes blazing in the darkness as he watched Rebecca drink and dance and laugh, before pulling her onto his lap, one arm around her waist. Possessive. He hadn't been important though. It was Becks Bray who shone that night, though Kate wonders now if she had been crying for help, and nobody had even tried to hear her.

Rolling onto her side, Kate wonders why she's remembering that particular night now. She only had one of the bottles her mum gave her, too nervous to get drunk and let go at a party full of people she didn't know. The group Rebecca was part of had seemed so much older, and Kate had been scared to get out of her depth. She spent most of the night sat on the living room floor with a friend, watching the rest of them.

She remembers bumping into Rebecca later that night, outside the bathroom upstairs. Although she'd watched Rebecca drink an entire bottle of vodka and smoke at least two spliffs, her step had been steady and her eyes had glittered as she held the bathroom door open for Kate, the edges of her mouth pulled up in a smirk. But there was something behind all of that, Kate thinks now, closing her eyes and feeling her body go heavy. Just like today, when Kate had sat in her living room, on that night all those years ago, Rebecca had had the look of a haunted woman.

Kate's phone rings as she pulls up outside Rebecca's house the next day. 'Kate,' DS Tremayne barks down the phone, and Kate rolls her eyes. *If anyone thinks I'm terse, they've obviously never met Tremayne,* she thinks wryly.

'Sarge,' she replies. 'I've just arrived at Blackwater House.'

'Well you won't find the father there. He's buggered off up country.'

Kate feels her eyes widen. 'Now?'

DS Tremayne blows out a breath. 'I know. A work emergency, and apparently it can't wait. I've told him to keep his bleddy mobile on at all times.' Kate's eyes are drawn by a flicker at the upstairs window, but the glass is too dark to make anything out. Is Rebecca standing there, watching her? She feels her skin begin to prickle and gives herself a shake. 'I don't like him,' DS Tremayne continues. 'What's your feeling?'

Kate hesitates for a moment. She doesn't like making a call so early on in an investigation, but she can't ignore her initial feelings about Daniel. 'I'm not sure,' she says, erring on the side of caution, 'but I think there's more to this.'

'You'll get a sore arse,' DS Tremayne says gruffly, 'sitting on the fence like that.'

Kate laughs despite herself. 'Isn't that in the job description? *I take the time to get to know others and their perspective in order to build rapport.*'

'Well bleddy build it quicker. It's only a matter of time until the media gets wind of this, and then we'll all be on trial.' Kate opens her mouth to speak, but her phone bleeps, the call apparently over.

Sighing, Kate locks the car and crunches over the gravel towards the house. Her eyes flick to the doorbell attached to the wall beside the front door. She'd received an email last night telling her that the cameras had been switched off between eight p.m. on the thirty-first and three a.m. on the first, capturing Ava's friends arriving and Rebecca going out to pick up some pizzas, but nothing else until the police arrived.

So she doesn't have an alibi, Kate had thought as she read the email over her first cup of coffee this morning. The footage from the camera was being saved into a folder on the cloud, accessible by Daniel through an app, which Rebecca said she doesn't have access to. Kate arranges her features as Rebecca opens the door, noting the difference in her demeanour today. Her shoulders are more relaxed, her hair has been brushed and arranged in a bun on top of her head, and her eyes are clear and bright. Kate can't help but wonder if it's because Daniel isn't here.

'I spoke to Ava's aunts today,' she says. 'One of them is heavily pregnant and due to give birth soon, so they haven't been able to come down yet.'

'Have they heard from Ava at all?' Kate asks as she follows Rebecca into the kitchen.

'No.' Rebecca appears to deflate. 'I had hoped she would go to them if, you know, if she did run away. She loves her aunts. I think they make her feel connected to her mum.'

Kate hasn't had a chance to look into Ava's mother yet, and she's hoping Rebecca will fill in more of the gaps today. Just as Kate opens her mouth to speak, a phone begins to ring, and Rebecca rushes over to the windowsill where her mobile rests. She snatches it up, holding it to her ear. Kate's heart starts to race, an adrenaline kick at the merest whiff of a clue, a lead to chase down.

'Hello? Ava? Is that . . .' Rebecca trails off, and Kate lets out a breath. 'No, wrong number.' Rebecca's arms drop to her sides, the phone held loosely in one hand, and she sits down heavily on a kitchen stool, head down. 'I thought that was her,' she says quietly, and Kate feels a wrench at the pain in her voice.

'Is there any reason why Ava might want to run away?' she asks, sitting down opposite. 'Any reason at all?' She's aware this question has been asked many times before, but if Rebecca thought Ava was calling, she must believe there's a chance that Ava left of her own accord.

Rebecca shakes her head without looking up. 'No. None. She's happy here, she likes her school, she's made new friends.' She sighs, getting up and pacing the floor in front of the sink. 'She misses her old friends, but none of them have heard from her since before New Year's. I've spoken to all of them, and their parents.'

Kate nods. She still suspects Daniel isn't who he appears to be, and DS Tremayne seems to agree. She wonders if Daniel is abusive, if not physically then certainly emotionally. Could he have been mistreating Ava? Has she fled for her own safety? Kate suppresses a shudder as she recalls one of the first cases she was assigned to as a DC. A three-year-old girl had been reported missing only to turn up five days later, buried under the shed in the back garden. Her skull had been fractured as a result of the father throwing her against the wall in a drunken rage.

Could Daniel have been abusing Ava? Or was she still grieving the loss of her mother? The sketch pops into Kate's mind, the large M scrawled across Ava's mother's chest. Had Ava done that? What did it mean? M for Meghan? Or . . .? She opens her mouth to mention it, then changes her mind. She needs to find out more about Ava's mother before she raises it with Rebecca. She takes two clean mugs from the draining board and drops a teabag into each of them, reminding herself of the key principles of her role while the kettle boils. *I understand when to balance decisive action with due consideration.*

'Was Ava seeing anyone?' Kate asks, trying to sound nonchalant. 'A boyfriend? Girlfriend?'

Rebecca looks up in surprise, her eyes narrowing at the question. 'Seeing anyone?' she repeats. 'No. She was too young.'

Kate remembers reading about a girl who tried to take her own life last year after someone at school circulated a nude photo of her. She had been around the same age as Ava. Kate takes in Rebecca's expression, the fire in her eyes, and decides to change tack. 'Have you seen many people?' she asks, placing the teas on the counter before sitting down opposite Rebecca. 'Since you've been back, I mean. It's a small village.'

'Not really,' Rebecca replies, avoiding her eye. 'We've spent a lot of time here, doing up the house. It was a bit of a state. The annex used to be a garage, but we're going to rent it out to tourists.'

Kate nods, remembering her first visit to Blackwater House. Had two days already passed? Time was slipping through her fingers, and she was still no closer to finding out what happened to Ava.

'Ah. Not Ava's "own space"?' She puts the words in air quotes, smiling as if to say, *teenagers*. She wonders if Rebecca can read her, whether she knows what Kate is doing.

Rebecca shakes her head, a smile tugging at her lips. 'We agreed that she can use it when it's not being rented out, but I think her bedroom is big enough. It's bigger than any room I had as a student.'

'I know what you mean. I had to share a poky flat with four other students and Christ, they were messy. I once opened the fridge to find my milk had been emptied out and the bottle filled with someone else's leftovers.' Kate grimaces at the memory. 'I think it was curry.'

Rebecca mirrors her expression. 'I had a few experiences like that. I couldn't wait to graduate and get a place of my own. Somewhere just for me.' She falls silent, her face serious now. 'Ava has never been like that, not really. She gets moody sometimes, especially during a certain time of the month, but she's generally happy to sit with us on the sofa to watch TV or eat dinner together. We do a lot of things as a family, when Daniel's here.'

'And when he isn't?'

Rebecca shrugs. 'It's just me and Ava. We have "self-care Sundays", and we go shopping and to the cinema together.' She pauses. 'Well, we did, back in Hertfordshire. We haven't done much of that since moving here – we've been too busy with the renovations. I've been meaning to take her over to Plymouth, actually.'

'There's not much here for kids that age,' Kate says. 'My weekends and school holidays were spent on the beach, weather permitting.'

'That's what we wanted for Ava. Want,' Rebecca quickly corrects herself. 'The great outdoors. Summers in the sea, walks along the cliffs. Days spent exploring, like I used to.'

Kate watches Rebecca as she speaks, wondering when Rebecca changed the word *escaping* to *exploring* in her mind. And whether she believes it.

15

Rebecca

Before – December 2019

The day before Christmas Eve, I greeted Daniel at the front door wearing my new festive jumper. He held me at arm's length to take me in. 'Foxes. Cute,' he said, kissing me on the nose. His lips were cold and he smelled like brandy, and I wondered whether he'd been drinking on the train from London. He used to drink more often during the day, but since moving to Cornwall it seemed to have stopped, which I was grateful for. 'Where's Ava?' he asked, dropping his suitcase in the hall and taking off his coat.

'Upstairs, in the bath. She had to wash her hair.'

Suppressing a yawn, he took off his shoes and put them on top of the shoe rack. His eyes were drawn to the living room and he smiled. 'Hey, you put the tree up! It looks great.'

'Ava helped,' I said, flushing with pride. It *did* look great. Perfect, in fact. It was something I'd worked hard at, being able to turn a house into a home. Candles, throws, perfectly placed photo frames. A well-dressed Christmas tree. It was something Daniel always liked about me, I supposed. That I always took care of those things, so he didn't have to.

A memory flashed across my eyes: the Christmas tree on its side, the star thrown across the room, Daniel's face red with fury. Aisha picking Ava up, her emotions written across her face as she stormed out of the front door; Ava watching me over her aunt's shoulder as I stood in the doorway, torn, helpless, afraid. It reminded me so much of my childhood, that simmering tension, the ever-present threat of violence. I was transported back to the house that was my home for fifteen years, with its peeling paintwork and mould around the windows. The kitchen cupboards bare, the oven smeared with grease, the walls stained yellow by cigarette smoke. The life I'd fought to escape.

I shook myself and smiled brightly at Daniel. 'Tea? Wine?'

'The second one,' he said, eyes twinkling with the reflection of the lights on the tree. 'It's Christmas, after all. I'll just get changed.' He bounded up the stairs, taking them two at a time, while I wandered into the kitchen to take the wine out of the fridge, grabbing two glasses from the cupboard on my way back to the living room. I placed them on the coffee table and poured two generous glasses before sitting down on the sofa, tucking my legs beneath me. The house felt cosy, the smart thermostat keeping it at a comfortable twenty-one degrees, and the lights were low, the light strip running behind the TV unit turned to a soft orange. We hadn't had the new fireplace installed yet, so I'd placed a basket of chopped wood in front, three lantern candles beside it to make it feel more homely.

Ava and I had spent the past few days putting furniture together for the annex. I'd ordered a king-size bed, a wardrobe, two bedside tables, and a dressing table with a large mirror. The truck hadn't been able to squeeze down the lane, so we'd helped the two men carry everything through on foot, shoes skidding on stones. Thankfully they'd carried it all up to the mezzanine for us and then we'd got to work, surrounded by cardboard boxes and bits of wood and tiny screws that liked to get lost amongst the detritus. It had been fun though, as most things were with Ava.

Before Daniel got home, we'd been to the supermarket and raided the shelves, packing a trolley full of crisps and sweets and bottles of Coke. We'd told Ava no alcohol as I didn't fancy looking after a group of drunk teenagers – or answering to their parents the next morning – so we overloaded on fizzy drinks instead.

'You should see the annex,' I said when Daniel came back downstairs. He sat down beside me and sighed. 'It looks amazing. Ava has done such a brilliant job.'

'Later,' he said dismissively, and I felt my heart sink. His good mood wasn't set to last, then. I only hoped he would perk up tomorrow, once he'd rested and switched off for the holidays.

I stayed up long after Daniel went to bed. I poured myself another glass of wine, finishing off the bottle and placing it in the recycling bin outside the back door. Then I rolled myself a cigarette and lit it, keeping the door closed behind me. Daniel didn't like smoking. He often looked down his nose at people we encountered with a cigarette between their fingers, but for some reason, I'd always found the smell comforting. Stale cigarette smoke never failed to make me feel sick though, the memories of the smoke-filled living room and the yellowing walls of my childhood rushing back. I pulled a hat over my hair, protecting it from the smell and the bitter cold. The sky above me was clear, stars twinkling against an indigo backdrop.

Our first Cornish Christmas. But not my first. My first eighteen Christmases were spent in Cornwall, the day rarely marked or even acknowledged. I couldn't recall ever believing in Father Christmas, or going out to watch the Christmas lights switch on in the village until I was a teenager and could go with friends. Or, more often, alone. Until I came here, to Blackwater House, Christmas was just another day. With Gwen it had been a quiet affair, a simple roast dinner with apple crumble for dessert, but it was calm and pleasant. She taught me how to make a parcel out of tin foil for the carrots, loading them with butter and garlic, and how to make my own Yorkshire puddings out of cornflour, which came in handy after my diagnosis.

I realised that I knew very little about Gwen's past, despite the years I'd spent with her, but we were alike in so many ways. I hadn't ever been the type of person to ask questions; even with Gwen, I'd been afraid I would ask the wrong one and find myself thrown out of this house as well. I couldn't risk it, this new, tentative refuge of mine. I knew that Gwen owed me nothing, that she didn't need to feed or house me, or encourage me to go back to school and then to college for A levels. I was nobody to her, a stray taken in from the street, and she could ask me to leave at any time. But she never did. She'd pushed me to apply for university elsewhere, telling me that it was my chance to have a fresh start, and she'd been right. In those three years, she did more for me than anyone had ever done in my entire life, a debt I could never have hoped to repay.

I heard a rustling in the garden and snapped my attention back to the present, peering out into the gloom. I waved my arm and the security light flicked on, illuminating the patio area and a patch of grass beyond, but the trees remained in darkness. *I must get more lights to put out there,* I thought, not for the first time. I remembered Ashleigh appearing out of nowhere, her shadow sliding out from between the trees, and I shuddered. Anything could be out there; anyone could be watching me.

Or it could be the Beast of Bodmin, I thought, chiding myself for being so skittish. It was probably just an owl or a cat, stalking its prey amongst the bare trees. The light went off and I listened intently but didn't hear the rustle again. After finishing my cigarette, I ground it out on the slightly damp grass and threw it into the bin before going back inside and locking the door firmly behind me.

I glanced at my phone to see a message from Cass had arrived a few hours earlier.

Hey lovely, are we still on for Boxing Day? xxx

I closed my eyes for a moment. I'd almost forgotten about Ava's aunts coming to visit. Ava's mother was someone I tried not to think about too often, but she was always there, a ghost peering over my shoulder, checking to see if I was raising her daughter right. *I'm trying, Meghan,* I wanted to say. *I really am.*

Of course! I texted back. *Let me know when you're nearby, I'll get the kettle on x*

The reply came back almost instantly, Cass being a night owl herself. *A woman after my own heart! See you then xxx*

I tidied the kitchen, switching off lights as I moved through the house, and paused at the door to the library. The newly installed shutters were open, moonlight filtering across the floorboards. I stepped into the room and ran a hand across the desk, the laptop turned off and closed, ready for when I went back to work.

A sound made my head snap towards the window, my eyes searching the shadows beyond. Something flashed across the grass and I gasped, my heartbeat pulsing in my ears as I tried to follow it. Was someone out there? It was so quiet out here; every sound was amplified. The front garden was in darkness; there were no streetlights on the road beyond the lane, and our security lights hadn't been set off. I peered through the glass, my eyes slowly adjusting to the light of the moon. My breath created ghosts across the glass as I tried to see if anyone was out there. It could be kids, or a lost tourist, I thought, noticing that the front gate was open. Did Daniel leave it open when he came in earlier? I couldn't remember. I wanted to go out and close it, but my feet were rooted to the spot, my eyes darting across the front garden. But there was no one there.

As I turned away, I heard a noise again, a low, mewling sound, and let out the breath I'd been holding. It was just a cat, prowling through the darkness beyond the house in pursuit of a mouse, but, for a second, I thought it sounded like a baby.

16

Rebecca

I woke on Christmas morning to Ava grinning down at me, 'Have a Holly, Jolly Christmas' playing softly on the Echo in the corner of the room, the sky beyond the window tinged light grey.

'Ah,' I said, rubbing my eyes, 'excellent. You've defrosted Michael Bublé.' I sat up, wondering why I was on the sofa and frowned before remembering the events of the day before.

I'd opened my eyes on Christmas Eve to Daniel placing a takeaway cup of coffee on my bedside table, his hair damp from a shower.

'Have you been out already?' I'd asked, turning over to check the time. Almost ten.

He smiled. 'Yes, sleepyhead. I went for a run then braved the supermarket. I thought two pensioners were about to have a scrap over the last cabbage.' He shook his head. 'Absolute chaos. And the driving! It's like everyone is hoping to spend Christmas Day in A&E.'

I smiled, sitting up and removing the lid. Toffee Nut, my favourite. 'Did you manage to get everything?'

'I'll be surprised if we manage to drink our way through four bottles of prosecco, three bottles of Buck's Fizz, and three bottles of red wine.'

I'd felt my heart sink as I remembered Cass's messages from the night before. It seemed that Daniel too had forgotten that they were coming to visit on Boxing Day.

'We'll probably need a bit more,' I said, my eyes on the cup in my hands. I felt the liquid slosh around as I fought the trembling in my hands. 'We're going to have company on Boxing Day.'

I felt Daniel's eyes on me and looked up, my heart beginning to race. 'When was this agreed?' His words were sharp, his gaze pinning me to the spot.

'Oh, ages ago,' I said, aiming for nonchalance, but instead I sounded shrill. 'They always visit around Christmas, you know that. And it will be nice for them to see our new house.'

'I had hoped, Rebecca,' he said slowly, drawing my name out, 'that we would avoid them this year. Having moved so far away.'

I forced a smile to cover my nerves. 'I'm sorry, darling, I suppose we both forgot. We've had so much going on, it's no surprise really.' I reached out a hand, meaning to place it on his shoulder, but he caught me mid-air, his fingers tightening around mine. I gasped, trying to jerk my hand away but he held on. Coffee slopped over the side of the cup and burned my leg through my pyjamas. I glanced down at the brown stain spreading across the sheet beneath me. He brought his face close to mine, his breath tinged with the scent of alcohol.

'I hadn't forgotten anything,' he hissed. '*You* neglected to inform me of your little plans.' He tugged at my wrist so our foreheads touched. 'As usual.' He took the cup from my hand and before I could move, dumped the hot liquid into my lap.

'Why are you sleeping down here?' Ava whispered now, and I tried to shake the memory away, but my thighs prickled and I knew the skin would still be red and sore.

'I couldn't sleep,' I told her, smiling so widely it felt like my face would crack. 'I was too excited for today.'

She didn't respond, her eyes fixed on her phone as her fingers flew over the screen. Who was she talking to on Christmas Day?

'Ava?' I reached out to touch her shoulder and her eyes snapped back to mine, her phone slipped into her pocket. I hesitated for a moment, wanting to ask, not wanting to smother her. 'Come on,' I said, 'let's have a cuppa before we wake your dad.'

An hour later we were on the sofa, Daniel and I with mugs of coffee cooling on the table before us, Ava sitting beneath the tree like when she was six, grinning from ear to ear. Tension rolled off Daniel in waves, but I tried to smile at Ava, thanking her for my gift of fluffy socks and a bath set.

Ava handed a present to Daniel, and I saw her smile slip as he ripped it open and grunted a thank you for his aftershave. I fixed my smile in place as I exclaimed over the gifts. He had been tired from the long journey down from London, I reminded myself, the train delays getting him home later than expected the day before yesterday. He'd had a busy week at work, wrapping things up in time for the holidays, and having to smile through the boozy lunches they were throwing for clients. It was my fault; I should have reminded him earlier about Meghan's family visiting tomorrow.

Though we sat just a few feet apart, I could feel the distance between us widening. When he was in London and I was down here, I felt like the string between us was stretched so thin it was almost invisible. His moods had started to become even more unpredictable, and I could feel the ice cracking beneath my feet. I knew Ava could feel it too. Would her childhood have as much impact on her as mine continued to have on me? Would she still be trapped in the past even in her thirties and beyond? I couldn't afford to wait to find out, I decided, staring out of the window and at the garden beyond, the sky still a dark grey. I needed to do something now.

Ava's voice brought me back to the room, her face bobbing before me. 'Becks?'

'Hmmm?' I blinked, and she rolled her eyes.

'I *said*, what's for breakfast?'

Breakfast? I glanced at the clock above the fireplace then jumped up and headed for the kitchen, glad to be out of that room and with something practical to do. Ava came up behind me as I opened the fridge, catching a bag of sprouts before it hit the ground. The fridge was packed with food and alcohol, an obscene amount for just a few days. I found a carton of eggs hidden behind a mountain of cheese and pulled it out. 'How about scrambled eggs?' I suggested.

'And bacon?' Ava asked, reaching into the fridge and rummaging around.

'Why not? It *is* Christmas.' While the bacon sizzled, I cracked the eggs into a saucepan, grating some cheese on top and beating the mixture with a fork until it was light and fluffy. I patted the grease from the bacon and started to plate up, asking Ava to call her father, who to our relief came in with a smile. We sat at the breakfast bar, Ava squeezing maple syrup over her bacon to Daniel's disgust, and we ate and laughed as if we were a normal family. And we *were* a normal family, weren't we?

Later, we headed out for Christmas lunch wrapped up in coats and scarves, hands shoved into our pockets. We wiped our booted feet on the mat as we entered the pub, relishing the warmth coming from a roaring fire crackling in the corner. Ava skipped over to a table next to it while Daniel ordered drinks at the bar, bringing over a glass of wine for me, a pint for him, and a Coke for Ava, who was chatting excitedly about the Kindle we'd bought her and the books she'd downloaded using the Amazon gift card Daniel received from a client. Ava had always been a reader, insisting I read to her every night before she went to bed almost from the first day I moved in with them. By the time she was five, she would end up taking over, reciting some of the words from memory, the stories firmly lodged inside her head. I cherished those moments with her. It wasn't always easy, moving in with Daniel so soon after meeting him, but Ava seemed to enjoy me being around when her father wasn't. And, before long, even when he was.

I reached out and gently tugged a strand of Ava's hair. She glanced up from her phone and smiled at me. 'Who are you talking to?' I asked, nodding towards her phone. To my surprise, she clicked the button on the side and the screen went blank.

'Just Cass. We're talking hair products.'

I remembered when Cass, the youngest of Ava's aunts, came over one day to teach me how to do Ava's hair. She showed me how to wash her hair with a cleansing conditioner, getting Ava to sing two songs while I gently scrubbed her scalp with my fingertips. 'Never brush her hair dry,' Cass warned. 'Only when it's saturated in conditioner. Some people detangle just with their fingers, but who can be bothered with that?' She laughed, reaching for the wide tooth comb and showing me how to work through the tangles.

'Moisture,' she said, holding up a leave-in conditioner in her left hand, 'and hold.' She indicated the tub of gel in her right hand. 'Do washday right, and you can probably get away with only washing once a week.'

I was surprised at the idea of only washing – and detangling – Ava's hair once a week. 'You'll see,' she said, smiling, using her fingers to rake the products through Ava's hair before cupping the strands and scrunching them. And she was right. Ava started looking after her own hair when she was about twelve, but it remained a way for us to spend time together.

Sundays became deep-conditioning days, Ava and I lying on her bed with shower caps on our heads, faces coated in garish green masks, painting our toenails whatever colour Ava wanted that week. It was our special time, while Daniel was at the gym or out running. Sometimes we listened to music or an audiobook, wriggling our toes as we waited for them to dry, or Ava would tell me about her week at school. I realised we hadn't done it in a while and felt a pang.

'Are you all right, Becks?' Ava said, bringing me back to the present, and I felt a jolt at the name. It was what my mum called me, her friends snorting with laughter as they held up a bottle of beer with the same name. When I escaped, I became Rebecca, or Becca, never Becks. But Ava didn't know my history, and I supposed, in Ava's mouth, the name was one of affection, of friends. Of family. It was time to move on, to leave that part of my life behind me. It was time to focus on the future, I decided as I smiled at her. On Ava's future.

The food arrived and Daniel clapped his hands together, grinning at me from across the table. He finally seemed to have broken out of his bad mood, and for that I was grateful. I had my own dark thoughts to contend with at this time of year, and it was always an effort for me to shake them off. But I tried. I always tried.

'This is delicious!' Ava exclaimed, with a mouth full of turkey. I took a bite of the potatoes and nodded while Daniel tucked into his beef. Even the gravy was gluten-free, and the Yorkshires were made from cornflour, so I could enjoy the meal without worrying. We listened to the Christmas music coming out of the speakers and the chatter of fellow diners as we tucked into our food. A waiter placed three crackers on our table and we grinned at one another as we pulled them, with Ava winning twice. We put the paper hats on our heads while Ava read out the jokes.

'Who hides in a bakery at Christmas?' she asked, already giggling. Daniel and I looked at each other, shrugging, smiles creeping onto our faces. 'A mince spy!' Ava exploded into laughter, as if it was the funniest thing she'd ever heard. She was at that strange age where she could seem like a child one minute, and an adult the next, and I found myself simultaneously excited and terrified for her future.

'I should have worn leggings,' I said as dessert arrived. 'I already feel like I'm going to pop!'

The waiter chuckled as he placed a bowl of apple crumble and an espresso in front of me, sticky toffee pudding for Ava and a pot of tea for Daniel. We barely managed to eat half of it and, defeated, I leaned back in my chair, hands on my stomach.

Ava mimicked me, tilting her head back towards the ceiling. Daniel shook his head at us, but he was smiling. 'I think a walk is in order,' he said, taking a sip of his tea. 'Try to burn some of these calories.'

'We'd need to walk for a hundred years!' Ava said, stifling a burp behind her hand. I caught her eye and we grinned.

Daniel went to the bar to pay while I visited the loo. I washed my hands at the sink, peering at my reflection in the mirror. My eyes were bright, my cheeks flushed from the wine. I swiped a finger under each eye, patting the skin beneath where the concealer had sunk into the creases. When did those wrinkles appear? I was barely thirty-four, but already life was leaving its mark on me. I'd had dark circles beneath my eyes for as long as I could remember, sleep often evading me as I lay awake in my childhood home, listening to the music pounding through the floorboards, the shouts and shrieks and smashing of glass. I turned away from the mirror, hoping to leave my memories with my reflection.

We left the pub and the past behind, walking back towards the sea. The wind was biting as we left the shelter of the village and emerged on top of the headland, the clouds in the sky above us full and dark, and the sea was grey, its white-tipped waves crashing onto the rocks below. Ava skipped across the headland and, as I watched her, I remembered sitting here when I was a teenager, a bottle of vodka in my bag, gazing out across the never-ending water. *How different our lives are*, I thought. *How different her childhood has been.* How different her life would be, if I had anything to do with it.

Daniel took my gloved hand in his and squeezed it, breaking me out of my thoughts. 'Happy Christmas, darling,' he said, bending down and pressing his cold lips to my cheek. 'I've been a beast, haven't I?'

I turned to him, studying his face in profile as he watched his daughter. He had fine lines around the corners of his eyes, and a streak of grey near his temple, but his skin was clear and slightly reddened by the wind, and his mouth curved into a smile as Ava turned back and called to us.

'Smile, Becks!' she called, holding her phone in front of her, and I did, turning my face towards her and feeling my lips tug upwards, as if on a string.

'Do you forgive me?' Daniel asked when Ava started taking selfies in front of the sea, the ends of her new scarf flapping in the breeze. I nodded automatically. I did, of course I did. I always did.

'There's nothing to forgive,' I said, kissing him on the cheek, feeling the rasp of his stubble against my lips. 'Happy Christmas.'

'Becks, Dad, look!' Ava shouted, and we picked our way over the cliffs to join her. A crowd of people stood on the beach, their pale skin almost blending in with the sand beneath them. 'What are they doing?'

'It's the Christmas Day swim,' I said, smiling as Daniel and Ava turned to me with matching expressions. 'I know, but it's actually not too bad. The sea retains some of the warmth from the summer. I don't think it dips below seven degrees, even in the winter.'

'Seven degrees?' Ava exclaimed, pretending to shiver.

'Some of them are wearing Santa hats,' Daniel said with a laugh, his eyes still on the crowd below. 'I wonder how many of those will be lost in the water.'

We watched in silence as the crowd started to move on some unheard command, bare feet slapping against the sand as they ran towards the sea. Ava cheered as they entered the water, waves lapping at their ankles.

'Isn't it dangerous though?' Ava asked, her eyes wide. 'The sea looks wild.'

The sea is always wild, I thought, my eyes on the grey-green waves topped with white foam. There is a wildness to Cornwall, a half-tamed beast that you're bound to fall in love with, and that tolerates you in return, if you're lucky.

17

Kate

Now – 3rd January

Kate's phone buzzes as she leaves Rebecca's house, the sky already turning a deep pinky-blue despite it only being three o'clock. Noticing the number, she climbs into the car and closes the door before answering. 'Can I help you?' she says, putting on a posh accent.

'Excuse me, Mrs Policewoman Officer, just a moment of your time,' Lauren responds, laughter in her voice. 'I wondered if you were free for some food.'

'Always. When?'

'Now? I'm, erm, I'm in the village.'

'Well you're not the only gay, at least.'

'Are you allowed to say that?'

'Probably not. I'll arrest myself promptly.' Kate grins. 'Where you to?'

Lauren gives an exaggerated sigh at the Cornish-ism. 'In the car park. Did you know it's free?'

'Erm, yes.'

'Cornwall will never cease to amaze me.' Kate hears Lauren take a pull on her e-cigarette. 'So. Food?'

'Yes'm. What did you have in mind?'

Kate meets Lauren at the car park and together they walk to the pizza place on the corner. They place their orders – margherita as always for Lauren, a more adventurous Wheal Phoenix, which features a local pheasant salami, for Kate

– and they wait inside, browsing the selection of Cornish beer and cider.

'I'd better get a Coke,' Kate grumbles, reaching into the fridge for one. 'What do you want?'

'The same, since I've got the car. Though I'll have a Polgoon for later.'

'Good idea, I do love a cider.'

They watch their pizzas being prepared, making small talk with the staff, then pay and wander back to the car park, boxes balanced on palms.

'Whoop, watch it!' Kate shouts, pretending to bump into Lauren. 'Don't drop your pizza!'

Lauren glares at her. 'I believe that's grounds for divorce.'

'You wouldn't.'

'Try me, Mrs Woman.'

As they're getting into her car, Kate has an idea. 'Have you ever been up to the tin mines?' she asks, placing her pizza box on Lauren's lap. Lauren shakes her head. 'Right then, how about dinner and a show?'

'If you're going to drop your trousers, I'll want my money back.'

Kate laughs as she pulls out of the car park and takes the road towards the old tin mine. She has always loved this part of the county, the rugged north Cornish coast with its wild seas and colourful landscape. The sky is leaden now, the wind buffeting the car, and Kate wonders what Lauren will think of this treasured place. This was Kate's mother's favourite place, before the cancer took over and she was too ill to leave the house, and so coming here has always felt bittersweet. But when she pulls into the empty car park and manoeuvres into a space, Lauren gasps, leaning forward in her seat, and Kate feels warmth flood through her veins.

'What a view!' Lauren's eyes scan the horizon, and Kate follows her gaze. Weak wintry sunlight ripples across the water, and the sea is a deep blue-grey. 'It's stunning.'

'Mum loved it here,' Kate says quietly, and Lauren turns to her, a sad smile on her face, but she doesn't speak. No words are needed; they have always had the ability to read each other's thoughts, and Kate can hear hers now, loud and clear. They turn as one back towards the glittering sea, their eyes drawn to the birds wheeling overhead.

'No shitehawks down here,' Kate says, using her favoured word for seagulls.

Lauren laughs. 'Good. I still haven't got over that time in St Ives, when one pinched my ice cream. I'd only had one lick!'

'And it shat on you, don't forget,' Kate adds helpfully. 'Hence the name.'

'Yes, thank you for that reminder.'

'Come on. Let's eat before it gets cold.'

Lauren passes Kate's box over and the car fills with the smell of pizza, the warmth steaming up the windscreen.

'We could pull a *Titanic*,' Kate says with her mouth full, reaching out to swipe a finger across the glass.

'What, hit an iceberg?'

Kate laughs, covering her mouth with a hand to avoid spraying crumbs across the dashboard. They finish their food quickly, then wipe their hands on tissues Lauren produces from her coat pocket, and sit back in their seats, full and contented.

'How's it going?' Lauren asks, pulling out her e-cigarette and opening the window a crack. 'The case?'

Kate sighs heavily. 'Slowly. Every time I think I'm getting closer to something, Rebecca pulls back.'

Lauren nods, blowing vapour out of the window. 'Is she a suspect then? Rebecca?'

'Everyone's a suspect.'

'You'll figure it out,' Lauren says confidently. 'You always do, eventually.'

The clock is ticking, Kate thinks. *Two days have passed already. I don't have time for 'eventually'.* But she knows Lauren is only trying to help. Sometimes she wishes she had a job like Lauren's, a normal nine-to-five office job that she could leave at the front door. A job that let her take normal holidays, regular time to spend at home or with friends. But she doesn't think she could ever leave the police. She loves it too much. And no matter how low she feels, how stressed the job makes her, spending time with Lauren never fails to lift her spirits.

'How about a walk?' she suggests, shaking herself out of her funk. 'Blow away the cobwebs.'

'You sound like a nan,' Lauren remarks as they get out of the car, the wind whipping her hair into her face.

'Button up, dearie, you'll catch your death out here.'

Kate leads Lauren down the narrow path, their shoes crunching on the loose stones. The wind slams into them, making conversation impossible, and when Kate reaches back to tuck her hair into her hood, she sees Lauren doing the same. They stop outside the first ruin, Lauren reading the sign that Kate almost knows by heart.

'Opened in 1802,' Lauren says, raising her voice above the wind. 'Worked until 1889, then reopened in the 1900s for a few years. Declared a World Heritage Site in 2006.' She looks up at the crumbling ruin. 'Incredible.'

Kate wanders across to the next site, jumping up on the ledge and peering down. Lauren leans against the wall, arms crossed over her chest. 'I'm half expecting Ross Poldark himself to come up out of there,' she says with a grin.

Kate rolls her eyes. 'Bleddy Poldark. Not you as well?'

'It came up on Netflix,' Lauren says with a shrug. 'What would you call him? "Ansum"?'

'I wouldn't call him anything,' Kate says with a sniff. 'He's not my type.'

'All right, what about Demelza? She's definitely "ansum".'

'I'll give you that.'

Kate jumps down and takes Lauren by the hand, leading her down the steep cliff towards the engine house.

'I've not got life insurance, you know,' Lauren yells as the wind picks up again. 'So there's no point in throwing me off the cliff.'

'What about for fun?' Kate shouts back, risking a glance over her shoulder. Lauren sticks out her tongue.

They make it down the cliff face unscathed, despite Lauren skidding on a loose piece of rock and nearly crashing into Kate, and climb into the engine house.

'When the tide's in, the water comes all the way under here,' Kate explains, pointing down the hole which has, thankfully, been covered over with a metal grate in recent years. She wonders how many drunk teenagers had fallen down there before. 'It kept the water out of the mine, I think.'

They sit on the cold rock, legs tucked up beneath them, gazing out across the sea. They watch a group of walkers make their way down the coastal path, red jackets making them stand out against the heather, and two birds dance above them, circling one another before plunging down towards the water. Kate looks up and realises she can just see the top of Blackwater House from here, the evergreens surrounding it like a shield. They've searched all along the cliffs here and down on the beach below, but nothing has been found. Like Rebecca, Kate doesn't think Ava was the type to go wandering across the cliffs in the middle of the night, but where else could she have gone? She must have been on foot, unless someone picked her up, but who?

'It's beautiful here,' Lauren says, shuffling closer to Kate and resting her head on her shoulder. 'Thanks for bringing me.'

'I came here a lot after Mum died. She loved it here. I'd sit here by myself, thinking, remembering. We had so many happy times.'

Lauren takes one of Kate's hands in hers, rubbing it gently as if trying to smooth the tension out of her. 'Sometimes those are the hardest to remember.'

18

Rebecca

Before – December 2019

I woke late on Boxing Day, my eyes bleary, the beginning of a headache behind my right eye. *Too many glasses of wine,* I chided myself as I climbed out of bed. Daniel's side was empty, as was the bathroom when I went in to shower, but I noticed that Daniel's gym clothes had gone from their usual place in the wardrobe as I got dressed. He must have gone out for a run. I could hear the opening music to a TV show coming from Ava's room as I pulled on a pair of the fluffy socks she had given me before padding downstairs to make coffee. Fifteen minutes later, Daniel came in through the back door as I was flicking through the news on my phone, damp hair pushed back from his face. He flashed me a grin as he poured himself a glass of water.

'It's freezing out there!' he said, taking a long sip. 'Anything interesting?' He nodded at my phone as I placed it face-down on the counter.

'Just news. Brexit.'

'Don't swear at me.' He winked and I smiled. Brexit had caused him no end of grief at work and he refused to discuss the topic at home, much to my relief. It only served to make me anxious. 'Have you just got up?' he asked. I smiled sheepishly and he wagged a finger as he drained his glass. 'Lazy bones.'

'I will never understand why you have to run at the crack of dawn,' I said, sipping my coffee.

'Crack of dawn?' Daniel said incredulously, looking at his watch. 'It's nearly nine!' He ruffled my hair as he passed on his way upstairs for a shower. I was surprised at his good mood, and hoped he hadn't forgotten the plans for today.

I decided to make another coffee and settled down on the sofa, scrolling absentmindedly through Instagram, enjoying the peace and quiet. An hour later, I heard the crunch of gravel and was surprised to see a car pulling into our drive-way. I hadn't expected them this early. I opened the door with a feeling of trepidation, a knot in my stomach that would undoubtedly stay with me for the duration of their visit, but I also felt the familiar warmth spreading through me at the prospect of spending time with them all, my adopted family.

Ava ran past me, hurtling towards her aunt Cass, who jumped out of the car as soon as it came to a stop. She hugged her niece, squeezing her tight and lifting her off her feet. 'When are you going to stop growing?' she exclaimed, pulling away to look at Ava. Her eyes met mine over Ava's shoulder and she smiled, lifting a hand in greeting. Cass's girlfriend Natalia ran up behind Ava and started to tickle her, and Aisha got out of the driver's side, her hands pressed against the small of her back, her seven-month-pregnant stomach straining against her trousers.

'That's some journey,' she said before saying hello to her niece, who was babbling excitedly about the house and her new room.

'What time did you leave?' I asked, remembering the journey from Hertfordshire to Cornwall. They had been closer to the M25, at least, coming from London.

'Five,' Natalia groaned, and I made a sympathetic face. Aisha was someone who liked to be punctual, usually arriving at least fifteen minutes early for anything, and I wondered how Natalia, someone who was often late, felt about such a rude awakening this morning.

Sierra, the matriarch, glided across the gravel towards me, a tin balanced on one hand. 'Happy Christmas, sweet pea,' she said, leaning in for a kiss on the cheek. She smelled like oranges and cinnamon, and I returned her one-handed hug.

'So glad you could make it,' I said. 'The journey wasn't too bad?'

She raised her eyes as if calling on the heavens. 'Aisha's driving is enough to make me never want to get into a car again.'

'But did you die, Mother?' Aisha called, grabbing her handbag from the boot and winking at me. I knew that Aisha was partial to a bit of road rage and colourful language. Sierra tutted, but she was smiling as she moved into the house, placing the tin that would no doubt contain her famous black cake, made gluten-free for me, on the console table in the hall. We didn't give each other presents as a rule, instead spending our money on the children in the family, but Sierra always brought something sweet when she visited.

'Come on in,' I said to the others, holding the door wide. 'Shall I put the kettle on?'

'I want to show you my room!' Ava said, bouncing up and down, the teenager coolness she'd recently adopted forgotten in her excitement at her aunts' arrival. 'And The Hideaway! It's so cool. I painted it you know.'

'The first thing I'm doing is using the bathroom,' Aisha announced, patting my arm as she went past. 'This child is seriously testing the limits of my bladder.'

'Opposite the stairs,' I said, pointing towards the downstairs toilet, and she waved a hand in thanks.

Ava skipped through the front door, holding hands with Cass, and led her family into the living room. I saw Daniel lurking in the kitchen doorway, his emotions written all over his face, and I forced a smile. 'Can you put the kettle on, darling?' I called, and he nodded, seemingly grateful for an excuse to stay out of the way. This was the role he would play today, lurking in the background, rarely engaging in conversation. The women were used to him, and they all seemed to prefer it when he was this way instead of his other, more grating self. It could be a struggle for them to hold their tongues when he was playing the other role: the man of the house, brash and elaborate. It would be more peaceful this way.

We settled in the living room, Aisha joining us and collapsing into an armchair, her legs resting on a stool, fingers spread over her bump. Ava perched on the stool at Aisha's feet, smiling up at her aunt.

'Lord, child, when's the last time you had a haircut?' Aisha said, snatching a strand of Ava's hair and examining it carefully.

'I found a curly hair specialist in Truro,' I said quickly. 'We're going in the new year.'

'Is she Black?' Aisha asked, raising an eyebrow at me. 'Because there's a distinct lack of diversity down here.'

'She's curly girl friendly, whatever the hell that means,' Daniel put in, placing mugs of tea on the coffee table. The two women exchanged a look and I closed my eyes for a second, but then Sierra reached out and patted my hand.

'I'm sure she'll be wonderful,' she said, her eyes crinkling as she smiled. I returned it, squeezing her fingers in mine.

'Remember how Dad used to brush our hair after a bath?' Cass said with a grin.

Aisha's laughter filled the room. 'Nana was worse! Pinning us between her knees, ripping through our *dry* hair with a *comb*! She really should've known better.'

Sierra chuckled. 'That woman never wore her hair natural in all the years I knew her. It's no wonder your father insisted on having his hair short. Until he went bald, that is.'

Ava, sitting in the middle of them all, giggled as they told her stories from their childhood, mentioning her mother as casually as if she was sitting right next to them. Meghan was a name we'd tiptoed around for years as if she was the mad wife in the attic, not the woman who died tragically young, leaving behind a small child. I realised now that I'd mistreated her memory, giving in to my guilt and my fear that I would never live up to her, that I didn't deserve to take her place in this life.

I'd always tried to do right by Ava, feeling keenly my inadequacy as someone who was neither Black nor her mother. In my naïvety, I didn't think it mattered what colour my skin was. It had never mattered to me, and at first, I failed to see how Ava being mixed race might impact her in ways I wouldn't – *couldn't* – understand. I was glad for these women, I thought to myself as I looked around the room at them. I was glad Ava had them in her life, and I was glad they'd accepted me and tried to bring me into their circle. Like all families, we had our moments, and I knew they didn't think much of Daniel, but they were here for Ava and she needed them. We both did.

Sierra caught my eye and smiled, as if she was reading my mind. She had that way about her, that quiet strength that emanated from her. Though softly spoken, I noticed early on that everyone listened when she had something to say. I knew she had been proud of Meghan, but I wondered if she had worried about her while she was at university, if her falling pregnant the year after she graduated had concerned her. Sierra never told me what she thought of Daniel, but I could tell by the way she looked at him that she didn't believe he had been good enough for her daughter. And maybe she was right.

I watched Daniel slink off upstairs like a grumpy teen, and I excused myself to make a start on dinner, leaving Ava to hold court. I was making *melanzane alla parmigiana* – which was a fancy way of saying aubergines, tomatoes, and lots of cheese – with a big leafy salad and gluten-free garlic bread on the side. I told the Echo sitting on the side, a Christmas gift from Daniel, to play my audiobook as I began chopping onions and garlic. I felt at peace, despite the full house. Or maybe it was because the house was full of people that I felt as if a weight had lifted. Daniel, Ava and I rubbed along together well enough, but I'd always sought comfort in crowds. A busy pub, standing squished on the Tube like sardines in a can. You would think, after the childhood I'd had, in a house always full of strange people, that I would seek peace and quiet, but the opposite was the truth. I couldn't stand silence. I needed other people to drown out my thoughts, silence the ghosts that refused to leave me alone.

Until now. Blackwater House had, for the second time in my life, become a sanctuary for me. A place I felt at home.

I sliced the aubergines and rinsed them before placing them in the griddle pan, quickly opening the window and switching on the extractor fan, not wanting to set off the overzealous smoke alarms. They were supposed to be smart, with an accompanying app to turn them off, but they really did take their job too seriously, shouting out a warning whenever someone fried as much as an egg. I flipped the aubergines and began to fry the onions and garlic together in some oil, then someone walked into the room and I told the Echo to stop the audiobook before turning around.

'Smells great! Do you need any help?' Natalia said from the doorway.

'Oh, no, I'm fine. Thank you though,' I said. 'Can I get you anything? Drink?'

She smiled. 'You're always looking after everyone else, Rebecca.' I felt my cheeks redden and turned back to the hob. 'Actually, I wanted to ask you something.' She came over and leaned against the side, her hands fiddling with her baggy jumper. 'How did you know when ... that Daniel was, you know. The *one*.' She put emphasis on the last word and I felt my stomach lurch at the memory of our engagement announcement a number of years ago. Daniel decided to tell everyone on Christmas Eve, a couple of months after he'd proposed and I'd accepted. Everyone was gathered in the living room, dressed in their finery, and Daniel waited until each person had a glass of champagne in their hand before speaking.

'To Rebecca,' he said, raising a glass aloft, 'who has just agreed to be my wife.'

I was surprised at the time. Knowing how close he and Meghan had been to getting married before she died, I would have preferred to speak to her family in private, but Daniel always liked to be the centre of attention, to make an impression on those around him. I'd caught the expression on Aisha's face that night, saw the look she exchanged with her sister, and felt my heart sink.

'I didn't, I suppose,' I said, choosing my words carefully. 'I mean, you never know, do you? You can never truly know another person. I'm not even sure I know myself.'

Natalia laughed. 'Yeah, I know what you mean.' She let out a breath. 'I just ... I want to ask Cass to, you know ...' She trails off as I turn to her, my eyes wide.

'To marry you?' I whispered the words. She nodded, and I clapped my hands together, the memory of my own engagement fading at my excitement. 'Oh, that's wonderful! You should! Of course you should! Shouldn't you?' An edge of uncertainty crept into my voice as she stared at me, her hands still fiddling with her jumper.

'I-I'm not sure. What if she says no?'

I stirred the passata into the saucepan and turned down the heat. Wiping my hands on a tea towel, I reached for her hands, fixing her with my gaze. 'She won't. She loves you. You can tell by the way she looks at you.' She had been with Cass almost four years now, after they'd met at work. I smiled. 'Ask her.'

Natalia's face broke into a grin, relief coming off her in waves, and we giggled like teenagers, hands clasped in excitement.

19

Rebecca

After dinner, while Daniel was in charge of grilling the crème brûlée pots for dessert, the rest of us gathered in the living room, glasses of wine in hand, the Christmas tree lights twinkling in the corner of the room. Sierra was dozing in the armchair, and Ava was telling Cass and Natalia about school and an upcoming trip to Jamaica Inn.

Aisha raised an eyebrow. 'Jamaica Inn?' she repeated.

'It's where the novel was set, by Daphne du Maurier,' Ava answered.

'Sounds like fun,' Cass said, sipping her orange juice. 'Is it haunted?'

'Probably.' I stifled a giggle. The wine was making me giddy; I could feel my cheeks flushing as I took another sip.

'There's no such thing as ghosts,' Ava said sternly, reminding me of the way she used to tell us off when she was a child, her face serious, her tiny fists clenched at her sides. I burst into giggles, setting off Cass and Natalia, Ava glaring for a moment before joining in. Daniel entered with the tray of desserts, Christmas oven gloves covering his hands, and we all turned to look at him, our lips still stretched into grins.

'What?' he said, slightly indignant, and it set us off again. Aisha snorted, holding a hand in front of her mouth, and Sierra started to chuckle, her eyes still closed, her hands resting across her stomach.

I waved a hand as I got up to help him with dessert. 'Nothing, darling. Nothing at all.'

Later that evening, Cass suggested we go for a walk, so we bundled into our coats, wrapped scarves around our necks and shoved our feet into boots. Daniel stayed behind, pleading a headache, and I didn't press him. The village was silent, lights twinkling in the trees and above shops with darkened windows.

'It's so peaceful here,' Sierra remarked, her words frosting in the air before her.

'Everyone is tucked up indoors,' Aisha said, her coat barely fastened across her large stomach. 'Not out in the cold like you maniacs.'

'You're out here too,' Cass pointed out, and Aisha stuck her tongue out at her sister.

We walked arm in arm through the deserted streets, stopping when we heard Christmas music drifting from the pub where the women were staying that night.

Sierra took my arm, her hand resting in the crook of my elbow, her shoulder bumping into mine as we walked through the garden of rest across the road. 'This place is beautiful,' she said quietly, pausing to read a gravestone half-hidden by greenery.

'Daniel says it's morbid,' I said without thinking, and Sierra flashed me a knowing smile.

'Daniel doesn't know everything.' She started walking again, her arm still in mine, eyes scanning the area for more gravestones. 'This is a wonderful example of Mother Nature reclaiming her land,' she said after a moment. 'Taking back what is rightfully hers.'

I considered her words, my eyes on the headstones and the untamed greenery. She was right; it *was* beautiful, wild and striking, just like so much of the Cornish landscape.

Sierra nodded as if I had spoken and we continued walking. I could see Cass and Natalia holding hands up ahead, Aisha leaning on Ava's arm as we followed the path through the gardens. I thought of Ashleigh then, and wondered whether I'd see her again. I didn't even know where she was living and had no way of getting in touch with her, but something told me that she would be back. Maybe then I would tell Daniel and Ava about her, my long-lost sister who was almost half my age. But how could I tell them about Ashleigh without telling them the truth about my childhood? How much did I really want them to know about my past?

The air was crisp, the sky full of stars, and the leaves on the trees rustled in the breeze as we passed. It was the last few days of 2019, but here, it could have been any time throughout history, submerged as we were in nature and the night.

I remembered a summer's evening spent here when I was a teenager, a bottle of cider shared between me and Stacey, who had one arm wrapped around her boyfriend at the time. We'd sat in the grass, sharing the cider between us, passing cigarettes back and forth, until Stacey stood and pulled the boy towards the privacy of the dense foliage. I lay back, my hair tangling with the weeds, a tiny spider crawling along my arm. I'd lifted my gaze to the sky, a patch of blue visible between the trees, a fluffy white cloud passing over. Birds sang, children giggled as they jumped off the bus, cars whooshed down the hill and through the village. *I could be anyone,* I'd thought, closing my eyes. I could have been anyone lying there in the shade, seeking respite from the relentless sun. My legs were crossed at the ankles, the grass beneath tickling my bare feet, and my arms were folded beneath my head. *I could run away. I could go anywhere I wanted. Go travelling, see the world. Stacey and I could go to college. I could learn how to do hair or plumbing or study media. I could become a journalist, a photographer. I could be anyone I want to be.*

The possibilities were endless. The world, I'd decided, was my oyster. But life had other plans for me, and it took moving into Blackwater House with Gwen for me to find my own path.

We parted ways outside the pub. Ava leaned against me as we said goodbye to Sierra and her aunts, her eyes heavy, and I wrapped an arm around her shoulders as we walked the rest of the way home.

'Becks,' she said as we entered our street. 'Why did we move here?'

I bit the inside of my mouth, considering my answer. 'Gwen left me the house,' I said. 'She wanted me to come here, I guess. She wanted us to live here.'

She sighed. 'But what do *you* want, Becks?'

She stopped and I turned to face her, her expression hidden by the darkness. But her eyes were glistening, and her words surrounded us, the accusation in her voice harsh against the quiet night air.

'I want what's best for you,' I said, reaching out and pulling her to me. 'That's all I've ever wanted. And I will see it happen, okay? You just have to trust me.'

The women left the next morning after a quick breakfast at the local café. Daniel didn't join us, choosing to go for a run instead, and I didn't miss the look that passed between Sierra and Aisha. Sierra caught my gaze, her eyes sparkling, and I tried to read the emotion there. Embarrassment? Frustration? Concern? She took my hand as they piled into the car, pulling me closer. I crouched down beside the passenger window, enjoying the warmth of her fingers in mine. If I could have chosen a mother, I would have chosen Sierra. She was kind, warm, and – although quiet – I knew she was both intelligent and fierce, commanding respect and love in equal measure. For some reason, I felt then as if it would be the last time I would see them, and I realised suddenly that I didn't want them to leave. Feeling a rush of emotion, I tried to swallow the lump in my throat as Sierra spoke.

'Take care of yourself, sweet pea,' she said, rubbing the back of my hand. 'You know where we are if you need us.'

'Just a text away,' Cass added from the back seat. Natalia caught my eye and we smiled at one another. I wondered when she was going to ask Cass to marry her. I hoped it would be soon. We could all do with a wedding to look forward to. Although Daniel and I had been engaged for years, I'd never felt it was the right time to plan a wedding, and he had never seemed fussed either.

Aisha bustled out of the front door, tugging at the buttons on her coat. She smiled at me as I straightened, Sierra releasing my hand. Aisha had always been the hardest one to read. Being the eldest sister, I supposed she was very protective over Meghan, and, by default, Ava too. While she had never been hostile towards me, I'd always felt as if I had something to prove. She came over and patted my shoulder, and I felt some of that tentativeness dissipate. Maybe I'd finally won her over.

'Be careful,' she said, locking me in place with her gaze, and I felt a shiver run down my spine. I wanted to ask her what she meant, why I needed to be careful, but the words stuck in my throat. She squeezed my shoulder once and turned to get into the car.

As Ava and I waved them off, I felt a prickle of anxiety on the back of my neck. A part of me wanted to run after them, to tear open the door and ask them to stay as we watched the car disappear down the road, and I couldn't shake the feeling that they were taking a piece of me with them.

I could almost see the black cloud trailing behind Ava as we went back into the house, her shoulders slumped as she walked. She went straight up to her room, and I found Daniel sitting at the breakfast bar, munching a slice of toast. A bubble of frustration rose in me as he looked up, swallowing his mouthful. 'They gone?' he asked. I nodded, not trusting myself to speak, and he sighed loudly. 'Thank fuck for that. God that was hard work.'

I stared at him as he popped the last piece of toast into his mouth and brushed the crumbs from his hands. *Hard work? What hard work did you do, exactly?* I wanted to say. It wasn't even as if they had stayed with us, so we had no extra sheets to change or towels to wash. Not that he ever did either of those things. I ignored him, turning to flick the kettle on before unloading the dishwasher.

'At least we won't see them for another year now,' he continued behind me.

'Ava likes seeing them,' I snapped, slamming a mug down on the side with more force than necessary. I heard his chair scrape on the tiles as he got up, putting his plate next to the sink.

'So she can visit them,' he said. I could feel his eyes on me and my skin prickled. 'At Easter, maybe. It'll be good for her.'

'Easter?' I turned to him, incredulous. 'That's months away.'

He raised an eyebrow at my tone, a tone I rarely used on him, but my emotions were too heightened to moderate the way I was speaking. 'So? I didn't spend much time with my extended family when I was a child. It's not normal.'

'Not normal?' I repeated. The memory of the coffee flashed through my mind, my instincts telling me to back down, not to cause a fight, but anger pushed them away. I knew he didn't like them, how little they had in common. But they had Ava in common, and she was the most important thing of all. She was always the most important thing. 'She loves them, and they love her. She's lucky.'

'Lucky?' Daniel scoffed. 'Yeah, right. Lucky to have that busybody Aisha, who acts as if she's the fucking queen of the world. And Cass as a role model? Yeah, really lucky.'

There was something in the way he said her name that made my hackles rise. 'Cass? What's Cass got to do with it?' I stared at him, comprehension dawning as I took in the look on his face. 'Because she's gay? I didn't know you were such a bigot, Daniel.'

His hand was in my hair before I realised what was happening, bringing my face closer to his. I tried to pull away, but his grip was like iron. 'I'm not a bigot, *Rebecca*,' he spat out my name as if it carried a bad taste. 'I don't give a shit who she fucks. But the way she dresses, her ridiculous makeup, her loose way of life.' He gave my hair a tug and I let out a gasp. 'I don't want my daughter around someone like *that*.'

'There's nothing wrong with the way Cass dresses,' I whispered, but I could feel the fight draining out of me. My heart beat with fear as he brought his other hand up to my face, gripping my chin. 'They're her family, Daniel. Her blood. She loves them.'

'Blood means nothing,' he hissed at me. 'You of all people should know that.'

He released me and I stumbled back, banging my hip against the counter. I stared after him as he stomped out of the room, his feet pounding on the stairs as the blood rushed in my ears. At that moment I saw Aisha's face, heard her words again inside my head. *Be careful.*

20

Rebecca

Before – December 2019

I woke early on New Year's Eve, padding downstairs to make myself a coffee. The house and annex needed a clean before Ava's sleepover, and I needed to go to the supermarket to pick up dinner for Daniel and me. I'd planned to cook steak, his favourite, and make some gluten-free brownies for dessert. I left the house before anyone else stirred, and when I returned, Daniel was sitting on the bottom step, lacing up his trainers.

'What's all this?' he asked, nodding towards the bags weighing down my arms without moving to help.

'Food. Dinner for tonight and to see us through the week.' I moved past him and deposited the bags in the kitchen. He followed, watching as I started unpacking them.

'Tonight? Is someone coming round?'

'Only the girls, but this isn't for them. They'll be ordering pizza. This is for us. I got steak and asparagus.' I held up the packs before sliding them into the fridge.

'Us? But I won't be here, Rebecca. I'll be in London.' I turned to him, my mouth open in surprise. He gave me a look. 'I told you I wouldn't be here.'

'Did you?' His eyes darkened and I forced myself to laugh. The house had been full of tension since Boxing Day; I couldn't afford to rile him up again. 'Oh, of course, how silly of me. Sorry, darling. Where is it you're going again?'

'Kensington. A client is throwing a party, and we're all stay-ing at the hotel. I told you this.'

'Of course you did,' I said brightly, transferring the steak from the fridge to the freezer. 'Sounds lovely. Are you off on a run?' But he had gone, the front door slamming in his wake.

I kicked the empty shopping bag at my feet. Had he really told me he'd be going away for new year's? Maybe he had. My mind was so full of the renovation and Ava and Christmas and Ashleigh. *Ashleigh.* I realised that I would be alone for new year's and wondered if she might like to come over. Ava and her friends wouldn't want me crashing their fun, but it might be nice to have some company. But I decided I'd rather be alone. I wasn't ready to let Ashleigh in yet.

Oh well, I thought, snatching up the plastic bags and shov-ing them into the larger one, which I deposited in the cupboard under the stairs. *It'll be fine. I'll be fine.* Twenty years had passed since that New Year's Eve party that changed my life. Maybe it was finally time to move on.

My phone buzzed in my pocket and I pulled it out.

My friend Holly is having a party tonight, the text read. *Do you want to come? Here's the address.*

It was from Lou. I'd texted her so she had my number, and we'd chatted a few times since we'd seen each other in the pub, but we hadn't arranged to meet up again. The address was on the next road, one of a few newer houses that had been built in the past decade or so. I didn't remember them being there when I was younger.

Ava's having a sleepover so I'm on parenting duties. Have a lovely time, and happy new year!

Oh, come on, Becks! Just for one drink? You'd be in shouting distance if anything happened. Mateo is having the kids so I'm looking forward to a night out!

I chewed my bottom lip. I couldn't go out and leave Ava and her friends here alone. Could I? She had been left by herself on a few occasions back in Hertfordshire, but that was usually when it couldn't be avoided: dentist appointments or when she was off sick unexpectedly. This was different. It was New Year's Eve, and there would be other people's children here, children I would be responsible for. I was an adult; I couldn't leave them to go to a party.

Memories of that party twenty years ago flashed into my mind. It had been peak 1999; girls glammed up with shiny lips and sparkly eyeshadow, boys with their overly gelled hair and overpowering body spray. We were drinking WKD and cheap wine, whatever we could lay our hands on, and someone had brought weed and tiny pills with smiley faces on. We lay on the cold grass in the back garden, music pouring out of the open windows, blowing smoke into the sky. The stars were out, the moon a mere sliver, and it was cold, too cold to be out with no tights and no coat, but the alcohol was doing its job, and we were lying side by side, sharing our warmth.

But we drifted apart during the night, lost in the music or in another room, fumbling at the zip of someone else's jeans, our cheeks flushed with anticipation. At one point I stumbled upstairs to the bathroom, leaning heavily on the banister, my vision blurring. The door was closed and I began to push it open, stopping short when I realised it was occupied. The whispered voices were just audible over the music, and I pressed my ear to the gap.

'You know her mum's a prozzie?' one voice said. 'She shags people for drugs. Always has.'

A giggle, the smell of weed floating through the crack in the door.

'Yeah. No wonder Becks doesn't know who her dad is,' another voice said. 'It could be anyone.'

I turned away, colour rising to my cheeks. I was about to leave when I heard the third voice.

'Like mother, like daughter.' Stacey's voice. I put a hand to my mouth in horror, unable to believe my friend – my *best* friend, the only one I'd ever had – was talking about me like that. 'Girls Just Wanna Have Fun' started playing downstairs, the party guests raising their voices to sing along to the words, and it covered the sob that burst from my lips.

'Why is she even here, Stace? Nobody likes her.' I recognised one of the other voices. Lou. 'She's so pathetic.'

Rage bubbled up inside me and I kicked open the door. The girls screamed as I launched myself at her, my fist connecting with her cheekbone, her head cracking against the sink as she fell. Stacey rushed over to her, gasping at the blood trickling from Lou's nose, before turning to me with fury in her eyes.

'Get the fuck out!' she screamed. 'Nobody wants you here, just get the fuck out!'

So I did.

When I think about that night now, all I can remember is the fear in Lou's eyes, and the disgust on Stacey's face. They were right: nobody liked me. I had no friends, no one I could confide in, and part of that was my fault. I couldn't let anyone in, couldn't tell them what was going on at home. I pushed everyone away, desperate to hide the truth.

I sat at the breakfast bar now with a cup of tea, hesitating over my reply to Lou. Despite our somewhat difficult past, part of me wanted to go. It seemed like Lou had put the events of our teenage years behind us, and I should do the same. I knew we had to start integrating with the local community, to truly make this place our home. Ava was already making friends, so why couldn't I?

'What's that?' Ava appeared over my shoulder, crunching loudly on a crisp and making me jump.

'First of all: yuck,' I said, locking my phone, 'and second of all: it's rude to read other people's messages.'

'You read mine,' she pointed out, moving away to lean against the sink, chewing.

'No, I don't. Besides, that's different. You're a child.'

She rolled her eyes and ate another crisp. 'Are you going out tonight then?'

'No, I am not going out tonight.'

'Why not?'

'Because you've got friends coming over and, again, you're a child.'

'Yeah but like, collectively, our age would be almost a hundred.' She paused, licking some crumbs from her finger-tips. 'Ninety,' she said decisively.

'Not quite. You're still fourteen.'

She shrugged. 'Anyway, I've been left alone before.'

'This is different. I've never met these girls before. I'm not sure their parents would be happy with them being left alone here.'

'You deserve to have some fun too, Becks,' she said, scrunching up the crisp packet and throwing it towards the bin. It bounced off the lid and she groaned as she went to retrieve it.

'I thought I'd add a pizza for myself to your order and just watch a film. *Mean Girls* is on Netflix.'

Ava made a face. '*Mean Girls*, really, Becks?'

'You love that film.'

'Yeah, but it's New Year's Eve. Surely you'd rather be doing something else? Where's Dad?'

'On a run.' I paused, remembering what he'd said earlier. 'Do you remember him saying anything about being in London tonight?'

'What? No.' She frowned. 'Not to me, anyway.' She looked at me then, her eyes narrowing. 'Why? Is something wrong?'

'Oh, no. Nothing's wrong. I must have just forgotten.'

21

Kate

Now – 4th January 2020

At HQ, Kate stares at the board in front of her, a printed photo of Rebecca dangling from her fingers. Her gaze is focused on the photo of Ava in the middle, on the wide, carefree grin on her face. *She really does look happy,* she thinks, but she knows looks can be deceiving.

She reaches for Daniel next. It's a photo taken from Ava's Instagram page, with the caption *Daddy Dear.* She hasn't been able to find a picture of Ava's mother yet, so she places a blank piece of paper with the words MEGHAN BIRD beside Daniel.

Building a family tree is something Kate finds therapeutic. As she pins photos of Ava's aunts on the left-hand side of the board beneath Meghan's name, she can almost feel something slipping into place. *But what?* Sierra, the grandmother, sits above Meghan, another one without a photo, and there is a large question mark beside Daniel, where his family should be. Kate knows his father had died a number of years before, but what about his mother? Siblings? Rebecca's mother, Gemma Bray, is looking particularly unkempt in her mugshot from an attempted shoplifting spree some years before, which Kate has pinned above Rebecca. She places another blank piece of paper beside Gemma, remembering the entry beneath *Father* on Rebecca's birth certificate. *Unknown.*

'Kate?' A knock on the door behind her and DS Tremayne steps into the room. Her eyes roam over the board for a moment before she nods. 'Good work.' Kate allows herself a small smile. 'We're going to do a press conference today,' DS Tremayne says, leaning against the table. 'The father is still up country, so it'll have to be Rebecca alone. Do you think she's up to it?'

Kate frowns. Rebecca was someone who always seemed tough, but she also had a kind of vulnerability to her that Kate saw even back when they were kids. She has seen it many times since joining the police; in the eyes of the neglected child being carried out to the police car; on the trembling fingers of the woman reporting a sexual assault. It is a vulnerability as old as time itself, an unbreakable bond between those who know.

'I'm not sure,' she says, deciding not to commit either way. 'I'll ask her.'

'Good,' DS Tremayne says, nodding as if Kate has just in fact committed herself.

'A press conference?' Rebecca's eyes are wide as Kate places a cup of tea in front of her.

'It's an appeal, really. To get the word out there.'

'But . . . me? I don't know, Kate, I . . .'

'I know it's not easy,' Kate says, sitting down and reaching out a hand to Rebecca. 'But it could help us reach Ava.' *Or whoever is holding Ava,* she finishes in her head. She doesn't want to put that scenario into Rebecca's mind. Or rather, bring it to the surface. Kate can only imagine what horrors have been going through Rebecca's head since Ava went missing.

Rebecca is silent for a moment, staring down into her tea. 'Daniel should be here,' she says eventually.

Yes, he should, Kate thinks. *I have no idea why he isn't.* While it isn't unlawful to go to work while your daughter is missing, it certainly is irregular, and it raised a red flag for Kate and her colleagues. *And it doesn't make him look very good, does it?* 'Would he come down if you asked him to?' she asks. 'Should I give him a call?'

'No,' Rebecca says, too quickly, taking out her phone and scrolling to find Daniel's number. 'I'll do it.'

Kate isn't going to hold her breath; a man who runs off up country during the search for his missing daughter doesn't seem like the kind of person to drop everything and come back for an appeal, even if he had mentioned it during Kate's first visit.

'Rebecca,' Kate hears a loud voice say on the other end of Rebecca's phone, just as Kate thinks it will go to voicemail. 'What is it? Is there news?'

'N-no, no news.' Rebecca's voice is small, and Kate wonders if she should have left her to make the call in private, but something keeps her in her seat, pretending not to listen.

'Then what?' Daniel barks. Out of the corner of her eye, Kate sees Rebecca jump.

'T-the police, they want us to do a . . . an appeal. A press conference. They think . . .'

'A press conference?' he snaps. 'What is this, a fucking circus?'

'Daniel, please, I—'

'No.'

'It's an appeal, for Ava. She might see it, she might—'

'She's not going to fucking see it.'

Kate's gaze snaps back towards Rebecca, and when their eyes meet, she recognises something in the other woman. Fear.

A second later, without realising she had even moved, Kate has the phone pressed against her ear. 'Mr Everley,' she says, her voice sharp, 'this is Kate Winters.' The man is silent, but a quick glance at the screen tells her he hasn't hung up. 'We believe an appeal like this gives us a good chance at reaching Ava, or someone who knows where she might be.' Another pause. 'Will you come back to Cornwall for it?'

Daniel makes a noise in his throat, and Kate isn't sure if it's a noise of frustration or concern. 'I can't. I'm needed up here.'

You're needed down here, Kate thinks. 'All right,' she says, deciding not to waste her time on persuading him. 'But if Rebecca consents, she can do it alone.'

'If *she* consents,' he repeats, an edge to his voice. 'What about *my* consent?'

'It's not required,' Kate says, before hanging up and handing the phone back to Rebecca.

'Just remember what we said,' Kate whispers an hour later, crouching down beside Rebecca's chair. The rows of chairs are still empty, the door to the press room closed firmly against the swarm of journalists waiting outside. 'Keep it simple, read from your notes. You're talking to Ava now. Nobody else.' She stands, feeling something click in one of her knees. *Grandma,* Lauren would say. The door at the back of the room opens and DS Tremayne slips inside. 'I'll be right over here, okay?' she says to Rebecca before stepping back.

DS Tremayne joins her on the edge of the room. 'All set?'

Kate nods. 'I think so.'

A retractable banner with Devon and Cornwall Constabulary emblazoned across it sits behind Rebecca. Kate can see her legs bouncing beneath the white tablecloth, her fingers twisting in her lap, and she feels a pang.

'Bastard, letting her go through this alone,' DS Tremayne whispers, reading Kate's mind. 'What an absolute shit.'

Bastard, indeed, she thinks, *but is he guilty of something other than being a shit? Could he know more than he's letting on?*

A woman from the force press office enters the room and begins fussing around the table, filling water glasses and tidying papers. Rebecca stares straight ahead while the woman buzzes around her, ignoring her inane questions, and Kate takes a step forward to intervene when the door opens again, and the room is suddenly full of people, their murmurs filling the air. *Rhubarb, rhubarb,* Kate thinks, remembering her trip to the theatre with Lauren and her dad last year. 'The background noise is actually the actors repeating the word *rhubarb,*' David told her with undisguised glee, which was even more annoying than his look of horror when he found out she'd never been to the theatre before. He didn't seem to think that the Minack counted.

DS Tremayne takes the seat beside Rebecca, her freshly ironed suit drawing attention to Rebecca's crumpled appearance, and reaches out for a glass of water. The press officer claps her hands and the room falls silent. Almost all the chairs are taken now, and dozens of microphones and cameras are pointing at the front of the room. *She looks so young, and so alone,* Kate realises suddenly, wishing she could step in front of her, read out the statement herself. She looks so much like the Becks Kate knew as a child, lost and in need of rescuing. *But she wants to do it,* she reminds herself. Or had Rebecca only acquiesced because DS Tremayne wasn't going to take no for an answer? For once, Kate is inclined to agree with her superior. She believes in the appeals, believes that they work, and hopes beyond hope that Ava is watching; that, if she left of her own accord, she sees the desperation on Rebecca's face and comes home. But what would she think about the absence of her father?

The press officer, now stood at the back of the room, gives DS Tremayne the nod, and Rebecca picks up the sheet of paper before her. 'Ava.' Her voice cracks on the second syllable, her eyes fluttering closed for a moment against the camera flashes, and Kate sees her fight to regain her composure. 'Ava, if you're watching, if you can hear me . . .' Another pause, and the room holds its collective breath. 'Please get in touch. We miss you so much. Ava, we . . .' A flash of light, her eyes glancing down at the statement then back at the cameras. 'We are beside ourselves with worry. You're not in any trouble. You're not . . . We're not angry, darling. We miss you so much. Please. Please come home.' Kate feels her eyes stinging with tears and she fights them back, focusing on Rebecca's straight spine, her hands now clasped between her knees. 'Please come home,' Rebecca repeats, this time barely a whisper, and suddenly she collapses, her body folding in on itself as her hands fly up to cover her face.

DS Tremayne clears her throat, her upper body leaning forward as she speaks into the microphone. 'Ava Everley was last seen at a sleepover at her house in the early hours of the first of January. She was wearing black jeans and a blue top, black trainers with white laces, and may have a black coat with a fur hood. She is fourteen years old.' She holds up an enlarged photo of Ava. 'If anyone has any information on the whereabouts of Ava, please get in touch with the Devon and Cornwall Constabulary. Thank you.' She stands, shifting her body so the crowd can no longer see Rebecca, and Kate rushes over to crouch beside her as the room empties.

'Well done, Becks,' she says, rubbing her arm, and she barely has time to register her mistake and the flash of anger in Rebecca's eyes before she is knocked to the ground, Rebecca stalking across the room, the door slamming shut behind her.

22

Rebecca

Before – December 2019

'Have a lovely time, darling,' I said, leaning in to kiss Daniel on the cheek as he pulled on his coat. 'And happy new year.'

He opened the front door then paused, turning back towards me. My heart sped up in anticipation, but his eyes were soft when he spoke. 'Are you going to be all right? I know you're not a fan of New Year's Eve. I don't like the thought of you being here alone.'

'Oh, I'll be fine. Ava and the girls will keep me busy, and I've decided to indulge in a pizza and some Buck's Fizz. I'll probably be asleep before midnight anyway.'

He smiled, and suddenly he reminded me of the man I'd fallen in love with all those years ago. His twinkling eyes, his generosity, the way he lifted my hair to kiss my neck. I closed the gap between us and kissed him then, tasting him as if for the last time. 'You're making me not want to go,' he said when we pulled apart. I watched as he walked backwards down the front steps and crunched his way across the driveway, pausing to wave before he got into the car. I waved back, leaning against the doorframe, watching until his car disappeared down the lane.

Closing the door, I exhaled. My hair was still damp, and I was under strict instructions not to touch it. Ava had painstakingly brushed through my hair after we'd washed out the mask earlier, gathering the clumps and scrunching them in the palm of her hand, fingers opening to reveal curls. She'd applied a tropical-scented cream, which I could still smell as I stuffed my feet into boots and went outside to check on The Hideaway. We'd worked hard to get it ready on time, carrying furniture downstairs once the laminate boards had been laid on the ground floor. The TV was up on the wall, and a few beanbags were spread out in front of it. The fridge was full of fizzy drinks and sweet treats, and I'd added a can of squirty cream for their hot chocolates. They had everything they could need and more.

I suddenly realised how much I wanted the night to be a success. Ava was always the kind of person to make friends wherever she went, but being a teenager wasn't easy, and I wanted her to form real, lasting friendships here. I wanted her to be happy.

I made a quick lunch of cheese on toast for us both, making the most of Daniel's absence by taking the plates into the living room and eating off our laps in front of the TV. Ava had persuaded me to start watching *Ru Paul's Drag Race*, another thing Daniel wouldn't have approved of, but we enjoyed it and besides, I'd probably watch anything just to spend time with Ava. We used to watch children's cartoons every afternoon, the high-pitched voices and unnecessarily catchy music playing over and over again. In comparison, *Drag Race* was rather soothing.

After we ate, Ava went upstairs and I cleaned the kitchen before making a cup of coffee and taking it out into the garden. We were protected from the worst of the wind by the thick trees standing guard on either side, but it was still freezing at this time of year and I shivered, wrapping my hands around my mug as I stared out to sea. The sky was thick with clouds, the threat of rain in the air. I walked along the back fence, checking for signs of damage. I knew the girls wouldn't be silly enough to try to climb the fence, but it was good practice anyway.

Gwen did this a few times a year, walking the perimeter of the property to make sure the fences were in good condition and would last through the next season. The ones hidden behind the trees on either side were normal-sized fences, six feet or so, but a four-foot post-and-rail fence ran along the back so as not to block the view of the ocean. A few feet beyond, the ground gave way to the cliff face, and, over a hundred feet below, sea.

I leaned out over it, catching a glimpse of the engine house, which sat further along the cliff. Almost twenty years ago, I'd staggered along the dusty path, fingertips clutching at rocks to haul myself back up, clothes sticking to my skin with sweat and blood. I stumbled through the adjacent field, tears blurring my eyes, and ended up here, on the edge of Blackwater House, faced with a choice. Did I keep going, clamber over the rocks to find the highest point and jump from it, give myself to the sea? I had been going to. I had nothing to lose, nothing to live for. I hadn't intended on being found.

I stared out across the water now, letting the noise fill my ears. It all would have been different if I'd jumped. If Gwen hadn't taken me in. If she hadn't encouraged me to make something of my life. I'd never have met Daniel, or Ava. I'd never have left this place, my ghost would have been trapped here forever. Just like Ashleigh.

I sighed. Just like when I was younger, I didn't know what to do with my sister. She must have her own life, I reasoned. She was no longer a child, and she had obviously managed without me for most of her life. And, I had to admit, I hadn't thought about her much over the years. I'd tried to bury that part of my life, shoving it deep inside a box and turning the key, locking it up forever. But it was all coming back now. Terry, Mum, Ashleigh. Lou.

Wasn't it time to move on, properly this time? Time to

accept my past as something I had lived through, and despite the odds became this new person, this version of me. I was no longer Becks Bray. No longer the kid with greasy hair and a house full of secrets. I had survived. I was still surviving. Could my two lives really meet? Could I introduce Ashleigh to Ava? Daniel might never accept my past, but Ava could. Kind, thoughtful, innocent Ava, who loved me despite it all.

'Hi, Poppy!' I said brightly, smiling at the girl standing on the doorstep. Her mother, Angela, stood beside her, laden down with Poppy's bags. It was already pitch-black outside, the security lights creating a halo around us.

'Thanks so much for having them tonight,' she said. 'I can't remember the last new year's I had to myself!'

'Charming,' Poppy said, rolling her eyes good-naturedly.

'Come and see The Hideaway!' Ava said, pulling on her friend's arm. 'Bye, Mrs Barton!'

'Goodbye, girls. Happy new year!' Angela waved at their retreating forms and sighed. 'Ah, to be fourteen again. Actually, scratch that, I was a horrible teenager.'

'I highly doubt that,' I said politely.

'Weren't we all?' she said with a laugh. 'Anyway, I'd better go. My husband has booked us a table for eight and I still need to sort out this mess.' She waved a hand at her almost perfect hair. 'One of us will be over to pick her up at eleven tomorrow, if that's still okay?'

'Of course. Should I take those?'

'Oh, yes, here. Thanks.' She handed me Poppy's bags with a smile. 'And you've got my number?' I nodded. I'd made Ava get me all of her friends' parents' phone numbers last week, though I already had Angela's from when Ava stayed at hers before. She blew out a breath. 'Great. Well, thanks again, Rebecca. We should have coffee sometime, or dinner. Let's set something up. Right, best be off. Happy new year – and good luck!'

I waved as she drove away, lifting Poppy's bags and carrying them over to the annex. Inside, I could hear Ava and Poppy upstairs on the mezzanine, their excited voices echoing through the space.

'I'll put your bags down here, Poppy,' I called up as I dropped her bags onto the sofa.

'Thank you, Mrs Everley!' she called back.

'Her name is Becks,' Ava said.

'No, it isn't,' I said, at the same time Poppy said, 'But *I* can't call her that!' I smiled and turned to go back outside when I saw another car pulling into the drive. 'Ava, someone else is here.'

The two girls thundered down the stairs, giggling, and charged out across the garden. The car doors opened and three more girls got out, the five of them jumping around and squealing. I followed behind, smiling at the man who got out of the driver's side.

'Hi, Rebecca?' he said. 'I'm Lara's dad. I brought Lois and Jess too. Thanks for having them.'

'No problem. Ava's been really looking forward to it. Do they have any bags?'

'Girls, don't forget your bags,' he called. He popped open the boot and the three girls grabbed their rucksacks, one of them – Lara, I assumed – pausing to kiss her dad on the cheek. 'Bye. Have a great time.'

'Bye, Dad!' she said, and the group set off towards the annex.

'You're brave,' he said, watching them go.

'Or stupid.'

He laughed. 'Your words, not mine.' He checked his watch. 'See you at eleven tomorrow, right? My husband will probably pick them up, same car.'

I nodded. 'Hopefully I'll still be in one piece by then.'

'I recommend wine,' he said with a grin, then got into his car. He tooted his horn as he drove down the lane. I followed, latching the gate behind him. It was a safe area, and it was unlikely there would be many tourists at this time of year, but Daniel was right to be so security-conscious. It was a symptom of modern parenting, I thought, realising what Lara's dad had meant when he'd said his husband might come to collect their daughter, and how Angela had mentioned that 'one of them' would pick Poppy up in the morning. I had to be careful into whose custody I released the girls. For the next seventeen-ish hours, I was responsible for them.

I exhaled, rubbing my hands along my arms as I walked back up the drive. I poked my head into the annex and was greeted with the excited chatter of teenage girls, and I left without disturbing them. They knew where I was if they needed anything.

Inside, the house felt empty, the corners darker than usual. I switched on the lamps to chase away the shadows and went into the kitchen to make a cup of tea, then sat down on the sofa and flicked on the TV, scrolling through Netflix to find something to watch. My phone vibrated and I opened it to find a text from Ava.

What pizza do you want? Ordering now x

Gluten-free pepperoni please. Do I need to go and collect it? x

Yes please! In like thirty minutes. Thank youuuuu x

I smiled and locked my phone, settling down to watch an episode of *Friends*. Although it was cold, the skies had cleared and it looked like the rain might hold off. Before the next episode automatically played, I shrugged into my raincoat just in case and, as I was leaving, I noticed one of the girls standing in the garden, the end of a cigarette bobbing in the darkness. I heard her say *shit!* and saw the red dot cast to the ground.

'I don't mind,' I said, hiding a smile. 'Just use that pot as an ashtray, please. I don't fancy picking up cigarette butts tomorrow morning.' *Or have the whole place set alight because you felt the need to hide it,* I added silently.

'Thanks Mrs Everley,' the girl said, her eyes wide with surprise.

'Becks?' Ava popped her head out the door, looking at her friend then at me. 'Are you going to get the pizzas?'

I nodded. 'Any more requests before I go?'

'No, thanks. I'll open the gate for you.' Ava jogged ahead while I got into the car. I rolled down the window as I passed her. 'Thanks for being cool about the smoking. I don't do it – you know I think it's gross – but Jess, well . . .'

I smiled. 'I know. Just make sure they smoke outside, okay? And put them out properly. The last thing we need is a fire engine trying to get down this driveway.'

She laughed. 'Okay. Thanks, Becks. See you in a bit.' She jogged back towards the annex and I drove down the lane, turning towards the village. The Christmas lights were still up, stars and icicles glowing brightly against the sky. The pub windows were lit, the sound of music and laughter pouring out as I parked up and walked towards the pizza place. Inside, the glass had steamed up, and a couple sat together on the stools, waiting for their order. They smiled at me and I returned it, recognising the woman from somewhere. The pub, probably, or the café. I paid and, arms loaded with boxes, made my way back to the car.

As I drove down the lane towards home, something flashed across the front of the car, briefly illuminated by the headlights. A cat, or a fox, maybe. Hopping out to lock the gate behind me, I parked up and found the box marked GLUTEN-FREE, placing it on the doorstep before delivering the rest to the annex. The girls flocked around me like seagulls, laughing and chattering as they opened the boxes, trying to find their order. Ava mouthed *thank you* at me as I turned to go and I nodded, leaving them to it.

Part of me wanted to stay, that half-buried younger self that never got to eat pizza and watch movies and drink hot chocolate with friends. The Becks who never had a friend, not a true friend at least, who spent her life behind a locked door, trying to disappear into fictional worlds. The Becks who had never truly been a child, who had had to grow up far too soon.

Dropping the pizza box onto the counter, I fished out a plate and opened a bottle of strawberry wine, pouring myself a glass. As I was settling down on the sofa, I heard a knock on the front door and frowned. It must be one of the girls, I thought. But when I opened the door I found Lou standing there.

'Surprise!' she said, holding up a bottle of rosé.

'Oh!' I said, glancing down at my leggings and oversized jumper. 'Lou, hi. I wasn't expecting you.'

'Obviously, that's why it's a surprise.' She grinned. 'I thought we could have a drink before I went over to my friend's party, and see if I couldn't persuade you to join me.' I started to shake my head and she pulled a face. 'Just one glass? I can see you've already poured your own.' I followed her gaze to the living room door and the coffee table beyond that held my dinner.

'Come on, then,' I relented, stepping back so she could enter. 'Do you want some pizza? It's gluten-free. I have coeliac disease.' My words were coming out too fast and I stopped, trying to take a deep breath. Why was I so nervous? It was only Lou, and she'd invited herself in. She would have to take me as I was. 'I'll get you a glass.'

Lou followed me into the kitchen, whistling as she poked her head into the library and dining room. 'Nice place. Was it a lot of work?'

'Not much,' I said, opening the cupboard and grabbing a wine glass before finding another plate. 'Mostly cosmetic. The annex, where the girls are now, used to be a garage, so that was the hardest bit.'

'Annex, eh? Will you be renting it out?'

I nodded. 'That's the plan.'

'Perfect location for it. And nice for your daughter, too. To have somewhere she can have friends over. Though the house is big enough!'

'She's my stepdaughter,' I said as we went into the living room. 'Ava. She's fourteen.'

'And where's your partner tonight?'

'In London. He has a work do.'

'Ooh, London.' Lou smiled as I offered her the pizza box. She took a slice, sliding it onto her plate, before opening the bottle of wine and pouring herself a glass. 'Didn't fancy it yourself?'

'Not really. I've never been a big fan of London.'

Lou wrinkles her nose. 'Why'd you move there then?'

'Oh, well I moved to Hertfordshire. For uni.'

'I never went to uni,' she said around a mouthful of pizza. I nibbled at my own slice. 'Started working for my dad as soon as I left school.'

'Oh? What do you do?'

'Electrician. I know, proper feminist over here.' She laughed. 'My mum died when I was little so it was just me and Dad. I used to go to work with him during the school holidays, you know, so I picked it up quite young and found I enjoyed it. Mateo works part-time and looks after the kids, which he also enjoys. He's *far* more diligent with the duster than I ever was.' I nodded as she spoke. We weren't that close, so I hadn't known about her mother dying when she was young. How many of us hid parts of our life when we were younger, pretending we were fine? 'Anyway,' she said, taking a sip of wine. 'What about you? What do you do?'

'I'm a freelance editor. I do some ghost-writing too.'

'Ghost-writing?' She wiggled her fingers and I laughed. 'Is that when you write a book for someone else?'

'Yeah, pretty much. It's fun, usually. I enjoy it.'

'And what about your mum? Does she still live round here?'

I paused, heart speeding up. How much did she remember? *You know her mum's a prozzie. She shags people for drugs.* 'N-no,' I mumbled, avoiding her gaze. 'She's dead.'

'Oh, sorry.' She finished her slice and went in for another one. 'What does your partner do? Are you married?'

I blinked, stumbling over the quick-fire questions. 'No, not married. He's an accountant. He has his own firm.'

She whistled again. 'Nice. Is that how you could buy this place? You'd have to be a cash buyer, wouldn't you, what with the subsidence.'

Fuck. Only a local would know about that, how the historic mining had affected the ground around it. 'Erm,' I said, trying to decide whether to tell her about Gwen, when her phone beeped.

'That's Holly. Christ, is that the time? Ah well, I'm always bloody late – she won't mind. She's used to it.' Lou winked and took another sip as I checked the time: almost eight o'clock. 'Are you glad to be back?'

'It's nice. I liked where we lived before, but there's something about Cornwall, isn't there?' I wiped my fingers on a napkin and picked up my wine glass. 'I think I always knew I'd come back.'

'You can take the girl out of Cornwall,' she said with a chuckle. 'I could never leave. It's in your blood.' We sat in silence for a moment before she spoke again. 'You know, Holly is probably your closest neighbour. You should definitely meet her.'

'I'd like to, another time,' I said with a smile. 'Maybe you could both come round for dinner.'

'Oh, she'd like that. She's a bit posh, though she hates it when I say that. They moved down from London a few years ago and had a couple of kids, you know.'

'How did you meet?'

'I was doing a job for her. It's this massive house that looks like a doll's house, you know, like proper toy town. She was there alone with two screaming kids, sick all down one shoulder, and she's got three dogs, these massive chunky black Labradors, which are pretty cute when they're not trying to run you over. Honestly, I nearly turned around and left.' She laughed. 'But I went in to do the job, asked where the fuse box was, and she just kind of stood there, her eyes glazed over. Then she burst into tears, saying she didn't know where it was.'

'Oh, dear.'

'Yep. I felt a bit sorry for her then, so I made her a cup of tea and found the fuse box myself.'

'Now that's what I call service.'

'Right? She called me up a few weeks later and offered to take me out for a drink as a thank you. I wasn't sure at first but I went, and here we are, four years later and firm pals.' She drained her wine glass. 'Though not for much longer, if I don't leave now. I've got her sodding Kettle chips.' She stood up, holding her glass and plate. 'I'll just put these in the sink.'

'That's okay,' I said, taking them from her and putting them on the table. 'I'll see you out. Don't forget those Kettle chips.'

'God, no, Holly would throttle me.'

Lou followed me to the door, the security light flicking on as she buttoned up her coat on the doorstep. 'Thanks for having me. We should definitely do it again, with Holly. She'd like that.'

I nodded. 'That'd be nice. Text me, we'll sort something out. Happy new year.'

'Happy new year, Becks,' she said, pausing on the doorstep. 'You know, I'm really glad we bumped into each other. We've still got so much to catch up on.' I smiled, trying not to show the flutter of anxiety at her words as she lifted a hand and walked down the drive. I turned to go back in then paused, remembering that she had knocked instead of ringing the doorbell, and noticed a red ring around the button, which was usually blue. I pressed it but nothing happened. Maybe the internet was down, or the bandwidth was being hogged by Ava and her friends. Shrugging, I closed the door behind me and went back into the living room, wrapping myself in a blanket and settling down on the sofa.

23

Rebecca

I must have fallen asleep, because I dreamed of Gwen. We were in the dining room, her sewing box open on the table, the contents scattered across the surface, while I stood on a stool before her, trying not to move as she pinned the bottom of my school trousers.

'You can get down now,' she said, slowly getting up from the floor and sitting at the table. 'And try not to disturb the pins when you take them off.'

I went into the downstairs toilet to change back into my jeans, carefully peeling the trousers off and folding them over my arm to take back to her. She threaded a needle and started to work, and I watched for a moment, transfixed.

'Is that the kettle I hear?' she said with a smile, and I jumped up and ran into the kitchen with my usual haste. I was making the tea when I heard her calling me. She looked up with twinkling eyes as I entered the room. 'I think I've got some French Fancies in the cupboard. Can you have a look for me?' I rummaged around until I found the box, and then took it into the dining room. Gwen smiled, taking it from me. 'The yellow ones are my favourite,' she said. 'What about you?'

'I don't know,' I replied. 'I've never had them before.'

Her eyes widened and she shook her head. 'Well, we can't have that, can we? Make yourself a cup of tea, dear, and we'll find out your favourite flavour.' Once I'd deposited the mugs on the table between us, Gwen opened the box and took out a pink, yellow, and brown cake.

'Which one can I have?' I asked, fingers twitching in anticipation of the sugar rush.

'You'd better try all of them,' she said, 'else we'll never find out which one you like best, hmm?'

I woke to a voice calling my name, dragging me out of the past. 'Becks? Becks, wake up.'

'Ava?' I mumbled, rubbing my eyes. My vision swam and the face appeared before me. 'Ashleigh? What are you doing here?'

'Happy new year,' she said, sitting down beside me, the sofa barely sinking beneath her weight.

'Is it?' I checked the time on my phone – 23:40. 'Not yet.'

'Not yet,' she echoed. 'Ooh, is that strawberry wine?' She picked up the empty bottle and I nodded, a pain shooting behind my right eye. Had I drunk the whole bottle? I couldn't remember. Then I saw another empty bottle on the floor and groaned. Two bottles? No wonder I felt like shit.

I realised I was desperate for a cigarette. 'How did you get in?' I asked as I got up slowly and padded across the hall to dig out my tobacco.

'Front door was open,' Ashleigh said, following me. I held up the packet and she nodded, so I rolled her one too before putting on my shoes and grabbing a coat.

'I should check on the girls,' I said, opening the front door. I paused, trying to remember if I'd locked the door behind me when Lou left. I can't have done, if Ashleigh came in that way. The annex lights were on, and I could see through the window that they were all lying around on the floor, pillows and sleeping bags strewn around the room, the TV playing a movie. I counted four heads before I noticed Ava in the kitchen, filling mugs with hot water. One of the other girls got up and started spraying whipped cream on top, before ripping open a bag of marshmallows. Tiny squares exploded across the counter and their laughter trickled out to where Ashleigh and I stood, invisible in the dark.

'Looks like they're fine,' she said, and we moved away, walking down the garden, the security lights flicking on as we went. We stopped at the end of the garden, the wind whipping our hair back from our faces, the night air so cold it made my cheeks sting. It was almost midnight, and the memories were crowding in, threatening to engulf me. I wanted to return to the memories of Gwen, of school trousers and cakes and the overwhelming sense of calm. On the night she found me, I must have seemed like a frightened bird, a rabbit caught in the headlights, something to coax out of the darkness and into the warmth of Blackwater House. I wanted to stay there, wrapped up in my memories. I didn't want to think of *him*, the man who had changed my life all those years ago. But every year, he came back to haunt me.

'What did you do for Christmas?' Ashleigh asked, her voice thick with smoke.

I opened my mouth to tell her, pausing at the last minute to wonder how discovering she hadn't been invited, hadn't even been thought of, would make her feel. 'Oh, just a quiet one. You?'

'Nothing.'

'You could've come here,' I said, but we both knew I didn't mean it.

'I don't like the time of year.' Her eyes met mine and understanding passed between us as the memory of the last Christmas I'd spent in that house flashed through my mind. It was my first year at university. We had broken up for three weeks and I wasn't due to work at the pub until the day after Boxing Day, so I decided to come back to Cornwall. In my naïvety, I'd imagined that things might have changed. I'd been away for almost four months, only speaking to Mum on the phone once. I hung up every time Terry answered, or whenever a random voice came over the line, slurring 'hello?' over the music.

I had jumped on the coach at London Victoria, armed with a coffee and a copy of *The Handmaid's Tale*, which I'd finished by the time we got to Bristol. I spent the rest of the journey watching the motorway flash by, the heavy feeling in my stomach as if I'd swallowed a rock. Every muscle in my body screamed at me to flee, to jump off the coach at the next stop and turn back. But it was Christmas Eve, and I didn't want to get stuck in a strange town with nowhere to sleep, and I didn't want to go back to my silent, empty student house. So I stayed on, finally arriving just outside Newquay as the sky was darkening. Another bus journey and I was walking up the path to my childhood home, the house that had never, not once in my life, felt like home. Home was supposed to be warm, comforting, a sigh of relief as you kick off your shoes and flop on the sofa. Like it had been with Gwen. Home was not supposed to be dangerous.

I held my breath as I knocked on the door. I still had a key, but something stopped me from riffling through my bag to pull it out. A face appeared at the window, just two eyes and a shock of hair visible above the cardboard covering the bottom panel, before the door flew open and Terry stepped out. 'Well, well, well. The prodigal daughter returns.' He reached up to scratch his chin, jagged fingernails rasping against the stubble. He grinned as he noticed the wrapped present poking out of my bag, his yellow teeth glinting in the light. 'Is it Christmas, then?'

I looked behind him into the house. There was no tree, no presents, no turkey roasting in the oven. Why had I thought there would be? I took a deep breath. 'Is Mum here?'

'Nah, she's off touring the country with her new rock band,' Terry snorted, flicking ash from the end of his cigarette.

'Who is it?' I heard a voice ring out from the living room.

'It's me, Mum,' I said at the same time Terry shouted, 'No one!' We glared at one another, eyeing each other up like animals in the wild. I hadn't changed much since I left, my body still thin, my head barely reaching his shoulders, but I bubbled with a rage that threatened to overspill, to engulf me entirely, and I saw his eyes flash as he recognised it within me. It was the same beast that lived inside him.

I pushed past him, feeling my rucksack knock into his chest, and made for the living room. I glanced up the stairs, cast in shadow by the dark December evening, and saw Ashleigh's face peering around the banister at me, her hair in a messy plait, her feet bare despite the chill. Then Mum was in front of me, her eyes clear for the first time in years.

'Hello, love,' she said, and I stupidly, despite everything that had happened, believed that things might be different. But then my gifts sat unopened on the floor while Terry gave Mum a hit and he opened can after can of beer. His voice got louder and louder, saliva spraying from his mouth as he declared me a traitor.

'You're no better than me,' he snarled, his pupils huge. 'You're nothing. And you always will be.'

When my mum passed out, I left and went to the only place I could've gone. Gwen had chided me for coming back, then listened in sympathy when I'd told her about my empty student flat, the loneliness. I hadn't understood why I couldn't come back to her for the holidays.

'Because you're not mine,' she said gently, squeezing my hand.

But I am, I'd wanted to say. I'd understood, in a way. She wanted me to find my own path, a new life elsewhere, away from this place and all its darkness. She'd wanted more for me than a life that mirrored her own. But I'd been young and afraid, and I'd needed her comfort one last time. I'd lain awake that night, torturing myself with the memory of Ashleigh's face at the window, her doll clutched to her chest, her eyes wide as she watched me walk away for the final time.

'I'm sorry,' I whispered now, my eyes stinging with tears. 'I'm so sorry I left you there.'

She reached out and took my hand, and we stood in silence, watching out over the water, until fireworks exploded in the distance, bright shards of light pouring down over the ocean.

'Happy new year, Becks,' she said.

'Happy new year, Ashleigh.' *And Gwen,* I added silently. *I wish you were here too.*

She left a short while later. I watched her walk down the drive, the darkness swallowing her whole, as I went over to the annex to check on the girls one last time. The TV was still on, but the lights were off and they looked like they were settling down to sleep. After locking up, I went upstairs to bed, my body heavy, my mind full. I half-heartedly brushed my teeth and took off my makeup, pulling my hair into a ponytail as I turned off the bathroom light, plunging the room into darkness, and padded barefoot across the small landing. I lay in bed, watching the shadows of the trees move across the ceiling, memories pressing at the corners of my mind, ghosts knocking on the windows, demanding to be let in.

I must have slept again, because a noise snapped me awake, and I could feel my heart racing as I strained to figure out where it came from. Was something outside? Then another noise, and this time I knew it was coming from inside the house. Maybe Ava had come back inside for something, and was creeping around so as not to disturb me? I got out of bed to peer through the bedroom window, but it was too dark to see anything. Grabbing my phone from the bedside table, I opened the bedroom door and went down the half-staircase to peer across the first floor.

A shaft of moonlight fell across the floor outside Ava's bedroom, trickling through the skylight above. All the doors were closed except for the bathroom, which was wide open. I made my way down, a cold breeze brushing against my arms, making my skin prickle. Did Ava leave the window open earlier? I went into the room and pulled the window closed, locking it with a click. A voice came from downstairs and I jumped, letting out an involuntary shriek. It sounded as if it was coming from the living room. I listened, fingers gripping the banister, until I realised it was coming from the TV. Sighing, I padded down the stairs and into the living room. The TV lit up the room, and I recognised *Mean Girls* playing on the screen.

'Weird,' I muttered as I switched it off. The room fell into darkness and I shivered. Going to the window, I could see the lights were still on in the annex, the girls not yet asleep. I'd expected it might be a late one, and I didn't want to be that grouchy parent who told them to go to bed. They weren't disturbing anyone and besides, they could sleep in until their parents collected them in the morning.

Turning away from the window, I saw something flash across the living room doorway and jumped. *It's just a shadow,* I told myself, unlocking my phone and switching on the torch app. I crept out into the hall, aiming the torch at the closed doors on my left. *There's nobody there.* As I turned, the torch beam fell on the stairs and I froze. There, perched on the bottom step, was a doll Ava had had since she was a child, its black hair carefully arranged around its shoulders, its top torn open to reveal the letter M scrawled on its chest.

And then there was a hammering on the door, and a muffled cry that I realised had come from me. I spun away from the doll and wrenched open the front door to find Poppy standing on the steps, her face wet with tears.

'Ava's gone,' she sobbed, and I felt the world tilt beneath me.

PART 2

24

Rebecca

I stand at the back fence, staring out across the sea as the sun turns the water's surface to diamonds. Three days. Ava has been missing for three days, and I still have no idea where she is.

I can almost feel Kate Winters staring at me, her eyes burning into me from her place at the back door. She is always watching me, watching us. She knows something isn't right between Daniel and me, but I've been careful around her. She always was perceptive. I remember when she came to my house when we were kids, back when I was still naïve enough to hope people could see past the filth. Her eyes hadn't missed a thing, finding the passed-out form of my mother on the sofa, the dirt coating every surface. She was kind enough not to say anything, but that was the last time I invited anyone back to that house.

And now she is here, at Blackwater House, those eyes missing nothing. She's here to support us, she says, as our family liaison officer. To interpret and inform. But really she's here to watch us, and to report back to her team. She thinks we had something to do with Ava's disappearance, and she is closer to the truth than she realises. Whatever happened to Ava, wherever she is and whoever she's with, Daniel and I are ultimately to blame. We couldn't keep her safe.

My hands shake as I try to light a cigarette, the flame catching and blowing out in the sea breeze. What if Ava is out there somewhere, trapped, injured? She wouldn't last long in these temperatures. I have to find her. I have to know she's okay. I close my eyes, trying to breathe slowly.

'Tell me about Meghan,' Kate said earlier, and I was glad Daniel hadn't been there. Perhaps she'd planned it that way. Perhaps she sensed that he has a temper, and that it'd be easier to talk to me once he had gone back to London. But she's wrong. I have more to lose, after all.

'There's not much to tell,' I said, picking at a loose thread on the bottom of my jumper. 'She died when Ava was a baby.'

'Car crash, was it?'

I nodded. 'That's what Daniel said.'

She looked at me for a moment before speaking. 'What's Ava's relationship like with her father?'

'Oh, normal, I think. She's a teenager, so they clash sometimes, but they love each other. He's always been really supportive of her art.'

'And is he an active parent?' I frowned, trying to understand her meaning. 'Is he here a lot? I know he works in London during the week.'

'Oh. Yes, well, he tries to be here as often as possible. But it's hard, you know. Tiring.'

'It's just you and Ava a lot of the time then? You must have quite a close bond.'

'We do,' I said, holding her gaze. 'We're very close.'

'So she'd tell you if anything was bothering her? If she needed someone to talk to?'

'Yes. She knows she can come to me with anything. She knows I'd be there for her.'

'Is there anyone else she might talk to? One of her aunts, perhaps?'

'Well. Yes, I suppose. But you've spoken to them, haven't you? They haven't seen or heard from her.'

She pursed her lips. 'I know. But, Rebecca—' she reached out as if to touch my hand, pausing at the last moment and splaying her fingers against the counter '—you need to help me here. You need to tell me if there's somewhere you think she might have gone.'

I shook my head. 'I don't know where she is. I would have told you, would have gone to get her myself if I knew. I swear, I don't know.'

I wasn't lying, but I haven't been telling the truth either. I haven't told Kate or even Daniel everything. But I suppose I should start now, if there's even the slightest chance it could help me find Ava. I think of the photos pinned on Ava's wall upstairs, the one of her and her mother. It all comes back to her. Meghan, and the night she died.

You see, I didn't meet Daniel by chance. We were brought together by Meghan, and the man who changed my life forever twenty years ago.

Sam Everley, Daniel's brother.

After the fight with Lou at that New Year's Eve party in 1999, I'd stumbled home, hurt and upset. I heard the noise as soon as I turned onto our street. The music pounding through the open windows, the shouting and cheering. The taste of violence in the air. I weaved my way between the people crowded in the front garden, sipping from tins of beer, the air cloudy with smoke. I kept my head down as I always did, my eyes focused on the path in front of me. One foot in front of the other. A man staggered into me and I almost tripped, righting myself by grabbing the doorframe and pulling myself through.

The house was even more of a mess than usual. Empty cans lay scattered across the hall, and a heap of coats covered the banister, hems and scarves trailing over the dirty floor.

The music pulsed through me as I stepped over a man who appeared to be asleep but might have been dead, slumped against the wall at the foot of the stairs. I ran up to my room, closing the door behind me and sliding down to the floor, my whole body heaving with sobs. I truly had no one, I realised then. I was alone. Mum was the only relative I had, and though I'd often dreamed of a kindly grandmother who would appear and welcome me with open arms, I knew she didn't exist. Or maybe she did, but not in my world. I had nothing. I *was* nothing.

Nausea rose and I threw open the door, just making it to the toilet before the contents of my stomach came up. My throat burned with the alcohol I'd consumed, tears stinging my eyes. Empty, I gulped water from the tap and quickly brushed my teeth, my tongue thick and furry. I was suddenly exhausted. I staggered back to my room and fell into bed, still wearing Stacey's clothes, darkness taking me as her words spun through my mind. *Like mother, like daughter.*

I woke to a shaft of light falling across my eyes, a shadow moving in the corner of the room. A hand across my mouth, fingers scrabbling at my clothes. The stench of booze and an unwashed body filling my nose. Music was pounding through the ceiling, the beat pulsing. Nails dug into my cheek, scratching my hip as my skirt was pushed up. I tried to scream, tearing at the heavy shape on top of me with my own nails. A slap, my face pressed into the pillow beneath me. Pain, hot, searing pain. I couldn't breathe.

I'm not here. This isn't real. I'm not here. This isn't real. Three little words repeated to myself as the horror of what was happening consumed me. Time stood still, but the song continued to play, counting out the minutes that I lay beneath the man, trapped and afraid. The music paused, and a few jeers went up before the countdown began.

A grunt, a blast of foul breath. 'You know the world's going to end?' he said, his face close to mine. I forced myself to look him in the eye, to take in everything I could as his face moved into the shaft of light. One blue eye, a shock of black hair, a scar through his left eyebrow. I would burn it into my mind; his features would be imprinted on my memory. I would never forget him.

'Four . . . three . . . two . . .' He grunted along with the people downstairs, counting down the seconds until the new year. The new decade. The new century. He shuddered, his grip tightening for a second, and then he was gone, his hand falling away from my face as he zipped up his jeans. He stood in front of the window, his face in profile as he looked outside. 'Boom,' he whispered, as fireworks exploded behind him.

He left the door open, my frozen body cast into the light. A shadow fell across the carpet, and I lifted my eyes to see my mother, her eyes finding mine for a moment, taking in the tears on my cheeks, my ripped clothes, the blood on my thighs. I saw the disgust in her eyes before she turned away. *Like mother, like daughter.*

From that point, I let myself believe that it was the only path for me, following in my mother's footsteps, stumbling from drink to drugs to men who hurt me. There was no way out, not for people like me. So I lost myself to it. I spent the first day of the new decade, the new century, curled up in a ball, my eyes red and gritty, my throat sore. I didn't eat or drink. I didn't move. I stayed in bed, the duvet wrapped tight around me, staring up at the ceiling. The curtains were shut tight against the wintry sky, but I felt chilled to the bone.

Much later, I managed to drag myself out of bed and into the bath, soaking that night away with water as hot as I could stand. I submerged myself in the water, my back pressed against the bottom of the bath, my eyes open as my head went under. I stared up through the murky water, hands gripping the edges of the tub as my lungs burned and my legs began to twitch. I burst through the water, gasping, fury and despair washing over me in waves. My path was set then, I realised. I couldn't go to the police. Justice wasn't for the likes of me. I had to find solace somewhere else.

Hours after darkness fell and a sliver of moon hung in the sky, I went out. My still-damp hair froze in the January air as I trudged through the deserted streets towards the end of the village. I emerged on top of the cliff, the sea dark and silent beneath me, the moonlight reflected on the calm surface of the water. 'I've come back,' I whispered to the waves. 'I'm not going to fight anymore.'

Nobody noticed when I stopped going to school. Nobody noticed when I barely went home, spending the night on the headland or the beach, running into the frozen sea, arms raised above my head, mouth open in a silent scream. But the sea did not take me. The stars were my only companion, the fingernail moon the only thing keeping watch. Days were spent in the houses of someone or other, hoodie pulled up over my head, my body curled into a ball against the hard floor. I crashed parties and took advantage of the free booze, or else I stole bottles from the local shop, paying for drugs with anything other than money. My already thin body became emaciated, my periods stopped, my hair hung lank around my shoulders. And I remained dry-eyed, never shedding another tear for what had happened to me, for what my life had become.

I blamed her, my mother. It was her fault that I had been born. She had brought me into this world knowing that she could not care for me, that she did not want to. I stole from her, from Terry, from the mass of bodies passed out on the living room floor. The world would give me nothing, I realised, so I had to take what I could. A hot rage had taken hold within me, and nothing could put out the flames. I was fifteen, my birthday having come and gone without notice, and I had no qualifications, no skills, no future. I was simply drifting through the life that had been forced upon me.

One night in September, the air still hot, the sky streaked with purple and red, I made my way to the tin mine as I often did, finding solace in the ruins of the engine house. Somewhat sheltered from the elements, there I kept a sleeping bag and an old torch for the times I found myself alone without an alternative. I hadn't been home in months by that point, and had taken to washing myself in the sea, swimming out to where the currents tugged at my legs, the siren song calling me to the depths. But still the sea did not take me. I sat on the exposed stone and smoked a cigarette, my feet dangling over the edge. Birds whirled overhead, dark shapes dancing against the sunset, and below, the water shimmered, the waves lapping gently against the sand.

The first pain shot through me and I gasped, my hands clutching my stomach. I felt wetness spread beneath me then and the muscles beneath my hands began to tighten. I fell onto my back, lay across the stone like a sacrificial lamb, and I wondered if that was how it would end. If the sea would take me now, and finally put an end to my misery. But it wasn't me she wanted.

Gulls circled above, the breeze ruffling the heather beside me, and the pains intensified, my breathing becoming laboured. I scrambled back, pressing my back against the wall, hiding myself in the shadows of the engine house, and reached between my legs. My fingers came away bloody, a crimson stain blossoming across the front of my thin tracksuit. I pulled my trousers down, blood dripping onto the bricks beneath me, and moaned as another pain engulfed me. The sound of my breathing filled my ears, the waves lapping beneath the cliff as the tide came in, keeping pace with me as I panted. My cries bounced off the walls and echoed back to me as sweat poured down my face; my fingernails scrabbled at the stone beneath me, my body shuddering as I gave in to the urge to push. The sea whispered to me between the waves of pain and, finally, I felt something give. A final scream tore through me as the child slid out from between my legs and into my waiting hands.

I stared down at the thing before me, a tuft of black hair sprouting from its head, its face blue, its chest still. Blood coated my fingers, drying beneath my fingernails, and splattered the ground around us. The sun had set, the sky above turning a deep purple as I sat, frozen, my dead baby resting against my knees.

A shout snapped me back to my senses. Finding a sharp stone, I cut through the cord, severing the connection between us. I staggered deeper into the engine house and fell to my knees, staring down through the dark hole, at the water lapping at the rocks below. Wrapping the body in my scarf, I lifted my arms and opened my hands. I whispered her name, and watched as the sea took her away, the waves cradling the tiny bundle. I imagined the scarf unravelling, the child drifting down to the seabed, her arms open, ready for the sea's embrace.

Hours later, as the sky darkened above me, I left the engine house and staggered back up the cliff, fingernails digging into rock, eyes swimming with tears. I had nowhere to go, no home, no real friends. I should follow my daughter into the ocean, where I could finally let go of my pain. I stumbled through the field, the sea to my left, the moon lighting my way, and stopped at a low fence. It was Gwen's house, I realised, seeing a light on in the kitchen window and a figure moving around the room. Gwen the witch, who hated us all. Who just wanted to live in peace. I watched her as she filled a kettle at the tap before bending to get something out of the oven. I imagined I could smell the pie or lasagne she'd made, could feel the warmth of the oven on my cold cheeks. I wondered what it was like, to live alone, to be comfortable in solitude. I wanted that, more than anything. I wanted to be happy by myself, to be able to live with myself in peace, and need no one else.

I turned back to the sea raging beneath me, the water black and infinite, and closed my eyes. It was a fork in the road, a rare opportunity to make a choice that would change my path. An opportunity to control my own life. I climbed over the fence.

25

Rebecca

Now – 4th January 2020

But where does Meghan come into this story? Whilst I gave birth alone in the engine house, Meghan had been starting her first year at university. She was a few years older than me and had accepted a place at the University of London to study law. Later, her sisters told me how she was the first in her family to go to university, her older sister, Aisha, having married at eighteen and becoming pregnant swiftly afterwards. Her mother, Sierra, was a nurse, her father a mechanic. They had had four children, three girls and a boy who had died in infanthood. Aisha was destined to have a large family, and Cass, several years younger, was going to study hairdressing, specialising in curly hair. And Meghan was going to be a lawyer.

I imagined that she was her parents' pride and joy. The middle child, she had been quiet but perceptive, a trait I see in Ava all the time. She had been kind by all accounts, if perhaps a little naïve, and it was her naïvety that led her straight to Daniel.

I don't know how they met. Daniel has never told me and I've never asked, but I can easily picture him wooing her. Her family had been proudly working-class, but Daniel had been able to give her everything she'd never had before. Foreign holidays, fancy dinners, generous gifts. He did the same to me, at the beginning. However it went, Meghan and Daniel were quickly engaged and, soon after, Meghan had fallen pregnant. The perfect love story, or so it seemed.

My mother's final gift to me was the name of my rapist. She had stolen his wallet during that New Year's Eve party and thrown his driving licence, one of the first photocards, into the bathroom bin. I took it, had it in my pocket when I gave birth and hid it at the bottom of a drawer when I lived with Gwen. But I never forgot about it, about him. I knew what I had to do. I couldn't move on until I found and confronted him. I was stuck, like a soul in purgatory, and only revenge could set me free. Gwen encouraged me to move away, to make a new life for myself, and I went along with it, but for my own reasons.

I learned to drive, passed my exams, and accepted a place at the University of Hertfordshire. I moved into a flat with three other students and worked shifts at a bar where men tried to touch me up. I scoured charity shops for clothes that I could hide inside, and changed my voice, rounding out my vowels to rid myself of my Cornish accent. I had my hair cut by student hairdressers at the local college, letting them turn my dirty blonde hair to a dark reddish brown. A flatmate waxed my eyebrows and let me use her nail polish, and suddenly, I was transformed. I became Rebecca, shedding Becks like a skin.

The first time I saw him was at the bar where I worked, standing with a group of men, all dressed in jeans and polo shirts. His shoes were smart, shiny, as if recently polished, and as I inched closer, I noticed that his hair was fashionably styled, his nails neat, his skin clear. I had been expecting a wreck, another druggy loser with nothing to live for, but he was the opposite. He looked clean, healthy. Well-off. I'd been waiting for this moment, dreamed of it, and now it was here, I suddenly felt deflated, as if everything I'd thought I'd known about him had been wrong.

I stormed into the staff room for a cigarette, trying to calm my breathing as I leaned against the lockers, blue smoke curling in front of my face. I decided then that my planned revenge, a quick knife in the darkness, would no longer do. I would need to be clever, to come up with a way of truly evening the score.

I went to the bar on the next night I wasn't working and sat at the end, my strappy black dress clinging to my new curves, my legs bare, my feet pushed into heels. My hair was swept up in an elaborate style, pinned away from my face, and my lips were painted blood red. I sipped vodka and Coke, and I waited. It didn't take long. One of his friends bought me a drink, slinging an arm around my shoulders and taking me over to their table. He watched me from beneath his dark lashes as I approached, and I stared into those blue eyes that had haunted me for years. The eyes of Sam Everley, the man who had pushed his way into my bedroom and raped me when I was still a child.

I learned that his dad had been a barrister in London, and that Sam had studied law and dropped out, much to his father's disappointment. He sold drugs for a living, often frequenting the student areas, and he had no girlfriend, no children. His father had died the year before, but Sam still lived in the family home with his younger brother, who had just started working as an accountant.

I decided to use my penchant for blending into the background. I started to follow him. I sat outside his house in my battered Ford, watching him from across the road as he sat on the sofa, one ankle crossed over the other knee, arms folded behind his head, football playing on the TV. I watched him as he stood at his bedroom window, dressed in boxers, unable to see me hidden in the shadows. I followed him on the train, sitting several seats behind, invisible in my plain clothes, my face free of makeup, my hair up in a ponytail. I followed him into his local pub and watched as he met a man who could only be his brother, and a woman with long legs and dark skin. I watched him put his hand on the small of her back when his brother wasn't looking, his teeth bared in a smile. Meghan, another woman he was going to destroy, though I didn't know it at the time.

I went to work, serving the men who had bought me drinks that first night, who didn't recognise me, didn't *see* me. I blended into the background, was something barely human that merely served drinks and presented an opportunity for a grope. I let them touch me when I approached their table, my skin rippling in disgust, desperate as I was for information. If I knew one thing, it was that once you got a drunk person talking, you can have a hard time shutting them up, and his friends divulged information without a care, telling me everything I needed to know about Sam.

After graduating, I moved out of my shared flat and into one by myself, closer to where Sam lived. I started working in his local pub, where he often went to watch football and catch up with friends, and he barely glanced at me as I took his orders, couldn't feel the rage that was pulsing through me. I followed his friends, listening to every conversation I could. Every spare moment was spent gathering information on Sam. I knew I was obsessed, could see how damaging this life was, but I couldn't stop. Not until I put an end to it, once and for all.

The end came on New Year's Eve. Poetic, I suppose. I was working in the pub on Boxing Day when I heard Sam's friends talking about a house party in Hertford on the thirty-first. Apparently, it was going to be the 'event of the year'. It was my chance, and I had to take it.

I wasn't scheduled to work that day, so I spent the morning in bed, staring at the ceiling, my mind full of ghosts, memories replaying over and over again. I got up as the sky was darkening outside, dragging myself into the shower. I blow-dried and straightened my hair until it shone, applied bold red lipstick, and pulled a black glittery dress over my head. I wriggled into tights and stuffed my feet into black boots, grabbing my leather jacket from the back of the door. I stood in front of the full-length mirror, one corner chipped, the glass warped in places, and took myself in.

I hardly recognised myself. With my dark hair and bright red lips, I could have been anyone. Not Becks, not even Rebecca. I turned away from my reflection and the name that was ringing in my ears and sat on the bed, staring into space until it was time to leave.

I found the house easily: an end terrace with a brown door, the paint scratched and flaking. The bushes outside were overgrown, the recycling box overflowing with empty bottles, and I could hear music blaring out of the open windows. It was in a nice area, and I wondered what the neighbours thought of these people invading their middle-class community as I parked further up the road. The other houses had tidy front gardens and new cars parked outside, curtains and blinds closed against the night. As I stepped into the road, a black cat shot past me, disappearing into a bush further along, and I thought I could hear a baby crying in a house behind me.

No sleep for them tonight, I thought as I approached the brown door. *Not with this going on across the street.* The front door was ajar, the hallway dark, and I slipped inside, silent as a ghost. To my left was a small kitchen, the counters covered in bottles and used glasses, the sink full of dirty plates. I wrinkled my nose at the smell as I passed. It reminded me too much of my childhood home, of the life I'd fled from. In front of me was the living room, with the stairs rising to the right.

The house was full of people, the air thick with smoke, and I coughed as I slid into the room, bumping into a young woman who offered me a bottle of cider. I took it, smiling my thanks, grateful it wasn't beer. I couldn't afford to gluten myself.

I sipped it, my eyes scanning the room. Eight or so people were crammed onto the two leather sofas, their thighs pressed together, elbows jostling as they passed around a bong. One woman sat on the lap of a man, his face buried in her neck, his hand up her skirt, and I looked away, my skin prickling. The TV was on a music video channel, light flashing across the darkened room. The small coffee table was littered with packets of tobacco and small plastic bags, lighters and an overflowing ashtray. I clocked the time on the TV – 23:03 – as I leaned against the wall, trying to blend in, surreptitiously searching for Sam or his friends. I heard laughter from the back garden and picked my way across the room, feeling the eyes of the crowd slide across me as I passed, barely resting their attention on me before moving on. I could be invisible here, too.

I breathed in the cool air, staring up at the stars for a moment as I tried to slow my racing heart. A group of men stood in the overgrown grass, smoke rising above their heads, and a trio of girls who didn't look older than fourteen sat squashed together on a bench, sharing a cigarette and a bottle of vodka between them. My heart lurched as I saw the faces of my teenage friends flash before my eyes. I made my way over to them, asking to borrow a lighter, and noted the fear in the blonde girl's eyes as she handed it over. I wondered how she had found herself in a place like that, which of her friends had encouraged her to go.

'What are your names?' I asked them, handing back the lighter and blowing a smoke ring.

One of the brunettes smiled, watching the ring disappear into the air. *You,* I thought. *You're the one who wanted to come.*

'I'm Casey. This is Kat and Emma.' She pointed at her two friends.

'Becks,' I said, my old name feeling strange in my mouth. 'Nice to meet you.'

We jumped in unison as a shriek rang out from inside, turning as one to see a woman on the floor, another reaching down towards her, laughing hysterically. Casey turned back and shook her head. 'That's my sister,' she said, her eyes on her scuffed trainers, and I suddenly saw her as the child she was, the girl desperate for the approval of her sister and her friends.

'Do you want to go home?' I asked, reaching into my pocket and fishing out my mobile. 'I can call a taxi?'

Casey shook her head. 'I should wait for her. I'm not supposed to leave her.' Her friends looked up at me, their discomfort palpable, and I opened my mouth to speak again when Casey's sister tumbled out of the back door.

'There she is!' she shrieked, her arms held out wide, her eyes trained on Casey. 'My little sister!' She dragged the word out, turning the i into a series of e's. *Seeeester.*

I saw Casey wince as her sister wrapped her in a hug. 'Can we go home now?' she asked, and I heard the whine in her voice. Something smashed inside the house and the girls jumped.

'Oi!' a voice yelled. 'What the fuck? Where is she?'

I heard Casey's sister mutter something as I moved towards the back door and poked my head inside. Two men stood in the hall, their heads close together, and when one of them pulled back, I saw who it was: Sam.

His eyes were wide as they searched the room, passing over me as I made my way inside. The man grabbed his arm but Sam pushed him away and bounded up the stairs, the other man on his heels. I hurried through the room, trying to squeeze through the crowd as I followed them, grabbing hold of the banister and feeling the stickiness beneath my fingers. I paused for a second, trying to regulate my breathing, before stepping over a woman slumped against the wall, her head tilted forward, her hair covering her face. I felt something crunch beneath my boot; shards of glass, the green of a beer bottle, lay in little pieces across the stairs. I kicked them into the corner and was about to continue when something grabbed my leg. Suppressing a scream, I turned to find the woman gripping my ankle, her eyes half-open, her face slack. She mumbled something, her nails digging into my skin, and I saw my mother's face in hers. I shook my leg, trying to free myself. My heel connected with her chin and she lurched backwards, hitting her head against the wall. Nausea rising, blood pulsing in my ears, I continued upstairs.

The landing was almost completely dark, with four doors leading off it. The first was open, the streetlight outside casting shadows across the wall. The room was empty of furniture except for a bare mattress on which three figures lay, their eyes closed, their limbs entangled. Empty bottles and crisp packets littered the floor, and the air was thick with the smell of bodies. I saw images of my mother among them too and I shook my head to clear it, shoving the memories away. I had to stay focused. I moved on, pushing open the next door and switching on the light. The bathroom was empty, the bath and tiles covered in mould, the toilet seat broken in two and discarded on the floor. The window was open and the freezing December air drifted in, making me shiver.

I found him in the next room. He was laid out on the floor, a needle sticking out of his arm, his eyes half-closed. In the corner of the room was a single mattress, on which a figure was slumped against the wall, head lolling to the right, left arm resting on a balled-up sleeping bag. I could see small packets of tin foil and empty plastic bags, and I knew, as I had always known, what had happened. Memories of my childhood home once again filled my mind, the figure in the corner transforming into my mother, and I felt rage bubble up inside me.

Something moved behind me and I whirled around to find the other man in the doorway, the man who had argued with Sam downstairs. His face half in shadow, he pushed past me, ignoring Sam and kneeling beside the shape in the corner. He tugged at something, and in the half-light I could see it was a silver necklace. He stuffed it into his pocket and got up, pausing in front of Sam.

'You fucking idiot,' he said, his face briefly lit by a streetlight outside the window before he strode out of the room. I heard his footsteps on the stairs and then the front door slammed. I breathed out. Later I would remember this scene, the memory slamming into me like a train. But for now, Sam was my focus.

My eyes were drawn to the needle sticking out of his arm. I pulled it out, watching the blood well up to the surface before throwing it into the opposite corner of the room, where it clattered against the wall. I squatted beside him and began to shake him, my hands on his shoulders. His head moved as if his head wasn't attached to his body; his neck was like jelly, and he refused to open his eyes. I shook him harder, before drawing back and slapping him across the face. He blinked, his mouth opening in surprise.

'Wake up,' I hissed as his eyes began to close again. 'You need to be awake for this.' I found a bottle half-full of unknown liquid and poured it onto his face, watching as he gasped and spluttered. His eyes flickered across my face but I saw no recognition there, and the realisation made me burn with fury. 'You have no idea who I am, do you?' I demanded, my hands on his shoulders, my nails digging into his flesh. 'You have no fucking idea what you've *done*.'

He stared at me, unseeing, his face slack. I shook him again, releasing a moan of frustration. Rage caused the edges of my vision to darken. This wasn't how I had planned it, but it didn't matter. What mattered was that he paid for what he had done, and I wasn't going to let the drugs do the work for me.

I searched the shadowy room, nudging objects with the toe of my boot, until I found a small round cushion. Weighing it in my hands, I made my way back over to Sam and after a second's hesitation, pressed it against his nose and mouth with both hands, my eyes on his. I felt him jerk beneath me, his legs kicking out, so I moved to straddle him, pressing down on the cushion with my forearm. His eyes met mine properly for the first time, and I saw it then, that flicker of recognition amidst the fear. I smiled as his flailing became weaker, and I stayed where I was long after his body stopped twitching beneath me.

Glancing up at the window, I saw a face peering at me from behind the pane of glass, a face I had tried so hard to forget. Her. I fell backwards, heart racing, and squeezed my eyes shut, my fingers digging into my scalp, trying to shut the ghosts out. A noise brought me back to myself. A low mewl came from the corner of the room. I moved across to the figure slumped there, reaching out and turning their face towards the light of the window, but it was too dark to make out her features. I dropped her chin and pressed my fingers against the side of her neck. The pulse was weak, and her breathing was shallow. My eyes landed on a needle beside her and I felt nausea rise. Again I saw my mother, the track marks on her arms, bruises on her legs, her hair limp and her skin greasy. Terry – no, Sam – passing her a small bag, his wolfish grin turning towards me as I hid behind the banisters.

I got to my feet, staring down at the woman in disgust. Whoever she was, it was too late to save her. She would be Sam's last victim. He wouldn't be giving anyone drugs anymore. He wouldn't hurt anyone ever again. Maybe now the cycle could end.

I had taken two steps away when I heard it again, the mewling sound, followed by the rasp of fabric. Something was moving inside the sleeping bag. My heart pounding in my chest, I moved the woman's hand and carefully unzipped it. A tiny hand shot out and I gasped, falling back and landing heavily on the hard floor. No, no. It wasn't real. It couldn't be real.

I reached out with trembling fingers and touched the hand. The baby mewled again, louder this time, and I knew I wasn't imagining it. I unwrapped the sleeping bag and peered down at the tiny face, the wide eyes that fixed me in place, fingers reaching for me. She was wrapped in a knitted blanket, her feet covered by tiny boots, and I felt my eyes fill with tears. The woman had brought her baby into this place, had taken drugs while her daughter lay beside her. And she would die if someone didn't help her.

Fumbling with my phone, I dialled 999, before quickly cancelling the call. I couldn't. I had just killed a man; his body on the floor behind me, the cushion still lying across his face, his eyes staring sightlessly at the ceiling. But I had to get help. I couldn't leave a baby there, lying next to its dead mother, surrounded by needles and drugs in a house full of danger. Just like the one I had grown up in.

The cycle ends now, I thought as I stood and stumbled out of the room, running down the stairs and out into the night. I couldn't take her, but I knew there was a phone box in the next street; I had passed it on my way to the party. I ran towards it, wrenching open the door and throwing myself inside. 'Ambulance,' I gasped into the phone, 'th-there's a woman, I think she's overdosed. She has a b-baby with her.' I gabbled the address, barely letting the operator speak before slamming the phone down. I ran back to my car, diving into the driver's seat and resting my head on the steering wheel. 'Fuck!' I screamed, pounding my fists against the dashboard. 'Fuck! Fuck! Fuck!'

I lit a cigarette, trying to stop my body from trembling as the car filled with smoke. I heard the sirens within minutes, the blue lights flashing as the ambulance rounded the corner. I slid down in my seat, watching as they pulled up and three paramedics jumped out, carrying a stretcher between them.

Go, I told myself, my eyes glued to the front door of the house. *You need to leave, now!* But I couldn't move. I was frozen, waiting, my heart hammering, the sea rushing in my ears, for the paramedics to bring her out.

A female paramedic emerged from the house, a tiny bundle in her arms, and I released the breath I'd been holding as she jumped into the back of the ambulance. She was safe. The baby was safe.

As I started the engine and pulled out onto the road, I saw the paramedics carrying the stretcher out of the front door, the body covered by a sheet, and I knew that the baby's mother was dead.

26

Rebecca

Now – 4th January 2020

I spent that night wrapped in a blanket, curled into a ball on the sofa, the TV on mute. My head was spinning, a lump forming in my stomach as I waited all night and all day for the news report. But it didn't come.

I drifted in and out of consciousness as the TV flickered in the corner of the room. The news finally came the next evening, the headline flashing across the bottom of the screen. *Two found dead at house party after overdose.* My throat constricted as I turned up the volume, my eyes glued to the screen.

'A woman was found dead at a house party last night after what has now been confirmed as a heroin overdose. The woman has not yet been named, but police say they are in contact with her family. An unnamed man was also found dead in the same room. Police believe drugs were also involved in his death and are not treating it as suspicious.'

No mention of the baby. Had I imagined her? I closed my eyes, picturing again the tiny hand reaching for me, the soft mewling sound. Memories crowded in, filling my mind; my hands covered in blood, the rushing of the waves. No. *No. It was real.* She *was real.* I wrapped my arms around myself, my eyes focused on an old stain on the carpet. I breathed in and out, trying to push the nausea away. I had done it, I had found Sam and made him pay for what he did to me. But all I could feel was an emptiness opening up inside me, threatening to swallow me whole.

Over the next few days, I read every article I could, the TV left on day and night. A week later, two things happened: I found out the woman's name was Meghan Bird, and I got my first glimpse of her fiancé: Daniel Everley.

'I am lost without her,' he told the local paper. The photo showed him holding a baby swaddled in a pink blanket, and I felt my heart lurch with the knowledge that I hadn't invented her. 'My daughter is now without a mother. She's only six months old and she's lost her mother. How will we go on?'

The article described how paramedics had found Meghan's lifeless body on a filthy mattress, and how Sam Everley was found in the same room, sprawled where I left him, a drug overdose suspected to be the cause of both deaths.

'Whoever called an ambulance that night saved my daughter's life,' Daniel said in the interview. 'I lost my fiancée and my brother that day, but I still have my daughter, and for that I will be forever grateful.'

I stared at the black and white image of Daniel, trying to piece it all together. How did Sam become who he was – drug dealer, addict, rapist – when his brother was, judging by the impression he gave in his interviews, a smart, decent young man? How come Daniel went to a good university and had a steady career, while Sam shot up with heroin in filthy rooms?

I needed to find out.

I spent time getting to know Meghan Bird, the woman who had been torn away from her young daughter. Guilt gnawed at me every time I looked at her photo. How had such a bright, promising young woman become mixed up in Sam's sordid life? How did she go from a newly qualified lawyer, engaged to be married and a mother, to a 'tragic overdose' headline? I too wanted justice for Meghan. Meghan had given birth to her daughter a year after she graduated from law school, the papers said. She had planned to return to work when her daughter was a year old, but had started engaging in charity work during her pregnancy and continued after giving birth. There were photos of her helping at an allotment run by a local café, which gave jobs to people with disabilities. She spent time reading to children and ran a marathon to raise money for a charity that helped inner-city kids stay out of gangs. And behind the scenes, she took drugs. I had seen the track marks myself. But there was no mention of the dark side of Meghan's life in the papers.

Could I have saved her? Should I have? I blamed myself, and my desire for revenge, for Meghan's life ending, leaving her daughter motherless.

Her name was Ava, I later discovered. Ava Everley, the girl who deserved better. Whose mother didn't make it because of me. The girl I now owed a debt to.

I don't believe in miracles or coincidences or fate, but something was influencing the course of my life during that time, and I was going along for the ride.

It took some time for the police to release the bodies of Meghan and Sam. January turned to February, the sky leaden and dark. Meghan's wake was held in the pub where I worked. I pictured her coming here with friends, a glass of Pimm's in her hand and a flower in her hair, her head thrown back in laughter, Daniel's hand on her lower back. I tried to forget the woman I had seen, with the sallow skin and sunken eyes, her arms covered in marks, and instead focused on the Meghan Daniel had known, the beautiful law student with a bright future ahead of her.

I laid out platters of food, carefully peeling back the cling film and placing a stack of plates on the end. I was behind the bar when the funeral party came in, shaking damp umbrellas at the entrance, wiping their feet on the mat. Daniel looked hollowed out, his gaze unfocused, and for a second he reminded me of his brother, the way he had looked at me as he died.

My skin prickled as I served drinks. Alcohol flowed, as it often does at a funeral, and the pub filled with mourners clad in black. Daniel sat in a corner, drinking glass after glass of white wine, staring at the empty fireplace. We usually had it lit, but winter was receding, spring making an early appearance, and the day was unnaturally warm. The rain had made it muggy, the clouds full and dark, and the landlady switched on more lights as the afternoon wore on. I caught snippets of conversation as I drifted through the pub, collecting glasses and dirty plates, keeping one eye on Daniel. He wore smart jeans and shiny shoes, his hair fashionably styled, but his face looked as if it were made from stone, all his efforts going into making it through his partner's funeral.

Later, as people were starting to leave, the door crashed open and a woman stepped inside, her hair and face drenched from the rain, her boots leaving muddy footprints on the floor as she strode through the room. Her eyes blazed as they found Daniel, but an older man stepped in front of her before she could reach him, his hands up as if in surrender. She pushed past him, stomping through the dwindling crowd until she stood in front of Daniel, hands on hips, water dripping onto the floor beneath her.

'How dare you,' she hissed. The room was silent and her words ricocheted off the walls. 'How dare you keep us away. Who do you think you are?' Daniel stared down at his drink as if he hadn't heard her.

'Aisha,' another woman called from the doorway, her eyes darting around the room. Heads swivelled towards her and I saw her straighten as if to show she wasn't afraid. She was similarly soaked, an umbrella held uselessly at her side. 'Come on.'

'She was my *sister*,' Aisha spat. 'Ava is my niece. How dare you keep us away from her?' Her hand whipped out to slap Daniel round the face. His head jerked to the side, and when his gaze finally turned to Aisha there was a hint of fire in his eyes. He stood so quickly he almost overturned the table; his glass of wine tumbled to the floor, smashing against the wood.

'Get out,' he growled, and as the other woman ran inside to drag Aisha away, I thought I saw fear in her eyes. I should have seen then who he was. I should have recognised him as the man from the house party, the one who had been arguing with Sam, but it had been dark and I'd been so focused on my revenge that I hadn't looked at him properly. It wasn't until years later, when I found the necklace hidden in his bedside table, that I remembered him snatching it from Meghan's neck that night and walking out, leaving her – and Ava – to die.

27

Kate

Now – 5th January 2020

Kate is sitting at her desk, drinking her third cup of what more resembles dishwater than an enjoyable coffee, but she is grateful for the caffeine boost at least. She couldn't switch off last night, staring blankly at the TV show she and Lauren were watching for an hour before finally giving up and going upstairs to run a bath.

She'd stared up at the ceiling, the water growing cold around her. She thought of Ava, of the grinning young girl now splashed across the papers, Rebecca's appeal circulating through the news channels. Closing her eyes, she recreated Ava's room, seeing again the collage above her bed. One particular photo came into focus; a woman holding a small child on her hip, both of them clad in navy jumpers and brown boots, both smiling widely. The child was staring at the camera, but the woman was looking at the girl, arms wrapped around her.

Ava's mother.

Kate's eyes snapped open and, suddenly galvanised, she pulled the plug and hopped out of the bath. Wrapped in a towel, she sat down on the end of the bed and opened her laptop, typing the name *Meghan Bird* into Google and skimming the headlines with growing unease. She still wasn't sure what relevance Ava's mother had, but something was telling her to keep looking. She clicked on one article, which brought up a photo of Meghan, the same photo Kate had been thinking of, with a young Ava on her hip.

Family of tragic Meghan Bird speak out

The fiancé of Meghan Bird, the young woman who died from a heroin overdose last month, opens up about losing 'the love of his life'. Father to Meghan's six-month-old daughter, Daniel Everley describes how they had been planning their wedding, which would have taken place next summer, and that Meghan had already chosen her dress.

He said: 'She was such a beautiful, happy person. She had everything to live for. Now our daughter is left to grow up without a mother, and I've lost the love of my life.'

Meghan, a twenty-four-year-old law graduate, was found dead in a house in Hertford last month. Daniel's brother, Sam Everley, was also found to have overdosed in the same room.

Daniel defended his brother, saying: 'I do not believe Sam had anything to do with Meghan's death.'

Police are not looking for anyone in connection with the deaths.

'She was my everything,' Daniel wrote in an emotional Facebook post. 'I feel lost without her.'

Meghan had not yet returned to work after giving birth to her daughter, but she had been dedicating her time to charity work and reading to underprivileged children.

'She loved kids,' Daniel said. 'She had such a big heart. She just wanted to help others.'

Meghan had two sisters, who did not respond to The Chronicle's *requests for comment. Her mother, Sierra Bird, shared her concern for her granddaughter, who she has been unable to see since Meghan's death.*

She said: 'Daniel has shut down, closing us off from our beloved granddaughter. She has lost her mother, and he is keeping her away from the rest of her family. It's breaking my heart.'

Daniel refused to respond to Sierra's comments, instead stating: 'My daughter has everything she needs.'

Now, after a long, sleepless night, Kate is checking the police national database for Sam Everley, Daniel's brother. A mugshot from 2005 shows a clean-shaven, fresh-faced young man, despite the class-A drugs he'd just been caught with. She reads through the rest of his file: more possession, shoplifting, assault. A rape allegation that didn't go anywhere after the victim retracted her statement.

Kate sits back in her chair, staring up at the ceiling. A light is flickering above her, the small square blinking on and off as her mind tries to digest everything. Rebecca lied to her about Meghan's death; that much is clear. Or did she tell her what she believed to be the truth? Had Daniel lied about how Meghan died, and Rebecca never thought to look it up? She'd tried to get Rebecca to talk about Meghan yesterday but she'd clammed up, so maybe that was all she'd known. And then there was Sam, with his history of drug abuse and violence. If Meghan and Sam both died in the same house on the same night, could they have taken drugs from the same batch? Could he have given them to her? Was it really a tragic accident?

She decides to put a call in to the Hertfordshire Constabulary. She drums her fingers on the table as she explains who she is and is passed along the chain, until she eventually ends up speaking to a DI Wood, who had been a PC at the time of Meghan's death. When she tells him about Ava, he sighs heavily.

'I remember it well,' he says, his Hertfordshire accent reminding her of her father-in-law. 'Awful, it was. We believed that the bloke who also died had been Meghan's dealer.'

'Sam Everley? Her would-be brother-in-law?'

'Yeah, him. We'd nicked him a few times over the years so he had previous, but he was just one of those people who was hellbent on self-destruction. Except he wanted to take every-one else with him.'

'What makes you say that?'

DI Wood sighs again. 'I think he saw himself as a bit of a rebel, an early noughties Kurt Cobain or what have you. He had money, came from a nice family with a nice house, but he was only interested in drink, drugs, and women. And a bit of violence thrown in for good measure.'

'How many times was he arrested for assault?'

'Twice, if memory serves. Got off with a caution. The victims didn't want to press charges.'

'And the rape charge?'

'Same again. His dad got him out of everything. So I suppose we were waiting for something to happen to him. Overdose, or a fatal kicking maybe. But we were all a bit surprised by Meghan. No record, decent education, nice family. Not the kind of person you'd expect to find dead in a house like that.' He pauses, taking a deep breath before contin-uing. 'I say, do what you want with your own life, fuck it up as much as you bloody well like, but just leave your kids out of it. That haunted me for weeks after, finding her like that.'

Kids. Kate feels her throat constrict as she processes his words. 'Kids? Do you mean ... Are you talking about her daughter?'

'That's right. Paramedics found her curled up beside her mother. Poor thing was dehydrated, but otherwise unhurt.'

Kate remembers the article she read earlier, how Ava had been just six months old at the time. 'Jesus. Ava was there?'

'Yup. We found a bag packed full of baby things and some clothes for an adult woman, so we assumed Meghan was running away. But that fiancé of hers swore up and down that she wouldn't do something like that, and her family – the mother, and a few sisters I think – seemed to agree with him. They said she would've gone to them for help.'

Kate thinks back to what they know about Daniel. He had never been known to the police, had never even got a speeding ticket, but something still wasn't adding up. 'How long had she been taking drugs?' Kate asks, her pulse racing as she pictures the scene: baby Ava, wrapped up in a dirty blanket; Meghan slumped against the wall, a needle hanging out of her arm.

'Track marks were found on her arms and legs so it wasn't her first time, but the family clammed up when we prodded them. Nobody would tell us anything. Meghan had a normal birth, by all accounts, and the hospital didn't raise any alarms, so we assumed it was after that.'

Even a 'normal' birth can be traumatic, Kate thinks as she scribbles down some notes. 'What could have happened to make her turn to drugs?'

DI Wood clears his throat. 'Postnatal depression, maybe. One of my colleagues suggested it at the time, but Meghan had never sought help, and like I said, the family wouldn't tell us anything, so we didn't know for sure. And it wasn't as widely spoken about back then. She was prescribed sleeping pills though, about two months after the birth.'

Depression. Sleeping pills. Kate pictures a young woman, purple rings beneath her eyes as she tries to soothe her crying child. She can imagine how helpful Daniel would have been in that scenario, doubting that he ever changed a nappy, let alone got up to do a night feed. But to go from exhausted new mother to dead from a drug overdose? Something just wasn't adding up.

After she hangs up, Kate rewinds the scenes in her head, from Meghan's death to Ava's birth, trying to picture their lives. She imagines Meghan hastily packing a bag, leaving most of her possessions behind, her daughter carefully wrapped in a blanket as they left the house. Was she running away? What was she running from – or who? And why would she go to that house? It had been rented at the time, by a couple who since moved to Thailand and are proving difficult to contact, but perhaps Meghan had been looking for Sam, for one last hit for the road. Or perhaps she had been looking for a friend.

Kate's phone rings, startling her out of her thoughts.

'Have you heard from him?' DS Tremayne barks down the phone.

'Who?'

'The father, Daniel Everley. I've been trying to ring him all day and his phone's off.'

'I last spoke to him before the appeal,' Kate says, thinking back. 'I'll go to see Rebecca.'

'Do. There's something not right about him, and I don't like it when people suddenly go quiet. Apparently he hasn't turned up for work today. Something's going on. Find out what it is.'

Tremayne hangs up and Kate sighs. *There's definitely something going on,* she thinks as she quickly gathers her things and heads out to the car. *But we haven't found it out yet.*

28

Rebecca

Now – 4th January 2020

It is Kate who first alerts me to Daniel's disappearance. I couldn't believe it when he left, pleading a work emergency when his daughter is missing, but now she says he hasn't turned up at work, and her colleagues haven't been able to get hold of him. I'm sitting in Ava's room while Kate speaks to someone on the phone downstairs. I can hear her boots clicking across the wooden floor as she paces up and down the hallway. I lie across the bed, turning my face to the wall and the collage hanging above the headboard. Pain shoots through me as my eyes land on Ava's face, her glittering eyes and carefree smile. *Oh, Ava.* My gaze finds the photo of Meghan next, almost buried amongst the years of Ava's life since she lost her mother. She looks so much like her, though Meghan's hair was styled differently, and Ava's skin is lighter. I sit up, peering closer at a mark on the photo, and then it hits me. Someone has drawn a circle around Ava's tiny fist, and I suddenly realise what she would have been holding on to. The necklace.

I go upstairs to my bedroom, tearing open Daniel's bedside drawer and fumbling for the pouch I know he keeps Meghan's necklace in. Gone. I know then she has found it, and that she knows far more than either of us could have imagined.

Oh, Ava. Why didn't you come to me? I press the heels of my hands into my eyes and try to control my breathing. Suddenly

229

it is obvious that this was planned. But she is only fourteen years old. How could she have pulled it off alone?

'She didn't do it alone.' Ashleigh is standing in the doorway and I jump, heart pounding.

'How did you get in?' I whisper. I haven't told the police about my sister. What good would it do? She couldn't have been involved. And yet . . . 'What do you mean, she didn't do it alone?'

'Exactly that. She had help.' Ashleigh raises an eyebrow at me. 'Are you really trying to tell me that you had no idea what she was planning?'

I shake my head. 'No. No, I didn't. Where is she?'

She smiles, tilting her head to one side. 'Where you were always going to take her.'

I run down the stairs, almost crashing into Kate in the hall. 'Where are you going? Who were you talking to up there?' she asks.

'No one. I need to go out.'

'I'll come with you.'

'No, no, I'll be fine. I just need some air.'

'But, Rebecca—'

But I'm gone before she can finish, out of the house and into the car, stones skidding beneath the tyres as I hurtle down the lane. Kate might follow me – she knows the area and is confident on the roads – but I can only hope I've got a good enough head start. Because now I know where Ava is.

I kept a close eye on Daniel over the months after Meghan's death, listening carefully to his conversations in the pub, watching him push his daughter on the swings at the local park, following him around the supermarket. We were soon on nodding terms, his eyes flashing with recognition when I wheeled my trolley down the same aisle, or as I poured him a glass of wine at the pub. I tried to tell myself to stay away, that I had got what I came here for. Sam was dead. He would never hurt another woman again. But I couldn't seem to cut the invisible string that tied Ava and me together, and Daniel was my way in.

After just six months of dating, I gave up my job and moved in with him. It would be easier, he said, to see one another if we lived together. He had a demanding job and Ava to take care of, and my shifts were irregular. That way, I could spend more time with both of them, he said, but I knew it was mostly because he was embarrassed to be dating a barmaid. But now I could get to know Ava properly. The first time I officially met her, it felt as if I was greeting an old friend. She looked at me with her wide, dark brown eyes and a slight tilt of the head as if to say, *What took you so long?*

I've often wondered if I ever felt anything for Daniel, or whether Ava was the only thing tying us together. The important thing was that Daniel believed it was real. I didn't realise straight away that he had been there that night, that he had left Meghan and Ava to die in that house, but when I did, it only confirmed that I had been right to move in with him. That Ava needed someone looking out for her.

I found the necklace by accident. Or rather, I was looking through his bedside cabinet for something else – Ava's passport – when a piece of paper slipped down the back of the drawer. Cursing, I pulled out the drawer to retrieve the paper when I noticed something taped to the underside. The letter M on a silver chain. The memory came flooding back: Meghan slumped against the wall, a man reaching down to take the necklace from her. Daniel.

You fucking idiot.

He had no idea who I was, of that I was sure. He could not link me to his brother or that night, but I started to worry that he might stumble upon something. I considered leaving, packing a bag and fleeing into the night, but then, one Sunday evening when six-year-old Ava was throwing a rare tantrum, I saw him grab her by the arm, his fingers digging into her skin. He shook her, his face close to hers, his teeth bared as he hissed at her to *behave*. She was startled into obedience, and so was I. I knew then how I could make things right with Meghan. I had to protect her daughter.

Becks is nothing if not a great actress. The subservient woman, quietly keeping house and taking care of his daughter, admiring her sparkling engagement ring and talking breathlessly about her wedding dress, which did not exist. Graciously accepting the apologies and flowers after his violent outbursts. Daniel started travelling more for work, and Ava and I basked in the freedom away from him and his increasing violence. We enjoyed our time alone, getting to know one another, and I watched her turn from an energetic toddler to an intelligent, ambitious eight-year-old.

Which was when I first tried to abduct her.

Ava left for school as usual that day, waving at me through the kitchen window as she walked down the drive. Her friend Alice's mum was waiting for her down the road; we took turns taking the three girls – Ava, Alice, and Adele, or the Triple A's as we called them – to school, and it was Melanie's turn that day. I felt a slight wave of concern at how she would take it, Ava going missing on her watch, but it was nothing in the grand scheme of things. Ava was growing up; soon she would become a teenager, with hormones and periods, and the risk of her enraging her father would become greater. I had to get her out. I now had a higher purpose than revenge; I had to atone.

The plan was simple; Ava would go to school as normal, but I would collect her early for an appointment. I would take her to a safe place, somewhere she could stay on her own while I went home and played the worried stepmother. It wasn't the perfect plan, but I intended to report her disappearance to the police, wait for Daniel to get back, and then flee. I told Ava we were going on holiday, a break for just the two of us, but I think she knew what I was doing. She knew, and she wanted me to succeed.

But I never made it to pick her up. Daniel came back early from work, bleary-eyed after a liquid lunch, and started an argument, resulting in a trip to A&E for my broken wrist.

When Melanie dropped Ava off after school and Ava stared at me with her wide eyes, the unspoken question filling the air between us, I placed a finger to my lips. 'Soon,' I mouthed, and she nodded, her eyes full of trust I didn't deserve. She must have lost that trust over the years, because this time she had done it without me. This time, she turned to someone who would act, who would protect her. Who would see the plan through. Her grandmother.

29

Kate

'Rebecca!' Kate watches as she drives away. 'For fuck's sake,' she mutters, digging in her pocket for her phone and pulling up Rebecca's number, but she doesn't answer. She dithers, unsure whether or not to go after her. Something is prickling at Kate, something to do with Meghan and how she died. There was something in the way Rebecca had left so suddenly too, and she'd definitely been talking to someone when she'd gone upstairs. It must have been someone on the phone, but who?

Her chance to follow has disappeared, so Kate goes back inside and heads for Rebecca's bedroom. It was searched when the police first attended, but she isn't sure how deeply they looked, or what they were even looking for. They would have focused on Ava's bedroom and the annex. She doesn't know what she's looking for now either, but she knows there's something in Blackwater House, something that will reveal the truth about everything. And she's going to find it.

In the bedroom, Kate pulls open a drawer on one of the bedside tables, which is empty but for a few wires and a packet of tissues, an unplugged lamp sitting on top, its cord wrapped around the base. The other has a tube of hand cream on top and the lamp is plugged in, so Kate surmises that it must be Rebecca's side. Crouching on the floor, Kate lifts the mattress so she can peer beneath it. Nothing. Beneath the bed sits a small suitcase, which is empty and covered in dust. When she shoves it back, one of the wheels snags on the edge of the rug that has been placed along the end of the bed and pulls up the corner, revealing a flash of white before the rug falls back into place.

Bingo, she thinks, scooting to the end of the bed and pulling back the rug. Poking up between the floorboards is the corner of a sheet of paper, which Kate extracts between thumb and forefinger, being careful not to touch it anywhere else as she lays it flat on the rug before her. It's a photocopy of a newspaper article. *Family of tragic Meghan Bird speak out* the headline reads, and Kate knows it's the same article she'd read the day before.

She knew. Rebecca had known the truth about Meghan, and probably about Ava too. So why had she lied and told Kate she'd died in a car accident? To protect Ava? To shield her from the judgement Rebecca herself had grown up with, as the daughter of an addict?

Flicking on the torch app on her phone, Kate shines the light through the gap in the floorboards. There's something else in there. She tries to lift it with her fingers and although it moves, she can't get the right angle. Remembering the paint supplies in the room downstairs, she runs down and rummages through, coming up with a putty knife that still has a thin layer of filler along the edge. Sliding it into the gap, she levers it upwards and the board pops up just as the knife breaks. Throwing the pieces to one side, Kate reaches in and pulls out what looks like a scrapbook. Inside, the pages are covered in cut-out articles about Meghan and a few photos of low quality. As Kate turns the page, a thick piece of paper falls out onto her lap. Putting the book to one side, she picks up the paper and opens it, holding her breath. It's a marriage certificate, an old one judging by the faded ink and yellowed corners.

She notes the date – 21st February 1955 – and tries to read the names. John Howard Ashe, 39, Bachelor. Gwendoline Bray, 25, Spinster.

Something slots into place then and she jumps up, dialling DS Tremayne's number, but it rings out and she swears, then almost drops her phone when it starts to vibrate in her hand, the name Smithy coming up on the screen.

'Did you find a death certificate for Gemma Bray?' she asks before he can speak. Cradling the phone between her ear and shoulder, Kate runs out to the car to find an evidence bag.

'That's weird, I was just ringing about that. No, I haven't.'

'Have you found Gemma's birth certificate?'

'Yeah, I've got that.'

'What's her mother's name?'

'Erm, hang on.' While Smith riffles through some papers, Kate hurries back inside the house, slipping on the gloves before carefully sliding the documents into the evidence bag. 'Jennifer,' he says, and Kate deflates.

'Are you sure?'

'Yep, definitely Jennifer. But, wait . . . Yep, here we are. Jennifer Bray had a sister called—'

'Gwendoline,' Kate finishes.

'That's the one. Gwendoline Bray. How did you know?'

'Instinct. So you've not found a death certificate for Gemma?'

'No, sorry, Sarge. Nothing within the past thirty years in Cornwall.'

'I'm not a sergeant,' Kate says distractedly, 'but thanks for looking.' A buzzing starts inside her head. Was it a mistake to take anything Rebecca said at face value? Had she known that Gwen had been her great-aunt, and that was why she'd left Blackwater House to her? *What if her mother isn't really dead?* She considers again the link between the two families, the

Brays and the Everleys. She's certain there is one, that there's something connecting it all together. *But what am I missing?*

'I want to check out her old house,' Kate says, sealing the evidence bag and hurrying downstairs. 'It's on the other side of the village.'

'I'm actually on my way to a property nearby. Someone called in about junkies – uh, sorry, that was the word they used,' PC Smith stammers.

'Never mind. Carry on.'

'A neighbour reported a disturbance, said it's a house well-known for use by—'

'Junkies, yes. Where is it?' PC Smith reels off the address and Kate nods, recognising it. 'I'll meet you there.'

Kate pulls up opposite the address and peers at the dilapidated exterior. She notices a Cornish flag fluttering from the top window as she gets out of the car to join PC Smith. Wordlessly, they pick their way through the overgrown weeds towards the front door, passing a rusting car sitting on bricks in the front garden. To their surprise, the door swings open as soon as PC Smith's fist connects, and he pushes it wider, reaching for his baton as he steps inside.

'Hello?' he calls into the darkness. They begin to move into the house, their footsteps too loud in the silence. 'Police!'

Kate can just make out the stairs ahead and, as her eyes adjust to the gloom, she sees a door to their right and another at the end of the hall. 'Police!' she calls, her boots crunching on a pile of takeaway leaflets. She hears a noise and they both pause, glancing at one another before PC Smith nudges the first door open with his boot. The room is empty except for a broken armchair in the corner. The window is covered by dark curtains, which are fraying at the edges; empty bottles and takeaway boxes litter the floor, and the light fitting sits empty. Kate leads the way towards the room at the back of the house. As she places a hand on the door, she hears a giggle and spins to see legs on the stairs above her.

'Oi!' she shouts, turning to follow, PC Smith on her heels. They climb the stairs, following the hushed voices and another giggle, which is cut short, as if a hand has been placed over a mouth. Kate kicks open the first door to find three children huddled against the far wall, their faces grimy with dirt, their hair greasy and lifeless. 'Oh, fuck,' she murmurs. She tries to smile reassuringly at them, her heart pounding in her chest, and she hears PC Smith gasp behind her. 'You see to them,' she whispers, and he nods as she turns to search the rest of the house.

She finds them in the next room, two women lying on a single mattress. The air is heavy with smoke, and Kate spots a man sitting on a hard-backed chair in the corner, a cigarette dangling from his lips. She recognises him immediately.

'For fuck's sake, Tony,' she spits. 'What the hell are you playing at?'

His eyes widen as he takes her in, but his eyes are unfocused, as if he's not sure whether she's really there. *He's probably used to seeing ghosts,* she thinks as he takes another pull, blue-grey smoke pouring from his nostrils.

'Ahh, Katie,' he slurs, 'what are you doing here? I haven't done anything, Officer. I'm innocent, honest.'

Kate sighs. She's known Tony for years, had known him by sight since she was a kid, his limp marking him out from the others. He'd fought in Iraq, he'd told her when she was a PC and the police had been called by a neighbour after they heard screaming. But it had only been Tony, screaming at the demons that had followed him from the desert. 'When did you move from Redruth?' she asks, glancing down at the bodies on the mattress. 'And where did they come from?'

Tony grins, his teeth brown and crooked. 'I'm always on the move, me. Can't stay still.'

'Whose kids are they?' she demands, jerking her head towards the room next door, and the grin drops from his face.

'Kids?' He frowns, the cigarette held in front of his face. 'I don't know nothing about no kids.' One of the women on the mattress groans and his eyes move to her. 'Could be one of theirs. Here—' he nudges them with his bare foot '—did you bring bleddy kids here?'

The women don't respond, their mouths slack, eyes still closed. Tony looks at Kate and shrugs.

'We'll have to take them,' she says, stepping out of the room and making eye contact with PC Smith, who nods and pulls out his phone.

'I'll make myself scarce, then,' Tony says, sighing dramatically. His eyes look remarkably clear now, and Kate wonders whether the drugs help, or whether they bring the demons back to life. 'Tisn't even a nice place, this.'

'Whose is it?'

'No idea, maid. Just one of those houses we all end up in.'

Kate shakes her head and turns to leave, when a light flashes inside her brain. 'When's the last time you saw Gemma Bray?' she asks him.

Tony frowns again, dropping the cigarette butt into a can of beer where it fizzles. 'Gem? Christ, it's been a day or two.' He squints up at her. 'Why? She in trouble? I tell ee, I never liked that Terry of hers. He was a nasty piece of work.'

'Where's he to then?' Kate asks, feeling herself slip into her usual Cornish-isms, which she tries to avoid when on the job. But Tony seems to respond better to Kate than to DC Winters. *I adapt my style and approach according to the needs of the people I am working with.*

Tony leans back in his chair. 'Dead, I heard, or disappeared, thank the Lord. Years ago now. Good riddance.'

'And Gemma? Did she stay in that house after he died?'

Tony wrinkles his nose. 'I don't know. I bumped into her a while ago in a house up Camborne way. She was her usual friendly self, throwing herself at anyone with anything going spare.'

'When was this?' she asks, impatience creeping into her voice. She tries to contain it.

'Is it Christmas time?' Tony asks, his eyes wide like a child's, and Kate feels her heart lurch with sadness. She wonders when he last had a proper Christmas, with a hot meal and presents under a tree. She thinks of all the people in the world who don't have the things that many take for granted, the people forced to live on the streets after they've had their benefits cut, the mothers standing in line at the food bank, those kids in the room next door, dragged from pillar to post to feed their mothers' addiction. She glares down at the women on the mattress in disgust, and is glad PC Smith is with the children. He's always the one to call when there are kids involved, with his never-ending patience and calm demeanour.

'No, Tony,' she says softly. 'It's January now.'

Tony's face falls. 'Oh.' He chews his bottom lip for a moment before lifting his eyes to meet her gaze. 'I saw her at Christmas, and I knew it was Christmas because there were carol singers in the street. They sang my favourite, "Let It Snow".' A smile creeps across his face. 'It never snows here though, does it? Too much salt in the air.'

'I saw it once, I think,' Kate says, remembering standing in the garden with her mum, watching the snow come down. 'It was nice.'

'It snows in the desert, you know.' Tony's eyes have glazed

over and Kate knows she has to pull him back from the black hole gaping at his feet.

'And you saw Gemma?' she prompts, holding her breath until he meets her eyes again.

'Yes, at Christmas.' Tony frowns. 'Was it last Christmas?' What year is it?

30

Rebecca

I drive, taking the narrow bends too fast, fingers tightening on the wheel. The private road is uneven, the car rumbling as I drive, fingers gripping the steering wheel.

I'd found this cottage a few years ago, chosen for its proximity to Blackwater House and Gwen should we need her help, and its isolated location, with its own private road and large forest surrounding it on all sides. The perfect place to hide.

She'd written to me the year before she died, finally telling me the truth. Although her sister, my grandmother, had kicked my mum out when I was born, Gwen tried to keep an eye on her. At first she gave us a place to stay, but soon my mother had started stealing from her. Gwen had begged her to leave me with her, but my mum disappeared one night, taking every penny Gwen had had in the house along with some jewellery. A widow with no children, Gwen stayed in the village to watch over me from afar, intending to make herself known when I was old enough to understand. And then I had appeared on her doorstep, as if fate had guided the way. I said I don't believe in coincidences, but something drew me to Blackwater House that day, and I like to believe it was the blood ties between Gwen and me. That like calls to like, and somewhere deep down I had known I belonged with her.

As soon as I pull up outside the cottage, I see Ashleigh leaning against a tree.

'How did you get here before me?' I demand as I roll down the window. She gets into the car, leaving the door open. 'This is it, isn't it? She's been here this whole time?'

She cocks an eyebrow at me. 'Yep. She's pretty smart, you know.'

'I know,' I snap. I stare at the house, suddenly nervous. What if she doesn't want to see me? What if she did this not just to get away from Daniel, but from me too?

'They're going to find her,' Ashleigh says, her eyes on the house. 'Mum.'

The word is like a shock of cold water, and I gasp as the memory floods through me. I think of the knife in my hand, my mother's eyes widening as she realised what was happening, and who was doing it to her. The memory is searing, and I close my eyes, trying to snuff out the flames. 'I know.'

'She deserved it,' Ashleigh says. 'After what she did to us. To you. She wasn't fit to call herself a mother. They both got what they deserved.'

Before I can speak, the front door flies open, and there is Ava, hands on her hips, eyes blazing. 'Where have you been?' she demands, glaring at me as I fall out of the car, my blood fizzing with a mixture of shock and relief. I take her in; she looks healthy, if a little tired, her lips pursed with worry or anger or both. I open my mouth to speak, to ask her the same question, to grab her and hug her and shake her, but a noise silences us both. Another car is rumbling down the dirt track behind us, the low winter sun bouncing off the windscreen, obscuring the driver's face.

'Who is that?' I ask, watching as the car comes to a stop and Sierra gets out of the passenger side.

'Hello, Rebecca,' she says, moving steadily across the mud and taking my hands in hers. 'You made it.' She smiles that same smile, the one that always radiates warmth and love, but

this time I see something else there too, and a shiver of anticipation runs up my spine.

Ava moves past me to greet her grandmother, who drops
my hands to wrap her granddaughter in a hug. 'Hello, sweet
pea. How have you been? Has your aunt been taking care of
you?'

Bewildered, I look at Ashleigh, who shakes her head, and I
turn back to see Sierra gazing at something behind me. Aisha
has appeared at the front door, a blanket wrapped around her
shoulders, her feet shoved into boots, her pregnant stomach
protruding above her hips. I feel the air leave my body at the
sight of her, as the truth finally hits me like a blow. *They know.*
They all know. Ava has told them everything. And they've
helped her, like I never could.

I try to take a deep breath as the world spins around me.
'You knew. Why didn't you tell me?' I cry at Ashleigh as the
edges of my vision begin to darken. Hands grasp my arms
and I allow myself to be led away from her, Ava's small hand
finding mine, Aisha reaching for me as we near the house, pity
in her eyes.

Ava turns back as we reach the front door, her cheeks flushing as she watches her grandmother open the driver door.
Cass steps out of the car then, pausing to smile at her mother
before turning to open the back door. Daniel tumbles out
onto the mud, his hands bound behind his back, his eyes wide
with fear. He screams, but his words are muffled by the dark
fabric stuffed in his mouth. Aisha grips me more tightly as I
stumble, holding me up as I take in the scene before me. I look
wildly around for Ashleigh, but she's disappeared. Where is
she? How could she have been part of this? *Why* was she part
of this? How could she have kept it from me? *I* was supposed
to help Ava. It was all I've ever wanted; all I've needed to do.
This was *my* debt to repay.

I watch Sierra stare down at Daniel as he lies in the mud, his body flopping like a fish out of water. His eyes find mine and I feel my knees begin to buckle. Aisha tightens her grip on my arm as I try to fight against the encroaching darkness.

'It's time to make amends,' Sierra says, stepping over Daniel's body and making her way into the house, Ava on her heels. 'We have a lot to discuss.'

They drag him inside, Aisha stepping forward to help her sister wrestle him across the driveway. She is strong, despite her condition, or perhaps Daniel has been drugged. His eyes are wild and his forehead is slick with sweat. Ava pulls me out of the way, guiding me inside and towards the sofa, where I sit trembling.

'Sit here, Becks,' Ava says gently, and I sit, my eyes glued to Daniel as he writhes around on the floor, trying and failing to get to his feet. Cass puts a boot on his back and he goes still, his eyes round with fear. Sierra breezes into the room, her skirt trailing on the floor, giving her the appearance of gliding. Her face is serene, her eyes crinkling as she looks at Ava, reaching out to touch her face. But her expression changes as she moves closer to Daniel, her eyes blazing as she takes him in.

'What are you going to do to him?' I ask, but she ignores me. We all stare down at him, this man with whom I have lived for years, of whom I had been so frightened. I had been planning to run away for years, slowly building my nest egg, trying to hatch the perfect plan to rescue Ava from him, but it seems she didn't need me at all. She's done this herself, reached out to her mother's family for the help she felt she couldn't get from me, and I am suddenly ashamed of myself, of my failure.

Sierra crouches beside him, her long skirt pooling around her ankles. 'Ava has told us everything,' she says quietly, her voice barely above a whisper, and I see Daniel's face go white. 'We know you were there, Daniel. When Meghan died.' She slips a hand into her pocket and brings out a necklace, the large M swaying on the end of the silver chain.

You fucking idiot. He had taken it from Meghan's neck that night at the party and kept it ever since, and now they know. But how did they find out he was there that night? Do they know I was too? That I could have saved Meghan and didn't? Fear floods through me as Daniel starts to struggle against his bonds, his eyes wide. Ava turns to face me, her eyes searching mine, and I try to keep my face neutral. *She doesn't know I was there. She* can't *know.*

'She never took this necklace off,' Sierra says, dangling the necklace above Daniel's face. 'It was a gift for her eighteenth birthday, and she wore it everywhere. She would have never taken it off, like the police suggested.' The photograph of Meghan and Ava flashes into my mind. The necklace hanging from her neck, the silver M clasped in the chubby fist of her daughter.

'You left her there to die,' Sierra hisses. 'You left your brother there to die. And you left your daughter.' She raises an arm and points at Ava. 'Your own flesh and blood.' She drops the necklace back into her pocket and stands, clasping her hands behind her back. I have never seen her like this; so strong, so powerful. She was always the matriarch of this family of strong women, firm and steady, but I have never seen this side of her before. She has become a lioness, transformed by the testimony of her granddaughter. 'And when you thought she was missing, you left to go back to *work*?' Her voice rises at the end, full of incredulity. She shakes her head as she paces before him. 'She's told us about the way you behave behind closed doors too. The snide comments. The cruelty you inflicted on her. And on Rebecca.' She waves a hand at me and I blink, my eyes darting between her and Daniel. He tries to speak, his voice muffled by the gag, but he is silenced by a wave of Sierra's hand. 'We have no interest in what you have to say,' she growls, her gaze locked onto Daniel. 'We know everything. And you will pay for it.'

She holds out a hand to Ava, pulling her to her feet, while Cass takes my arm and guides me out of the room, closing the door and locking it behind us. Through the glass pane, I watch Daniel start to struggle against the rope binding his wrists and ankles, and see the ghost of Meghan drifting in the corner of the room.

'How did you get him here?' I ask Cass, extricating myself from her grasp.

'I met him at the house, in Stanstead Abbotts,' she says, avoiding my eyes. 'Mum ... Mum called him, told him to come up.'

I shake my head, realisation dawning at what has happened here. I look at Cass, and when her eyes meet mine I see they are full of sadness and pity, but there is a softness there too, a gentleness I hadn't expected. I had never imagined, in all the years I'd lived with Daniel, all the years I'd been planning to take Ava away, that Meghan's family would help me. I knew they loved Ava, but I hadn't expected them to understand. How could I have explained to them how I had come into Ava's life? How could they ever understand it? And so I tried to do it alone, as I have done my whole life. And I have failed.

I pace the hall, leaving the others to discuss their plans in the kitchen. I have to think. I have to know what Sierra knows, whether she blames me as she blames Daniel. As I deserve to be blamed. I spot Ashleigh in the front garden and rush to the door, pulling it open. *Why is she here?* 'Where did you go?' I hiss through the gap. Her eyes meet mine and I feel a shiver pass through me. Her eyes, so like Mum's, so like mine, are bloodshot, the rims red and puffy. Had she been crying? 'Did you know about all of this?' I jerk my head towards the closed door and Daniel beyond, still lying on the floor.

'Of course I didn't. I only know what you know.' Her voice is steady, almost monotonous, without character or feeling, as if she is in a trance. I stare at her, my pulse beating in my ears.

'What do you mean? You knew to bring me here.' Frustrated, I wave a hand at the house behind me. 'You knew where she was, didn't you? This whole time?'

'You did, too. You knew it all along.' She holds my gaze, life suddenly coming back into her eyes, and I see my own face reflected there, my eyes wide, my skin pale. She smiles. 'She saved herself.'

My throat constricts at her words, so like those three little words I'd repeated to myself over and over again as I lay awake in the spare room at Blackwater House. *I'll save myself.* My hands go to my head, which has started to pound, and the edges of my vision begin to darken.

Ashleigh keeps smiling, her expression fixed in place like a doll's. 'You know what you have to do now, don't you, Becks? You remember how it felt to kill our mother, how right it was?' I shake my head, my heart pounding in my ears. She leans in, her lips brushing my cheek as she whispers into my ear. 'You need to kill him, Becks. Before he kills you.'

'No! I can't—'

'What's going on?' A voice behind me makes me whirl around, my eyes flying open. Ava stands in the kitchen door-way, her hand on the doorknob, her brow furrowed. She peers beyond me at the open front door. 'Is someone out there?'

I turn around to see Ashleigh taking a step back as Ava moves towards me, and I want to tell Ashleigh to go away, to leave us alone. I want to erase her from my mind, erase the memories that haunted me for years, that followed me across the country and back again, ever since that night at the engine house. She opens her mouth to speak again but I close my eyes, my hands pressed tight over my ears, trying to block her out.

'Becks,' Ava says slowly. 'Who are you talking to?'

I open my eyes and feel the world tilt. The garden is empty.

31

Rebecca

Now – 4th January 2020

I wake in a strange bed, a musty blanket pulled up to my chin. My body feels heavy, my eyes dry and scratchy, and when I try to move, my head swims, nausea rising in my throat.

'Shhh,' Sierra says, moving from the window to sit beside me. 'Rest, child.'

'Wh-what happened?' I croak.

'You took a nasty tumble,' she says. 'You have blackouts a lot, don't you?' I hesitate before nodding, my eyes filling with tears. 'Oh, dear.' Sierra tuts softly, placing a hand on mine. 'I see her all the time, you know. Meghan.' The breath catches in my chest as she smiles sadly. 'You never get over the loss of a child. Never.' Guilt floods through me and I long to tell her, to explain, to beg for her forgiveness. But I could never ask that of her. 'I often talk to her, even now,' she continues. 'I spent more than twenty years talking to her, listening to her, loving her. You can't just switch that off, sweet pea, no matter how long you have them for. I think you know that too, Rebecca.' She smiles sadly, but as I open my mouth to speak there is a knock at the door. I turn my head to find Ava standing in the doorway, her expression unreadable.

Sierra pats her granddaughter's shoulder as she moves back to the window. Ava sits at the end of the bed, legs crossed, playing with a stray thread from the hem of her T-shirt. She is silent for a moment, her eyes on her lap, and I watch her,

251

wondering how we got here. How I could have missed what was going on inside her head. I swallow the lump in my throat. I want to ask her why she'd made her own plans, why she hadn't come to me, but I know the answer. I'd let her down too many times, and I would have done so again.

'It was Grandma's idea,' she says quietly, looking up and meeting my gaze. 'Aunt Aisha wanted to take me back with them on Boxing Day, but Grandma told her that wouldn't work. That they'd know straight away.' She smiles again. 'So we adapted your plan instead.'

'But why didn't you tell me?' I whisper. 'Why didn't you call me, later, so I could join you?'

'The police are monitoring the phones,' she says simply, as if this is a normal thing for her to be discussing. 'They would have known if I'd made contact with you.'

'But then how . . .?'

'I found your scrapbook. One of your boxes got mixed up with mine when we moved, and I kept it beneath my bed.' Her words hit me like a blow, the memory of finding Ava shoving something beneath her bed suddenly takes on a new meaning, and I feel my heart start to race. *'Family of tragic Meghan Bird speak out,'* she says, reciting a newspaper article I'd photocopied and kept, but her voice is barely audible above the rushing in my ears, the contents of the scrapbook flashing before my eyes. *She knows. She knows what I did. She knows.*

I gasp for breath, suddenly feeling as if I am under water. My vision blurs and I see Ava's lips moving again, but her voice sounds so far away.

'It was Aunt Aisha who told me about my mum's necklace. She told me to look for it, that it was mine now. After I found it in dad's drawer and realised my mum had been wearing it in the photo in that article, I put the pieces together. You were there that night, both of you. But it was you who called the ambulance, wasn't it? That's why you followed the case in the news.' She smiles again, reaching out and taking my hand. 'They said it was a woman who called. He left me – left us – to die. But you didn't.'

I stare at her, uncomprehending. 'But she still . . . I didn't . . .'

'You tried.' Sierra's voice comes from her place by the window, her eyes soft. 'You did what you could.' I shake my head, trying to clear it, but, misunderstanding, she moves across the room and takes my other hand. 'I don't know how you got involved in it all, but you saved her,' she says, her eyes flicking towards Ava. 'You saved my granddaughter. I can never repay you for that.'

'You tried, Becks,' Ava repeats. 'And then you moved in with us.' She raises an eyebrow. 'I'm not saying it all makes sense,' she says, 'but it's worked out in the end.'

'Has it?' I whisper, gripping their fingers in mine, the mother and the daughter of Meghan Bird, and I feel her in the room with us, her eyes watching the scene play out. 'Has it all worked out?'

Sierra squeezes my hand. 'It will.'

I drift in and out of sleep, feeling as though I am floating out to sea, the waves cradling me, taking me further and further away from land. Just as it took Ashleigh, when I whispered her name to the sea. Am I strong enough now to accept what she is? A ghost, a figment of my imagination. The child Sam Everley left me with, who I'm not sure I could have loved. Only Gwen knew what happened that night, the story told once and never again, pushed to the deepest recesses of my mind. Gwen had encouraged me in this, I realise now. She hadn't known how to deal with such deep trauma, and so she had thought it best that I try to forget about my daughter. But I could never have erased her completely. She became a sister instead, so I could remember her without having to endure the pain of her birth. It's no surprise she reappeared when I moved back to Blackwater House, which sits above her final resting place. We are tied to Blackwater House, to one another, and I don't know how to sever the connection. I don't even know if I want to.

A scream rings out and my eyes fly open to find the room in darkness, the sky outside leaden. *Ava.*

I throw back the blanket and hurtle down the stairs, Ava's scream still ringing in my ears. Aisha bursts out of the kitchen as I reach the bottom, and together we run towards the living room door, almost crashing into Sierra. We enter to find Ava standing in the middle of the room, her back to us. Daniel is lying at her feet, his face hidden from view. I look up to see Cass slumped against the far wall, blood trickling from her nose. I stare at her unseeing eyes, the breath held in my chest until, finally, she moans, her eyelids flickering.

Ava doesn't turn, her spine rigid, eyes trained on the body of her father. And then her arms drop, the blood-spattered knife falling from her hand as she finally turns to face us.

'He attacked her,' Ava whispers, her eyes wide. 'Aunt Cass. He was going to kill her.' Ava holds her hands out as if in supplication, her fingers coated in blood. Daniel's blood. Aisha gasps, her hands pressed against her mouth, as I fall to my knees, my brain unable to take in the sight before me. Unable to comprehend what Ava has done.

Sierra walks slowly towards her granddaughter, taking her hands in hers, the blood transferring to her own fingers. 'Well,' she says, her eyes locked on to Ava's, 'this changes things. We need a new plan.'

'We need to dump him somewhere,' Aisha says, and I see Ava flinch.

Sierra glares at her eldest daughter before squeezing Ava's hands. 'We'll think of something. Don't worry, sweet pea. This wasn't your fault.'

And then it hits me, the part I can play in all of this. How the debt can finally be repaid. 'I know a place,' I say, and all heads turn towards me. 'I know where we can take him.'

32

Kate

'Can one of you please tell me why I'm dirtying my new boots in a place like this?' DS Tremayne demands as she stands in the hallway, glaring at the officers in front of her. Kate glances at PC Smith before speaking.

'Tony says he last saw Gemma Bray around Christmas, but he isn't sure when.'

DS Tremayne raises an eyebrow. 'And he's to be trusted, is he?' A shriek comes from behind them and the trio turn in unison to see one of the children fighting against the officer who is trying to wrestle her into the car. 'Go and help them out, will you, Smith?' Tremayne barks.

'Sarge.' PC Smith trudges towards the pair, palms up, and Kate watches the child go still as he crouches in front of her, her fear evident.

'Rebecca told me her mum has been dead for years,' Kate says, and Tremayne turns back to her. 'But PC Smith said he couldn't find a death certificate for her. I want to check out her old house. I think I might find something there.'

Tremayne sighs, her face softening as another child is brought out of the house. 'You do realise that PACE doesn't cover gut feeling, don't you, Winters?' Her lips curve into a smile as she speaks, and Kate relaxes a fraction.

'I do, Sarge.'

'Do you have reason to believe that Ava Everley might be inside this house?'

A slight hesitation, then: 'Yes, Sarge.'

DS Tremayne nods. 'Off you go, then. Give me the address; I'll send uniform after you.'

Kate nods at PC Smith as she slides into her car. She still remembers the address, all these years later, of the house she visited only once. But it left a mark on her, those few moments she spent in Rebecca's shoes. She remembers going home to her mother and telling her what she saw, but the thing that got to her the most had been the smell. Rebecca's house hadn't just smelled of unclean bodies and cigarette smoke and congealed food. It had smelled of unhappiness.

Kate parks across the road on a grass verge and gets out, her eyes drawn to the sky as she pushes open the rusting gate. Clouds have rolled in and the sky above her is leaden, heavy with rain. The gate squeals as it swings wide, hitting the overgrown hedge beside it. The path is covered in weeds, and a crisp packet scuttles towards her, pushed along by the wind. She pulls the collar of her coat up around her ears as the chill bites into her.

Raising a gloved hand, Kate knocks on the door, paint flecks showering the step beneath her. The front panel of the window is still boarded up, just as she remembered it, but it is graffitied now, the spray paint barely covering the word CUNT written in thick black marker. Kate knocks again, then steps back and tries to peer through the filthy glass at the side. Years of neglect have left the glass smeared and opaque. Stuffing her hands into her pockets, she walks back to the gate and looks up at the house. A dark sheet is hung over the upstairs window, a splat of seagull shit crusted over the right panel. Kate kicks an empty beer can and watches it spin across the grass and onto the uneven concrete beside the house. She follows it, taking in the wooden gate that sits to the right of the house. A bin store? Or access to the back garden?

She chews her bottom lip. She doesn't have a warrant, or even a reason to be here, not really. Whoever owns this house has clearly decided to abandon it, and Tony said that he'd last seen Gemma in Camborne. But something niggles at the back of Kate's mind, what Lauren calls *intuition*, and what the DS calls *gut feeling*.

'PACE doesn't cover gut feeling,' she murmurs to herself, 'but it does cover reasonable grounds.' And although she doesn't actually believe Ava is in this house, she knows that *something* is. So, when Kate reaches out to push open the gate and finds it unlocked, she makes a snap decision. She goes inside.

The alley is dark, the sky blocked by a piece of tarpaulin, and Kate has a sudden vision of walking into a huge spider's web. She takes out her torch and flicks it on, looking around before directing it at her feet. Something moves next to her left boot and she jumps. Rats. She pulls out her baton, holding it against her thigh as she begins to creep through the alley. There's a putrid smell coming from somewhere. Holding her forearm against her face, Kate moves faster through the alley, finally breaking into the weak January light of the garden. The air is clearer here and she takes a deep breath, her eyes trained on a bird flying overhead. Her heart is pounding, her stomach clenching. She should call someone. Tremayne, Allen, Smith. Anyone. But she doesn't. Instead, she moves towards the back door, her pulse roaring in her ears, instinct pushing her on.

The back door slams in the breeze before creaking open again as she approaches. She puts a foot to the crack and shoves the door open, flicking her torch around the kitchen. The smell is even worse in here: rotting food, oil caked into the surfaces, cans and bottles sticky with liquid lying on the floor. It fills her nose, making her gag. It seems to be everywhere, crawling inside her. The overflowing bin is covered in flies, which startle at her presence, rising in a black cloud towards her. Kate bats them away and moves into the hall. Her boots stick to the carpet, peeling away with a sucking noise as she creeps towards the living room. Graffiti covers the walls, overflowing ashtrays litter the coffee table, and the sofas are ripped and full of cigarette burns. There is no TV, no photographs on the walls, no sign of this ever being a family home. A place where a child once lived.

Kate creeps out of the room and into the hallway. The wallpaper is peeling, the carpet worn through, and the headless body of a child's doll is propped up on the bottom step, arms outstretched, legs akimbo. The letter M has been carved into its chest, just like the sketch of Ava's she had found. M for Meghan. M for mother. M for murder?

Kate shudders and begins to climb the stairs. She doesn't know what to expect as she steps onto the landing, her eyes flicking to the three closed doors. LEAVE is sprayed on the furthest one, and she wonders if it's a threat, a warning, or the demand of an overzealous Brexiteer. Carefully, she opens the first door off the landing, bracing herself for whatever might be waiting for her, but each room is empty.

She enters the bathroom, switching on the overhead light which, miraculously, works. An ancient extractor fan starts to whir as she moves the rotting shower curtain aside to find an empty, filthy bath. Something moves out of the corner of her eye and she spins, but there is nothing there. Turning off the light, she goes back out onto the landing and stands in the darkness, her heart pounding in her ears. She knows something is in this house. Something is waiting for her, but what?

A noise from downstairs makes her jump. She peers over the banisters to find a figure standing in the hallway, their face hidden by the shadows.

'Kate.'

For a moment, Kate feels as if she has gone back in time. She is twelve again, and Becks Bray is in the bedroom behind her, digging through her wardrobe for a pair of shorts Kate will wear once then throw away a few years later, wrinkling her nose as she fails to remember where they came from. But Becks Bray isn't there. Rebecca is downstairs, waiting for her.

33

Rebecca

Now – 4th January 2020

I wait in my old bedroom, crouching like a hunted animal beneath a bush. When I hear Kate go into the bathroom, I slip down the stairs and into the kitchen, pausing to scoop up the doll on my way down. She needs to check, to find the house empty, before she will come with me. Before I finally tell her the truth.

The light goes off upstairs and I move out from the shadows to stand in the hallway. 'Kate,' I say, and I see her move to the top of the stairs. 'Kate, it's me. Rebecca.' The beam of her torch hits my eyes and I blink away the stars.

'What's going on?' she demands, but her voice is weaker than usual.

'I need to . . . You'll see.'

I hear her footsteps on the stairs as she makes her way down, one foot after the other, like she is approaching a wounded animal and is afraid of being attacked. 'What's going on?' she asks again, lowering her torch so I can see her face. She is afraid, and for that I am sorry.

'Follow me,' I tell her, and start to move towards the kitchen. She follows me out of the house and down to the bottom of the garden, to the small outbuilding that had, when the house was first built, served as an outside toilet. I take out a key and slide it into the padlock, then pause. 'I'm sorry for what you're about to see,' I say, and pull open the door.

The light from Kate's torch finds Daniel first. He is propped against the wall, his eyes closed, the wound in his neck glistening, and I hear her sharp intake of breath. 'Did you . . .?' She trails off as she takes in the rest of the surroundings. 'Wh-who's that?'

'That's Terry,' I say, pointing at the skeleton in the far corner. 'And that's my mum.'

The memory of that day eighteen years ago is still fresh in my mind. It was Christmas Eve, the village twinkling with lights as I walked through the familiar streets. I went with the hope of making amends with my mother, the hope of a Christmas spent together without the drinking and the violence. I should have known better.

'Well, well, well. The prodigal daughter returns.' The words had stung, but I tried not to let it show. I pushed past Terry into the house and saw my mother passed out on the couch, needles and other rubbish littering the floor. I turned to see him looming in the doorway, his eyes narrowed. 'What?' he said with a shrug, as if it didn't matter. As if none of it mattered. 'Did you expect anything else?'

A flash of movement on the stairs behind him; Ashleigh, a toddler then, her feet bare despite the cold. She had a deep purple bruise on her arm in the shape of a hand, and her eyes were red, her cheeks hollow. I know now that she was a figment of my imagination, or perhaps a projection, a memory of myself at that age and the horrors I had lived through, but a sudden rage bubbled up inside me at the sight of her, a spark catching and filling me with fire. I reached into my pocket and pulled out the knife I had taken to carrying since that New Year's Eve, and in one quick movement, thrust the blade into Terry's throat.

He died quickly. It was surprisingly easy, to watch the light go out of his eyes. I felt nothing but a sense of calm righteousness, a sense that this was always going to happen. As he slumped to the floor, I sat down in his chair and waited for my mother to wake up.

'Terry?' she croaked, her eyes blinking against the glare of the overhead light as she searched for him.

'He's dead.' My voice was low, almost a whisper, and her eyes widened as she took me in, huddled in the chair Terry had ruled from for so many years.

'What? Becks?' She pushed herself up, slowly rising from the sofa until she was sitting upright. 'Hello, love,' she said, and for a moment, I hesitated. For a moment, I thought she would see the pain her daughter was in, had always been in, and come back to herself. To me. And then she saw him. Terry's body, lying on the floor between us, his eyes wide and sightless, and she started to cry. I hadn't seen her cry in years, and her tears for him made the fury bubble up again. I told her then about Sam, about what he had done to me. About what this house, what *she*, had allowed him to do. And I told her about Ashleigh, who was stood in the doorway, watching the scene unfold. Ashleigh came over to me then and placed a hand on mine as if trying to give me strength as my mother shook her head, her tears gone now and replaced with her own kind of anger. The anger that comes with being confronted, with denial. She called me a liar as she struggled to her feet, trying to reach the door, but I was quicker and knocked her to the ground.

'You're mad,' she hissed as I stood over her, the knife clenched in my fist.

'Like mother, like daughter,' I said, and plunged it into her neck.

'It was about eighteen years ago,' I tell Kate now. 'I came home for Christmas.'

'And you killed them?' Her eyes are wide; I have surprised her, scared her even, but I can see her instincts are kicking in.

I won't fight her. I know what I have to do now. It's better that she knows the truth, the whole truth. I am ready for Kate to arrest me, and to face the consequences of what I have done. I brought the knife from the cottage with me, wiped clean of Ava's fingerprints and replaced with my own. The clothes I'd been wearing earlier are smouldering in the back garden of Blackwater House, smeared with Daniel's blood.

Our story is straightforward. I will say that Daniel had left his party and drove here, snatching Ava in the middle of the night. Earlier, I'd dug his phone out of his pocket and sent myself a text, telling me to meet him here, and that's how the police will think I'd found out what he'd done. They will think there was a struggle out here in the garden, that Daniel had tried to kill me, and I'd stabbed him in self-defence. They will think that Daniel had discovered my sordid past and wanted to get Ava away from me, but he wanted to confront me here, in my childhood home, as one final way to hurt me. And so I had to come back here, one last time.

'I killed them,' I say, holding out my hands. 'I killed them all.'

Things move quickly. Kate handcuffs me as she calls it in, and soon a police car is pulling up outside the house, lights turning the world blue. I am led to the car, a hand on my head as I am pushed into the back seat, the door shut firmly behind me. I breathe out, my breath creating ghosts on the window. I look up at the house and notice Kate standing on the path, watching me. But it is not her I see. It is Ashleigh, standing in the doorway, suddenly a child again. Her hair is soaked through, strands plastered to her skull, and there is a scarf around her neck, the scarf I'd wrapped her up in the night she was born. As she moves towards me, she begins to grow into the adult I have been seeing these past few months. The scent of the sea fills my lungs and I can hear the rushing of the waves in my ears. I reach out, my fingers pressed against the window, my chest so tight I fear it will burst. Then the car starts to move and she disappears, and I know it is the last time I will ever see her.

'Goodbye,' I whisper.

I am processed, the officer behind the desk sucking on a mint as he asks me questions, the sweet clicking against his teeth. My fingerprints are taken, and the camera flash makes my eyes water as they tell me to turn this way and that. I'm told to remove my clothes and jewellery, and they give me a shapeless grey tracksuit, which smells faintly of antiseptic. I wonder who wore it before me, what they did. Whether they were guilty.

My mind drifts to where Ava might be, whether she has presented herself to the police yet. She will be too traumatised to tell them anything of note, like where her father had been keeping her, only that she had been blindfolded and escaped by pure chance. I glance at Kate as she escorts me to my cell, a job that is no doubt beneath her, and I feel sorry that she won't be the one to find Ava. I find myself wanting to reassure her, that it wasn't her lack of skill or passion that stopped her from finding out the truth. It was Ava herself who has been driving this story.

A uniformed officer opens a cell door and I step inside, Kate stopping on the threshold as I sit on the mattress and feel it give beneath my weight. She doesn't look at me as she speaks. 'Are you sure you don't want a solicitor?'

I shake my head. What's the point? I have framed myself so perfectly. I will tell them that Daniel attacked me first, that he has always been abusive towards me, and Ava will be tearful as she explains that her father had abducted her. But it will not save me, and I don't want it to.

'But what about you?' Ava cried before I left the cottage, throwing her arms around my neck, her tears soaking into my hair. 'What about our happy ending?' I couldn't speak, just held her close before releasing her back into the arms of her grandmother, her mother's sisters looking on as I drove away towards my destiny.

I curl up on the hard bed, my knees tucked up beneath my chin, the sleeves of the jumper pulled over my hands. The door slams shut, and finally, *finally*, I am alone.

PART 3

7 years later

34

Ava

I have almost come full circle. I sit at the kitchen table and read the email from my agent again, trying to process the words. 'Ava, I am pleased to introduce you to your new editor, Nicky, with whom I have agreed the deal memo today . . .'

I sit back, my hands pressed to my face. My rescue dog trots into the room and sits beside me, her head cocked to one side. 'We did it, Ash,' I say to the dog, named for an aunt who never existed. 'We bloody did it!' She barks once and I laugh, reaching out to scratch behind her ears.

I am almost twenty-two years old, around the same age my mother was when she had me, and I have just received a contract for the book I have spent the past two years writing. It is a book about four fictional women and how their lives are entangled through one single act that binds them together forever.

I look around the flat I bought last year when I inherited my father's money and sold the house in Stanstead Abbotts. I wanted somewhere central, surrounded by other people, and I have been happy here, but it's time to move on now.

I decide to take Ash down to the common, the water rushing past as we cross the bridge. She is excited, her tail wagging as she trots ahead of me, turning her head every so often to check I'm still there. She bounds ahead to say hello to another dog and I smile at the owner as we pass, before calling Ash back to me. She walks beside me for a while, panting softly, and I reach into my pocket for her ball, throwing it across the open grass. She catches it mid-air, bringing it back and dropping it at my feet. We continue through the common, the river trickling along to my right, Ash running across the grass to my left.

I adopted her almost a year ago, after seeing a post on Facebook about a local sanctuary rescuing her from a kill centre in Greece. She is part golden retriever, part something else that nobody has been able to identify, and I immediately felt a connection with her. I am part victim, part killer. There are two sides to me, one which is hidden beneath my new, carefully constructed reality. I am my mother as she should have been: a young Black woman making my way in the world, trying to make a difference. I am Becks as she should have been: putting my past behind me, not letting it decide my future. But I cannot suppress it entirely, and I realise now that I have let Becks down.

Grandma didn't want me to go to the trial. 'You're so young, sweet pea,' she said, cupping my cheek with her hand, the skin soft against mine. But I smiled that winning smile that has still never failed me yet, and so I went, sat between Grandma and Aunt Cass, my palms slightly damp in theirs. I remember looking at Becks, her hands clasped before her, her head bowed. She did not give evidence, did not speak a word in her own defence, just like she'd promised, but her lawyer was a good one, paid for by a domestic violence charity, and so there was hope. For a while.

It was her final gift to me, taking the blame for my father's death, and how have I repaid her? With years of silence, never once visiting, never even writing a letter. I feel the weight of that now, as I realise that we are bound by secrets, Becks and me. She took the blame for me, telling the police that she stabbed my father after he attacked her. I told them that I ran away when he left to meet her, somehow finding my way back to Blackwater House. I had been unable to direct the police back to where my father had kept me after being kept blind-folded, and the officer who interviewed me after, Kate Winters, didn't seem to believe our story. She'd looked at me as if she could see into my soul and all the lies printed there.

I think of that night, slipping out of the annex and into the house to grab the bag I'd packed a few days before. It was during their visit over Christmas that Grandma and I made the plan. We decided it would be easier, and more confusing, for me to disappear the night of the sleepover, when I was unlikely to be missed straight away. In the end, I only got about an hour's head start, but it was enough.

Months earlier, Becks had shown me the place she'd chosen for our escape. It was close enough to Blackwater House for me to get to on foot, even in the dark. I climbed over the fence, accidentally dropping my scarf as I slipped through the trees and walked along the cliff edge until I found the coastal path. Aunt Aisha met me at the house and we waited for Grandma to arrive. The days dragged by, and every minute I felt guilty at what Becks must have been going through, wondering where I was. Grandma had been adamant that it was too risky to involve her, that it was better if we confronted my father alone, but Becks found us anyway, as I'd secretly hoped she would.

Throughout my life, she had done so much for me, even more than I'd realised, and so I had to attend the trial. I had to see the story unfold, that chapter of my life closing for good. Becks' lawyer was a large man, tall and broad, and his voice boomed across the courtroom. He began to speak about 'sustained domestic abuse', 'a childhood of deprivation and poverty', and 'diminished responsibility', and as he spoke in detail about her childhood, I felt a lump begin to form in my throat. I watched Becks' face as her lawyer spoke, her mouth set in a grim line, her head bowed as she absorbed his words.

'In 1999, Rebecca Bray was raped by an unknown man, which resulted in a pregnancy, of which Rebecca was not aware until she gave birth, alone and afraid, in an old tin mine, aged fifteen,' the lawyer said. 'Her baby was stillborn, never taking a breath.' He glanced at us, the audience, the people filling the hard, wooden benches, before turning back to the jury. 'And yet, she continued to live in Rebecca's mind. She buried the trauma, unable to cope with the reality of what had happened, but, at the same time, she was unable to forget her daughter entirely. She created a sister instead, forging memories of her, adding her into every scene, removing her from those that did not make sense, until her fantasy collided with reality.'

I remembered the way Becks had shouted at the empty front garden that day, her hands over her ears, her face screwed up as if in pain. I remembered asking her who she was talking to, the way her eyes had widened, her mouth dropping open before she fell, her body crumpling to the ground before I could catch her. Ashleigh, the baby who did not live, who Becks could not save. The ghost in the corner of the room, always there, always haunting her.

I feel my stomach clench as the images engulf me, pulling me away from the sunlit park. I cannot imagine what it must have been like for Becks, growing up in that house with a mother who didn't care about her. I suppose I can understand now how she must have viewed my mum, when she saw her the night she died. A mother neglecting her child, like her own had done. And how wrong was she? At first glance, my mother was no better. The fact that she was trying to flee doesn't change the fact that she put me in danger. Does it?

In my worst moments, this is how I view my mother. Selfish and weak. When I am alone in my flat, drinking my way through a bottle of wine as I stare out across the water, I hate her. I hate her for falling in love with my father, for staying with him when he began to abuse her. I hate her for relying on drugs to get her through, for allowing the postnatal depression to drag her under. I hate her for taking me to that house with her, for having one last hit for the road, and I hate her for dying, for leaving me with *him*.

These are not charitable thoughts. Most of the time, I know I am being unfair, blaming the victim of domestic abuse for staying, bringing out the typical *but why didn't you leave?* bullshit, which is exactly that. Bullshit. I know better than that. When I was at university, I volunteered for a refuge, wanting to get closer to people who might understand what my mother went through. I learned from them what I could not understand before: how people can get caught up in these abusive cycles, how completely and utterly helpless they can feel. I learned how abusers work, and slowly I managed to put the pieces of my childhood together. My mother was trapped and afraid; Becks was trapped and afraid. But neither of them were weak. Both of them made sacrifices for me, incredible sacrifices I could never hope to repay.

We are entwined, and now I am coming full circle to finally confront the past, to welcome it with arms wide open. Now we are becoming whole again.

35

Ava

I moved in with Grandma after Becks was arrested, living with her until I went to university. One day in August, a few days after I'd received my A-level results, Aunt Aisha sat me down to tell me all about my mother. It was time, she said, for me to learn about Meghan, who started reading at three and taught Aisha, older by two years, how to tie her shoelaces.

'She was always quick,' Aisha said, her eyes fixed on the wall behind me, staring into the past. 'If you thought she would take two hours to do something, she would take one. It was always the way. She showed us all up.' She smiled, tears brimming in her eyes, and I reached out to take her hand. 'I never expected her to end up the way she did.'

She told me how my mother and father met, how naïve Meghan was at the time, how young and vulnerable. 'He seemed all right to begin with,' she said, sighing. 'Smart, a bit posh, polite to Mum. He was always taking Meghan out to fancy dinners, weekend trips to Paris or Edinburgh or Dublin. A two-week holiday in the Maldives, that kind of thing. We didn't have a lot of money growing up. Mum did her best after Dad died, and we didn't really want for anything, but Daniel came from an entirely different world. I suppose Meghan found it exciting.'

I thought of Becks and her childhood, and I realised then that sometimes things are out of our control, despite our best intentions. That our past can decide our future, and we are often powerless to stop it. But I would not be that way. I decided that day that I would not follow my mother's path into addiction and helplessness. I would not follow Becks' path either, forged by a desire for revenge. I would set my own path, live the lives they both should have led. I would do it for them.

'I should have noticed what was going on with her,' Aisha continued. 'I should have seen it. I was her big sister.' I squeezed her hand. 'She hid it so well, the abuse. We saw a few things, I suppose, but we didn't really think anything of it. I remember one Christmas when Daniel made a remark about what she was wearing – I can't remember what he said, but I remember the look on her face. She looked crushed, as if he had really hurt her. She went upstairs and got changed, and we all said nothing.'

I remembered similar exchanges between my father and Becks, and Aisha nodded as if I had spoken. 'We should have warned Rebecca,' she said. 'We should have realised he would do it again. I'll never forgive myself for that.' She took a deep breath. 'Meghan became depressed, losing her passion for all the things she loved. We tried to pull her out of it, but every time we suggested she leave Daniel, she would close up. But when she fell pregnant with you, she changed. She almost became her old self again.' She fell silent, a smile still on her lips, her memories dancing across her eyes, and I pictured my mother as she was, as she should have been. 'Then as her pregnancy progressed, she became really protective over you,' Aisha continued, the smile dropping suddenly from her face. 'And when you were first born, she would barely let anyone hold you. I should have realised what was going on. I visited about a week after you were born, and I saw then that I had lost my sister. She wouldn't put you down, wouldn't even let me touch you, and she was constantly checking that you were breathing, placing her ear against your little chest to hear your heart beating. I'd never seen her like that before. My calm, bright little sister had turned frantic and obsessive. She had postnatal depression – it's so obvious to me now. She was prescribed sleeping pills, then painkillers for her headaches, and then . . . then your uncle Sam appeared.' I took a deep breath. I had been waiting for his appearance in this story, but until now, I hadn't realised the significance.

'He had been away for a while, a good few years I think. I don't know where. Daniel was often working away at that point and Sam had nowhere to live, so he moved in with them. Meghan got worse, locking you both in her bedroom, often going without food and water because she was too paranoid to leave the room. We tried to visit, but there were times that nobody answered the door.' She closed her eyes for a moment. 'We tried, but not hard enough. We were shut out, Daniel refusing to take our calls, Meghan trapped inside that house, inside her own mind. We were so worried for you. We knew she would never hurt you, but she needed help. By the time we managed to get to her, it was too late. She was hooked.'

Aunt Aisha sat back in the chair, her eyes fixed on the ceiling. 'Long story short, she was gone by the time you were three months old. First it was the painkillers, then the alcohol. Then the hard drugs. We later discovered that Sam had been giving her drugs after her prescription ran out. And it was Daniel who was funding him.'

My father had been the cause of my mother's death. I thought of the articles I'd found online after Becks' trial. I'd scoured the internet for all sources of information about my mother, torturing myself with the imagined image of her collapsed on a filthy mattress, a needle sticking out of her arm, me lying beside her dead body.

'We don't know what went on in that house. Meghan never told us anything, and by the end, we barely had contact. Mum was devastated. She'd had such high hopes for Meghan – for all of us, really, but Meghan was special. She was going to be a barrister, fighting for justice and change. If anyone could do it, if anyone could fight her way into a space that excluded her, Meghan could.'

I watched a tear trickle down Aunt Aisha's face, and I reached out to pass her a tissue.

'The day before she died, we organised an intervention. I had just had Anton, and Cass was still a teenager, but Mum's brothers were going to help her take Meghan to rehab. I was going to look after you.' She smiled at me. 'You were such a quiet baby, nothing like my kids. They were all a handful, always needing something. You, though. It was as if you were content in your own company, calm and steady, just like Meghan had been when she was younger.'

She wiped her eyes before continuing. 'Despite everything, she loved you more than anything else in the world. I believe that's why you were with her when she died.' Her eyes glazed over as she spoke. 'She had a bag with her. It had clothes for both of you, some ready-made bottles for you, a few jars of the food you liked, some toiletries. It was a bag to run away with.'

I sat back, stunned. My mum had been trying to escape, and Becks had stumbled upon us in her quest for revenge. I remembered what she had told me about Sam before she took my father's body to her childhood home, how he had been the one who raped her. I pictured the scene over and over again; Sam laid out in the middle of the room, Mum collapsed against the wall, my father walking out and leaving them, leaving us all. And I knew then that I had done the right thing by plunging that knife into his neck.

My phone rings as we cross the bridge back towards the flat. 'Hi, Grandma,' I say, raising my voice over the rushing water.

'Hello, sweet pea,' she says, her voice cracking. She is ill, has been for a couple of years now, and I feel a flicker of fear every time she calls. 'How are you?'

'I'm good. Just taken Ash for a walk, heading home now for some food. We're both ravenous.'

'You're always hungry.' She chuckles, then coughs, and I hear the phlegm rattle in the back of her throat. She sounds worse. Aunt Cass said she will need oxygen soon, an argument none of us are looking forward to having. Grandma is strong-willed and stubborn, and she will not be told what to do. 'Are you still coming this afternoon?' she asks once the coughing fit has passed.

'Of course. Three o'clock, isn't it?' The summons came a week ago, all of us – me, my aunts, and my cousins – are to meet at Grandma's house this afternoon. We've talked about it non-stop since, wondering what she's going to tell us.

Maybe she has a secret fortune, my cousin Anton joked in the WhatsApp group.

Or a secret lover, his sister Cora said, her message followed by emojis and an admonition from Aunt Aisha.

Cass: *Should I bring Natalia?*

Aisha: *I don't see why not. I'm leaving Sean at home with Robert though. He's too young for this.*

Cass: *What about Caleb?*

Natalia: *You're not leaving me behind to look after him. We'll bring him with us.*

Cass and Natalia have been married for six years now, and their adopted son, Caleb, is almost four. He's such a sweet child, and he adores Ash more than any of us, but Aunt Cass is allergic to dogs.

What about Ash? I typed, and laughed when the responses came in.

Anton: *You've got a death wish.*

Aisha: *What's wrong with you, child?*
Cass: *You're no longer my favourite niece, Ava.*
Cora: *Hey!*

We like to goad one another, our family, but always in a light-hearted way. My aunts tell me I remind them of my mother. Despite her studious ways, she also liked a practical joke, leaving fart cushions on Grandma's seat, or planting a fake spider in Aisha's bed. She used to hide their dad's slippers, and once bought him a mug that said *World's Best Farter* for Father's Day.

I like hearing about this side of my mum, the young girl who hadn't yet found the path that would lead to her death. The intelligent girl who read to the rest of her class at primary school, a habit she carried on as a university student and after she had me, reading to kids in underprivileged areas of London. The carefree girl who always went barefoot in the garden, lying in the grass with a ladybird on her finger. The happy girl giggling with her sisters, arm in arm as they ran towards the sea, their parents watching from a spot on a beach in Margate, the windbreaker erected precariously into the sand.

I open the door, Ash shooting ahead of me into the flat. She laps at her water bowl, her tail wagging, as I open the fridge to make a sandwich. I'm not sure what Grandma wants to talk to us all about, but I have a feeling it has something to do with Becks. We are coming full circle.

36

Ava

As I pull up outside Grandma's house, I see Anton's car turn the corner and I stand in the way, blocking his entrance to the driveway.

'Ten points!' Aisha shouts from the passenger seat, and Anton revs the engine until I move out of the way.

Cora opens the front door, her hair in braids, a new tattoo snaking up her arm. She pats my shoulder as I go inside and make my way into the living room. Grandma sits in her usual chair, her feet resting on a stool, a magazine in her lap. She looks up as I enter, pushing her glasses up onto her head. 'Ava,' she says, and I bend down to hug her. I breathe in her scent of oranges and cinnamon, a combination that always reminds me of this house.

'How are you, Grandma?' I ask, sitting on the stool at her feet.

'I'm fine, sweet pea. Never better.' But I can see the pain in her eyes, and her breathing is shallow. Grief hits me like a blow. I'm not ready to lose her, this woman who has been constant in my life, who has loved and protected and cared for me. I turn away to hide the tears in my eyes and find Anton standing in the doorway, waiting for his turn. I move so he can greet her, heading for the kitchen to make a cup of tea. The kettle is always on in this house, our favourite cups hanging from a mug tree on the counter. I take down enough mugs for everyone – there's no point asking if they want a cup of tea, the answer is always yes, sometimes with an edge to the word, as if I have offended them by asking – and fill the kettle.

Once everyone is settled in the living room, mugs in hand, I stand in the doorway, watching Natalia place Caleb on Grandma's lap. He chatters away about some television programme he loves, Grandma nodding sagely. Cora's sitting at the dining table and I go over to join her, setting my mug down on the table.

'I heard the news. Congrats, Baby Bird.'

I smile. Even though I'm older than Cora, everyone's called me Baby Bird since I changed my surname a few years ago, reclaiming my mother's name, discarding my father's like an old skin. 'Thanks. How are you?'

She smiles. 'Tired. I only got in on Tuesday, and I'm due to fly back out in a few days.'

'Back to Thailand?'

She shakes her head. 'Bali. I'm going to save some turtles this time.' Her smile slips as she looks over at Grandma, who is handing Caleb back to Natalia. 'Do you know why we're here, Baby Bird?'

I don't answer, grief settling over me like a shroud. Sierra, mother, grandmother, matriarch, is dying. She was a nurse for almost fifty years, starting work when she was a teenager after her parents brought her over from Trinidad and Tobago, and only retiring when I came to live with her, so she knows enough about medicine to understand her own condition. COPD, or more specifically, emphysema.

'She's not even eighty,' Cora whispers. 'It's just not fair.'

'I hope you're not killing me off over there,' Grandma says, her eyes settling on me as the room falls silent. 'I'm not ready to go just yet. But I do need to discuss something with you all.' A smatter of nervous laughter ripples across the room before silence falls again and Grandma looks at us all in turn. 'I know I'm not well,' she says levelly, 'and the time has come for me to move somewhere else, where I can be taken care of.'

'We can take care of you, Mum,' Aisha protests, sitting forward in her chair.

'I know you can. But I don't want you to.' Aisha goes to speak again, but Grandma raises a hand. 'You all have your own lives – jobs, children – and I will not become a burden.'

Now I open my mouth to speak, but she fixes me with her gaze and I fall silent. As always, she has chosen her words carefully. She knows we all feel guilty about not spending enough time with her, stressing ourselves out about making sure someone is always available for her. We do it without thought, because it is what families do, but it isn't what she wants.

'I cared for my own mother before she passed, as Aisha may remember, and I know how difficult it can be. I want you to live your lives, as I have lived mine.' She smiles then, her eyes twinkling. 'What a good life I have had. How lucky I am to have you all, and how lucky I was to have those who are now gone. My family.' I feel tears prick my eyes as I think of my mum, and I can tell Grandma is thinking of her too. 'I've organised a place, not far from here, and I expect to be kept in black cake and Quality Street.'

We laugh, eyeing the tin on the coffee table. She always has a tin of Quality Street open, no matter the time of year. The air in the room seems to grow calmer then, the tension fizzling out as the dreaded news settles on our shoulders. *It's not so bad,* I think. *It's not the end, not yet.*

'And I have one last thing to ask of you.' Grandma lifts her arm, holding out her hand, and all eyes in the room turn to me. 'Ava. My dear, sweet Baby Bird.' I stand, my legs feeling unsteady, and cross the room to take her hand. 'It is you who will suffer the most from my request, and for that I am sorry.' Her eyes are glistening with tears. 'But I must ask this of you.' She lifts her head to look around the room, still holding my hand in hers. 'Rebecca will be released next year.'

The room takes a collective breath, and blood rushes in my ears as I struggle to take in her words. *Rebecca. Becks. Released.*

'She has done her time,' Grandma continues, 'and the treatments have been successful. She is much better now.'

'Good for her,' Aunt Aisha mutters, and Grandma narrows her eyes at her. I realise again how wise the decision was not to tell the others the whole truth about Becks and her involvement in my mother's death. They wouldn't understand as we do. As always, Grandma knows best.

'I understand your concerns,' she says, 'but Rebecca stepped up for us. She protected Ava, and shouldered the consequences alone.'

I see Aisha nod, and feel my stomach unclench slightly. Cass is smiling at me, and I remember the look on her face when the knife fell from my hand. Relief that I had saved her; terror at the consequences.

Grandma looks at me then, her eyes meeting mine, and I feel something pass between us. I know what she is asking of me. I sit up straighter, squeezing her hand in mine. 'What do you want me to do, Grandma?'

A few weeks later, I am shown into a waiting room, my bag having been taken and my pockets searched. The defence of diminished responsibility worked; the charge was commuted to manslaughter, and the court made a hospital order, sending Becks to a secure hospital instead of to prison. She has been here ever since.

I look around the room, the stiff seat cold beneath my thighs, and tap my foot on the linoleum floor. The air outside is chilly, the early November sky grey when I pulled into the car park, the trees shedding their rust-coloured leaves, suspended in that space between the beauty of autumn and the barrenness of winter.

Soon I am collected and taken to another room, with two grey sofas and a table between them. The walls are painted light blue and there are posters on the far wall. I sit on one of the sofas, my hands folded between my knees, my head bent forward, breathing in and out. I can do this. I *can* do this. I have to.

Since Grandma's request, I have thought of nothing but Becks. I'd tried to put her out of my mind over the past seven years, focusing on school and friends and trying to be a normal teenager, but she has always been there, a spectre in the corner of the room. I know she tried her best for me, and I know she loved me. I loved her too, I still do, and it is only now that I can allow myself to realise it. She was kind and thoughtful, the complete opposite of my father. Where he dictated, demanded that I go along with his plans, Becks was considerate, making sure I had what I needed. While my dad might have paid for everything, Becks was the one who organised it all. Food, clothes, trips out. She did the washing and the cleaning, cooked my favourite meals and treated me to new art supplies. She was a mother to me, and she deserves better than what I have given her.

The door opens and a woman enters, her hair pulled back in a neat ponytail, her skin fresh and clean. Her eyes meet mine and I stand, moving towards her without thought. There's something in the way she looks at me that makes me feel as if I am being pulled towards her, this woman who sacrificed herself for me over and over again. It is I who owes her now, and I'm not sure if I will ever be able to repay her.

'Becks,' I say, my voice barely above a whisper, and she smiles, holding out her arms. I step into them, breathe in the scent of washing powder and citrus. I feel her body start to shake, and my eyes prick with tears. 'I'm here, Becks. I'm here.'

37

Ava

We have come full circle. I am back at Blackwater House, giving the place a thorough clean with the forced help of Cora and Anton. We will spend Christmas here, just like we did all those years ago. Grandma insisted on joining us, despite our concerns about her being able to travel, and I'm glad. We need to lay this to rest now, and the only place to do that is here, the home Rebecca gave me.

The two of us will live here together when she is released next year. They are allowing her to visit for Christmas, as they have allowed me to visit every week since that first time, making the long journey from Hertfordshire to Cornwall in a strange echo of my father's journeys. We are building bridges, and it will take some time, but I know we'll get there.

Rebecca will live in the annex, for it is the only place that doesn't hold any memories for her. It was her choice – there's plenty of room in the main house, after all – but I understand. After years of living in a hospital, the idea of moving back into Blackwater House must seem daunting. I have cleansed the house of all reminders of my father, his clothes and shoes given to charity along with other bric-a-brac. Though Rebecca said I should take the main bedroom, I'd prefer to stay in my old room. It's large, with a view over the garden and the ocean, and I feel at peace here. Rebecca's office will become mine, though there is space for a second desk and I hope, one day, she will join me in there, sitting together as we write. *Baby steps,* I remind myself. For now, it is enough that she is coming for Christmas, and that this house will be full of joy and laughter for the first time in years.

I hear Cora swearing at the hoover and poke my head out of the office, where I have been cleaning the windows. She looks up at me and scowls. 'How ancient is this thing? It's bloody stopped working again.'

I check my watch. 'Cass and Natalia will be here soon. Why don't you have a tea break?' Despite Cass's protestations, they are bringing Ash with them, who will have revelled in Caleb's company over the past few days, and Grandma, who will arrive with her famous black cake. It will be her final Christmas with us, for in the new year she will be taken to the home she has chosen, to, as she continues to remind us, 'finally get some peace'. I will drive over to the hospital tomorrow to pick Rebecca up, and take her back on Boxing Day morning.

Cora pretends to kick the hoover as she heads into the kitchen. 'Do you want one?' she calls as I hear her flick the kettle on. I follow her and grab my phone from the counter.

'No, thanks. I'd better get to the shop, actually. Is there anything you want me to add to the list?'

'Have you got vodka?'

I roll my eyes. 'Yes, Cora. I've got vodka.'

'I could do with one right now,' she says, filling her mug. 'I bloody hate cleaning.'

'Didn't you spend five months cleaning toilets in a hostel in Australia?'

'Exactly.'

I laugh. 'All right, I'd better be off. Anton!' He pops his head out of the living room, where he's been putting up the Christmas tree. 'I'm off to the shops.'

'I'll come with,' he says, placing a bauble on a branch before stepping back to admire his handiwork. 'This is done.'

'Looks great.'

'You're not the only artist in the family, you know,' he says with a wink. We put on our coats and crunch across the driveway to my car. 'I wonder how she's managed in there,' he says as I park up outside the supermarket. 'Being coeliac, I mean. I hope they've catered for her.'

'She always looks well,' I say, getting out of the car. 'But we'll make sure she's got lots of choice for tomorrow.' Everyone has their own shopping list, but I'm in charge of buying the gluten-free food and the alcohol, much to Cora's delight. I pick up a few boxes of mince pies, which I'll take with me when I collect Rebecca tomorrow and offer them to the staff and other patients. I wonder how many of them don't have families, what Christmas must be like in a place like that, and feel guilt begin to seep in. *No*, I tell myself firmly. *It's time to look forward, not back.*

I snatch a box of After Eights from the shelf, one of the remaining two boxes, and drop it into the trolley. The supermarket is heaving, people panic buying loaves of bread and pints of milk in preparation for the one day the shops will be closed. Anton picks the box back up. 'Are they gluten-free?' he asks, peering at the ingredients. 'What am I looking for here?'

'BROWS,' I say, and he frowns at me. 'Barley, rye, oats, wheat, spelt. BROWS.'

He laughs and wriggles his eyebrows. 'Handy, that.' He nods, placing the box back in the trolley. 'Looks good.'

'And also *may contain*.'

Another frown. 'May contain?'

I sigh. '"May contain traces of gluten" or something. It's when they're made in the same factory.'

'What a pain in the arse,' he says, snatching up the box of After Eights and glaring at the back, as if daring it to have any such warning.

I laugh, taking the box from him. 'These are fine.'

We take the shopping home and load up the fridge and pantry before settling down with a cup of tea and a packet of biscuits. Cora is sprawled across the sofa, one foot dangling off the end.

'Did Anton tell you his girlfriend is coming tomorrow?' she asks. Anton gives her a look that could kill.

'No,' I say, grinning at him. 'Who is she? What's her name?'

'She's *vegan*,' Cora says, wrinkling her nose.

'Her name is Ellie,' Anton says, still glaring at his sister. 'And, yeah, she's vegan.'

'What's she going to eat?!' Cora exclaims, as if it has only just occurred to her that we might have to feed this extra guest.

'Brussels sprouts?' I offer, and Anton lobs a biscuit at me.

Christmas Eve. I take Ash for a walk along the cliffs, her lead held tightly in my hand. She isn't used to this terrain and the drop is over a hundred feet, so I don't dare let her off. She sniffs at some heather, entranced by all the new scents, and I know she'll be happier here with a big garden to run around in and new places to explore instead of my tiny flat. We nailed up some chicken wire across the back fence to stop her from escaping, Anton whacking his thumb with the hammer at least twice, and I think I'll need to find a way to block off the vegetable patch if Rebecca wants to try to grow anything without Ash digging it all up.

It is early, and there is nobody else here. Although I liked living in Hertfordshire, Cornwall has definitely got under my skin. I love the way it is simultaneously quiet and loud at the same time. Up here, you can't hear any cars or people, but the sound of the sea crashing against the rocks fills the air, the cries of gulls twirling above, the wind whistling across the headland. It is peaceful, and it feels like home.

I wonder if my mum would have liked it. Though I don't remember her, I have always sought my mother's presence, keeping hidden her old hairbrush I'd found when I was a child, and pinning her photos on my wall. My favourite photo is of the two of us, with matching navy jumpers and brown boots, the truth of her pain hidden behind her smile. I reach inside my coat and pull out her necklace, the letter M on a silver chain, and close my fist around it, trying to conjure up her face.

Ash pulls on her lead then and I look up to see two figures approaching, bundled up as I am in coats and scarves, with a puppy trotting just ahead of them. I move Ash aside to let them pass, and am surprised when recognition dawns.

'Kate?' The word is out before I can stop it. The woman pauses before smiling.

'Ava? Is that you?'

I nod, suddenly shy. 'This is Ash,' I say, watching as the two dogs sniff one another.

'Vixen,' Kate says, indicating the fox-red Labrador. 'And this is my wife, Lauren.'

'Hi,' the other woman says with a smile. 'It's nice to meet you.' I smile back at her, then laugh as Vixen and Ash begin to play, tangling the lead around my legs in the process.

'Are you here for Christmas?' Kate asks once I've extricated myself.

'Yeah, well. I'm moving back, actually. Rebecca is . . .'

'Rebecca?' she cuts in. 'Is she okay?'

'She's good. Better. She's due to be released next year. She's . . . she's sorry, you know? For what happened. We've spoken about you a few times.' I feel my cheeks heat up as I remember the lies we told. 'Are you still a police officer?'

'I'm glad. She deserves to get better,' she says, ignoring my question.

Ash strains at her lead, wanting to run off with Vixen, but I pull out a bag of treats to distract her. The Labrador is suddenly sitting at my feet, grinning up at me and the treats in my hand. 'Can she have these?'

'If you've some to spare.' Lauren laughs. 'She'll be your friend for life now.'

'She's moving here with me,' I say, holding out a treat for Vixen. 'Rebecca, I mean, next year. To Blackwater House. It'll be a fresh start.'

Kate smiles. 'That sounds lovely. I'd like to visit sometime, if she'll let me. I'll give you my number.' I take out my phone and tap in the numbers she reels off. 'Let me know.'

'I will. Thanks. Merry Christmas.'

'Merry Christmas.' They both smile and Lauren whistles for Vixen to follow them.

I watch them go, reaching out to scratch behind Ash's ear. 'Looks like you've already made a friend,' I murmur. We continue on down the cliff, pausing at the engine house Rebecca gave birth in all those years ago. I think of how traumatic it must have been for her, still just a child herself. No wonder she suffered for so long. She had no support, no one to help her through it, except Gwen. I am grateful for her, that woman I never knew, for taking Rebecca in and giving her refuge. Despite everything that has happened since, Rebecca is finally free of her past, of the ghosts that have haunted her since she was a child, and I am glad.

Down on the beach, I let Ash off the lead and throw a stick into the water for her, thinking about how we are all entwined. The future may look different now, but we are bound together by our shared past and memories, and we can never let each other go. Each of us are waves in the same sea, forever overlapping, undulating, restless. Every event a ripple, rico-cheting off us; every undercurrent pulling us apart, until we rise again, together, breaking over the sand.

As I turn back towards Blackwater House, I look up to see a figure standing on the cliff edge, hair rippling in the wind, and hear a name whispered on the waves.

THE END

Acknowledgements

This book has truly been through the wringer. Originally written in 2019, it has been rewritten so many times I've almost lost count, and had so many near misses that I was about ready to give up and consign it to the drawer. But I sent it to my agent instead, and she found it the perfect home with Hodder. As they say, it only takes one yes.

My thanks and gratitude to the indomitable Emily Glenister at DHH Literary Agency, and to my wonderful, sharp-eyed editor, Bethany Wickington, who was one of those near misses. It feels a bit like fate that we ended up working together on this book, and I couldn't have dreamed of a better outcome. My thanks also to Mireille Harper for the much-needed sensitivity read and guidance on how to do better now I know better, and to Helena Newton for the thorough copyedit. A lot of things go on behind the scenes, and so I want to say a huge thank you to the incredible Hodder team: Lewis Csizmazia for the amazing cover, plus Katy Blott, Ellie Wheeldon, Katy Aries, Simon McArt, Rebecca Mundy, and Ollie Martin. Thank you for everything you do.

Many thanks to Ricky Carter for his help with all things policing during that evening in Starbucks back before the world imploded, and to Georgina Carter for facilitating and reading a very early draft. Thanks to Amy Fergus and Rachel Allen (as always!) for the extra guidance on procedures involving the coastguard and sentencing guidelines, as well as the Cornish-isms. All errors are entirely my own. To my wife, for championing this book from the very beginning and being with me through the (sometimes extreme!) highs and lows. And to Clive and Jean for their continued support.

Writing can be a solitary profession, but the support which comes from the author community is truly second to none. Here's to the Psychological Suspense Authors' Association, the Authors with Disabilities and Chronic Illnesses group, the Retweeters, the Savvy Writers, and all the incredible, lovely authors I've met along the way.

Return to Blackwater House is set in a fictional Cornish village which locals will recognise as being very similar to St Agnes. I hope you don't mind the liberties I've taken with your beautiful village. There is nowhere quite like Wheal Coates on a warm evening, especially with a pizza from the Cornish Pizza Company or a coffee from The Sorting Office. I studied policing at Cornwall College before completing my criminology degree at Plymouth University, where I met some of my dearest friends and spent three of the best years of my life. Cornwall will always hold a special place in my heart, no matter where I am in the world.

Readers who have been with me since the beginning might have noticed that Kate and Lauren Winters appeared in my debut novel, *The Diary*. Since then, I've been looking for an opportunity to explore Kate further as a character. I hope you've enjoyed getting to know her better.

This book explores some sensitive topics, and while I was editing, Sarah Everard was kidnapped, raped, and murdered by a serving police officer. As someone who has a complicated relationship with the police and criminal justice system, as well as a woman and survivor myself, I couldn't not mention her name. This book is dedicated to all of the women who were just walking home, or who were at home, or who were dancing or having a drink with friends or simply existing. To us.